M000170360

CIRCUS ACTS

DAVID ZINI

Copyright © 2021 David Zini
All rights reserved
First Edition

Fulton Books, Inc.
Meadville, PA

Published by Fulton Books 2021

ISBN 978-1-63710-758-4 (paperback)
ISBN 978-1-63710-759-1 (digital)

Printed in the United States of America

CHAPTER I

John St. Claire yanked the Navigator's seat belt across his Brooks Brothers suit coat. Tiny beads of sweat dotted his forehead in rebuff to the unwelcome morning heat. Glancing at his house as he backed out of the driveway, St. Claire felt a pang of anxiety. *Lots to pay for and the well is running dry. Damned Saudis.* A month of negotiations and a night of (very expensive) wining and dining had fallen apart like a two-year-old plowing through a carefully constructed Lego montage. Now what? John's private and professional financial status were collapsing faster than a pricked balloon.

St. Claire puffed out a sigh and focused on how he was (first and foremost) going to breathe some life into his now "tower of horrors," otherwise known as the Independence Republic Bank of Minneapolis, of which John was the CFO. The lifeline of money needed to keep his bank afloat in the wake of the 2008 mortgage meltdown crisis was about to wave goodbye as it departed MSP for the desert kingdom.

Hope they choke on the sand and dust. John hit the accelerator and swung out of his driveway, nearly crashing with a kid on a bike. The incident was resolved with a finger wave by one party (kid) and a dirty look by the other (John). *Okay, settle down.* Not to be.

Two blocks from his house, St. Claire begrudgingly stopped for a man standing in the middle of the street frantically waving his arms. Next to him was a van with its hood raised. Hurrying over to St. Claire, the frazzled man stammered, "I'm sorry to bother you. But my wife had a seizure, and I was following the ambulance to the hospital... And...and then my van broke down, and... I forgot

3

my cell phone." He clasped his hands together. "Please, help me." Although acts of human kindness weren't in St. Claire's playbook, he nonetheless reached for his cell phone. That was the last thing John remembered until a part of John St. Claire's altered consciousness emerged from the drugs that "desperate vanman" had administered. John's mind-bending hallucination now solely focused on chasing a balloon release of earthly cares into the far beyond. An illusionary release of his grip on the door handle of the abduction van into which he had been forced had propelled St. Claire's vault through earth's outer reaches. Swirling higher and higher, the deep space astronaut reached out to touch heaven's door, powered not by rocket fuel but by a chemical soup of drugs. Unfortunately for John, the mind-altering "booster rockets" were about to experience a flameout.

Envious of his captive's chemically induced bliss, but not so much the future of victim in hand, John's abductor nervously tapped out a meaningless cadence on the steering wheel of the parked van, his anxiety foreign for a man who normally circulated blood colder than an Antarctic ice shelf. But then, this was the maiden voyage.

The momentary pause soon caved to the task at hand. The kidnapper pulled in a deep breath and peered through the van's windshield into the busy downtown Minneapolis intersection. He reviewed his genius plan one last time. No argument, it was over-the-top dramatic. But then, it was meant to be. The risks? A fool's bet. Forthcoming rewards? At the moment, ambiguous. At the very least, sweet revenge. For sure, this was not your garden-variety kidnapping.

Money wasn't the issue—well, actually, yes, it was about money, but not in terms of exchange for St. Claire. No, John's sins would soon enough be displayed for all to see, as this campaign was about revenge, redemption, and reward; and if all went according to plan, the latter would, at the very least, be welcomed as a moral victory with the script reading, "Lord knows I've earned a recompense of some kind, selflessly crusading for the millions of my fellow citizens who have been victimized by the John St. Claires of the financial world." Then again, maybe not.

The platitude stuck in his craw like a doomed rodent glued to one of those sticky traps. *Crusading for the common good?* Likely as a cloudy day on the International Space Station. No, this was about him, and only him, and how to capitalize. So to which scandal did this insane crusade owe its conception?

It was labeled as the Great Recession of 2008, also peddled as the Mortgage Meltdown. The kidnapper disdainfully referred to it as the gutting and fleshing of America, of which he (also) had been financially scalped, skinned, and hung out to dry. For the first time in his life, Mr. Kidnapper was "financially naked." No jingle in his pockets. No wallet wads of currency. It was sobering. It was (ugh) living like his fellow Americans. And he didn't like it, deeming himself far too smart to have been conned. Oh yes, these legitimized crooks, aka the heart and soul of the financial world, would soon be exposed in ways never before experienced in these here *Yoo*-nited States of America. Welcome to the dark world of one pissed-off sociopath.

The kidnapper folded his hands over the steering wheel, slowly rocking it back and forth. Waves of adrenalin pulsated through his cold veins, welling up even colder thoughts of revenge. After reviewing the gory plan in his head one last time, he turned his attention to the task at hand and scanned the busy downtown Minneapolis intersection. Flagging no roadblocks to delay the premier of his very first "circus act of justice," he set the wheels in motion.

The kidnapper wrapped a clammy hand around the back of John's neck, drawing his face tight to the rearview mirror. John countered with shallow, stale exhalations onto the glass, evidence enough to confirm the drugs were steering the ship. "Take a good look, John," his abductor snarled. "Take one long last look at the big-shot investment banker." St. Claire posited no reaction. The kidnapper placed a finger on John's forehead and circled his face with it. "I have a present for you, Johnny. Consider it your 'scarlet letter.'" Again, no response. The man reached behind his seat and retrieved a clown mask complete with a white face, sullen dark eyes, wild red hair, and topped with a small black hat. He pulled the hideous mask over St. Claire's head, declaring, "What's a circus without a clown." Like a cat tormenting a captured mouse before he crunches it and slides it down his throat, St. Claire's abductor was enjoying his endgame antics, as the hate welling up in his soul spewed onto his hapless captive.

"Okay, m'boy, it's time to account for of all those pus-filled schemes you and your low-life cohorts invented that crashed the American economy and wiped out my life's savings. And when the schemes went south and the money spilled out of your bank like water through a ruptured dam, you looked to your deep-pocketed uncle for a life ring. But that didn't work so well cuz you weren't high enough on the totem pole. Well, I'm sure you know the adage, John, the one where sympathy stands in the dictionary, but for you, it gets worse because you see, I'm the self-appointed avenger for the good citizens of this country blindsided by your greed." St. Claire's fear receptors awakened. He felt a twinge of panic.

The kidnapper pulled in close, all but whispering in John's ear. "Quick business meeting, Johnny. Have you given so much as a passing thought to the lives you've ruined for the sake of stuffing your pockets? How about the 401(k)'s up in smoke? Oh yes, and don't forget the heart-wrenching scores of cancelled retirements. Think those folks don't have hopes and dreams? And while we're on the subject, how about the millions of empty houses your greed engineered? Ever wondered what's happened to the people who turned the lights on in those houses? I'll give you a hint—it's no fun living in your car."

St. Claire turned to the kidnapper, his lips quivering. The abductor waved a finger. "Oh, now don't go getting all slobbery with me. You've had plenty of time for repentance. No, John, today we're gonna be circling that other *r* word—*revenge*."

The kidnapper reached behind his seat and retrieved a PC. He fired up a program and turned back to his captive, forcing John to make eye contact—very close eye contact. "Look at me, John; remember my words. I am your worst nightmare. I am your personal grim reaper. It's not by accident I've chosen you to be featured in my first circus act of justice." Tiny bubbles of froth gathered in the corners of the kidnapper's mouth. "It's payback time, John—and as they say—paybacks are a bitch!"

St. Claire's eyes flashed a spark of fear. The kidnapper fell silent, but his cold stare spoke volumes. After a few uneasy moments, he loosened his grip and then gently brushed invisible lint off John's suit coat. His sneer transformed into a disarming smile, and his voice mellowed, dripping with insincere sweetness.

"Do I have your attention, John? I hope so because this is important. You see, unlike you, I do have a heart, and so I'm going to give you a chance to change your ways. Call it an opportunity for redemption. Now pay close attention to what I'm saying. Your wife is waiting for you across the street. She will take you home if you can find her. But you have to cross the street. Do you understand me, John?" The kidnapper leaned over, opened the passenger door, and gave St. Claire a shove. "Do you understand what I'm telling you, John? Go! Now!" The drugged abductee tumbled out of the van, clinging to the door for support. His eyes reached back into the cab. The man was gone.

St. Claire struggled to cross the busy downtown Minneapolis intersection, alternating sideways stumbles with forward advances. He ignored protestations from squealing brakes and screeching horns; his one and only thought was to obey the order—*find wife*. Pedestrians shot puzzled glances his way, but the stares and glares had less to do with St. Claire's staggered jaywalking than his clown face. Ahead, a parked car beckoned as a welcome island of stability, and like a desperate, drowning swimmer flailing to set anchor on the beach, St. Claire lunged forward, slapping a trembling hand on its shiny red hood. Safe. For the moment. And his wife? She would not be coming.

John steadied himself against the car and took stock of his foggy, detached world. People, cars, and even the surrounding buildings circled like buzzards over a fresh kill. *But what's this?* The building in front of him—there was something about it—but... *Look for wife—need help.* St. Claire threw feeble, awkward waves at passing pedestrians. He tried to shout out for help, but rebelling vocal cords squeezed out nearly inaudible grunts. All took notice. All moved on. Wife—a no-show.

John refocused on the building. He separated himself from the car and heaved a foot over the curb and onto the sidewalk. He lifted his other foot alongside, stretching out his arms for balance. The public gave him an even wider berth. After all, it would be a push to reach out to a person sporting a clown mask planted on a man staggering around in a Brooks Brothers suit. Additional attempts to secure help were unsuccessful.

Deciding there was to be no charity among the public and not making the connection that the building in front of him was the Independence Republic Bank, St. Claire reversed direction and flopped his way back onto the street. Ensuing gridlock drew in a patrol car. Wading between snarled traffic, a visibly irritated cop spotted the man with the clown face and shepherded him back onto the sidewalk. "What's going on, buddy? I didn't know the circus was in town."

St. Claire attempted a coherent sentence, but his hallucinating mind focused on the surrounding buildings swaying and twisting into giant pretzel shapes. The grotesque scene threw him off balance, causing him to teeter forward, exposing a manila envelope pinned to his back.

The cop took notice. "Well, well, what do we have here, a 'clowney backpack'?"

St. Claire struggled to embrace a second run at dialogue, only to spit out a few unintelligible words. The patrolman pitched a hand into the envelope and retrieved a sheet of paper. He read the note, stared at John, and read it again. His throat drew tighter with each line scanned:

If you are not the police, call them—NOW!
If you are the police, cuff me to the nearest meter.
I am wired with explosives.
Any attempt to not follow these instructions will result in their detonation.
DO IT NOW!
You are being watched.

The cop pressed a hand against St. Claire's rib cage, his fingers confirming the presence of long, hard-like sticks. He looked hard into John's eyes. The eyes ricocheted a blank stare.

The now dead-serious cop nervously tugged at his mobile radio, nearly dropped it. "37 to dispatch. I… I'm downtown in front of the Independence Republic Bank. I've got a guy who may be wired with explosives…"

A sharp discharge interrupted the call; shards of glass from an exploding window sprinkled down on startled pedestrians.

"Cuff me to the meter… Cuff me to the meter… Cuff me to the meter…" A voice repeated from—where? The cop shot St. Claire a nervous look. His eyes settled on the clown hat.

There's a speaker in the hat! Fearing the next bullet could have his name on it, the bewildered patrolman slapped one cuff on the clown's wrist and the other to the meter post. The speaker fell silent.

*****

Sergeant Mark Truitt stared, for a long minute, at bloodstained cartons of cigarettes, front-row witnesses to the grizzly events perpetrated by an as yet unidentified assailant the previous evening. The dynamics of three 9mm bullets slamming into the cashier on duty had initiated an initial trajectory forward followed by a reversal into a tobacco case. Tragically, the young woman who had circulated that blood would no longer have need of it. On the opposite side of the counter, an older gentleman had been relieved of his earthly boundaries courtesy of a slug piercing the back of his skull. A third victim, female, was expected to survive two non-life-threatening wounds— the lone asterisk to the Twin Cities' latest act of deadly violence, the recent uptick in crimes, a not-so-nice stepchild to the state's proud mantra of "Minnesota nice."

Truitt pushed out a heavy breath and scanned the scene a final time. Before stepping into the warm, humid morning, he extended his condolences to the store's owner who was recreating the horrid event to a group of patrons.

Mark took a moment to reset as he settled into his car. The day had barely progressed beyond a shave and first cup of coffee, yet muscles in his back were tensioned like banjo strings. Tight enough to play "Deliverance." Before long, sultry air enveloped the car's interior, mounting a challenge to his morning's hygiene efforts. Mark started the engine, turned up the air conditioning, and pointed his car in the direction of Minneapolis Metro First Precinct headquarters.

Two red lights and one green down the road, a call from dispatch diverted him to downtown Minneapolis. Something about a man with a clown face wrapped in a bomb. *Clowns and bombs in the same sentence?* Whole muscle groups pitched up to the A scale.

Mark scanned the perimeter as he pushed his way through a gathering crowd. Had the word *bomb* not been attached to the subject, who, at the moment was attached to a parking meter in front of the Independence Republic Bank and surrounded by police tape, the scene would have hinted at a performance about to begin. Keeping an eye on clown man, Mark passed a contingent of emergency personnel including cocooned bomb-squad members, first responders, and firefighters. Restricted to a safe distance, members of the news media strained for a closer look. Mark pulled up to a makeshift police command post and settled in alongside his supervisor, Lieutenant Guy Lompello.

"A new adventure every day," Truitt sighed.

Lompello shrugged. Peeling back the crusty layers of this old crime fighter, one would uncover a soft, lamby heart that the lieutenant took great pains to keep from showing up on his sleeve. What Lompello wasn't uncovering at the moment was an explanation for the odd scene displayed in front of him.

Training a pair of binoculars on the clown was Mark's new partner, Sergeant Sylkie Maune, a twenty-something firebrand and first rounder to grace police promotional posters.

Mark shot a glance at the young investigator. "Where's this bomb supposed to be?"

Sylkie lowered her field glasses. "Wired to the vic."

"Has it been confirmed?"

Lompello said, "No, but he was carrying a note saying he's wired with explosives. The cop who cuffed him to the meter echoed that possibility."

"Why did he cuff him to the meter?"

"Cuz the note said to cuff him to the meter."

"Uh-huh. So what now?"

Lompello scoffed, "You tell me. I don't have a protocol for pseudo-clowns wrapped in bombs and cuffed to parking meters. What I do have are uniforms on the street and snipers in place."

"Poor guy," Maune lamented. "I think the bomb squad should make a move."

Before *anyone* could make a move, a sharp "pop" preceded the ejection of a two-foot panel from the side of the abduction van, which was parked directly across the street from St. Claire. A few tense seconds later, a short burst of circus music radiated from the opening created by the missing panel. The music abruptly surrendered to static akin to tuning through an AM radio band. A prolonged *sssssss…bzzzzz…*gave way to a deep-throated announcement: "A public service message: Do not attempt to approach either the clown or this van. There are explosives attached to each." The circus music returned, only to once again fade.

"I don't like where this is going." Mark scanned the van with Sylkie's field glasses.

"*Sssssssss…*" An energetic voice poked through the static: "Heeere's Johnny… St. Claire… [crackle] CFO, Independence Republic Bank. …*bzzzz…* You go, Johnny…"

Mark made a call to track down the whereabouts of St. Claire. He recognized the name as prominent around the Twin Cities business and social communities.

Lompello shouted into his mobile radio, "Can anyone see movement inside the van?"

"*Bzzzzz…*" A parrot imitation squawked in cadence, "Johnny gets the bo-nus. We all get the bo-own…*ssssst…* Woo-hoooo. Bad Johnny, bad Johnny, you stole our mo-ney…hmmm."

Maune shook out a shiver. "This is downright spooky. I don't see a happy ending here."

"I don't see anything but the clown…or St. Claire…or whomever that is." Lompello cued his radio again. "Somebody's got to be monitoring this charade. Spread out; look for *anybody* or *anything* suspicious." The lieutenant turned to Truitt. The old veteran's face contorted to the point where it looked like he might be trying to hold back a gigantic gas release. "I'm having visions of animals and acrobats marching down the street cuz I can't believe this is for real."

Mark pocketed his cell phone. "St. Claire didn't show up for work this morning...so it could be him under the clown mask. But why?" Mark kept his focus on St. Claire. "This is way too elaborate to be either a joke or to embarrass the man. I don't think we have much time to defuse this nightmare."

"Yeah? And who do we negotiate with?" Sylkie reflected with a dose of sarcasm as she brushed back renegade strands of blond hair.

Mark pointed to St. Claire. "He looks like he's becoming more aware of his surroundings."

Sure enough, the drugs were releasing their grip. St. Claire tugged at his cuffs like a varmint straining to pull its paw out of a leg trap.

"*Sssss*...[crackle]..." A soft female voice broke through the interference. "Pork bellies futures took a tumble yesterday, following...*bzzzzzz*... And now, let's sing along with Mitch Miller... *sssssssss*..." Once again, the professional voice said, "Tip your hat to the crowd, John, and say goodbye. It's time to go."

A now quite-alert John St. Claire stopped pulling at his restraints and stared at the van. He knew his nightmare was about to reach its climax. In a final, desperate gesture, St. Claire extended his arm toward the crowd and pleaded for help.

Mark grabbed Lompello's mobile radio. "Hit the van with everything you've got! Do...it...NOW!"

At the same time, a distinctive John Wayne imitation cut a parting shot: "And this, pilgrim, is how we handle polecats 'round here... *sssssssss*."

The concussion from the explosion imploded several windows in the surrounding buildings. Simultaneously, a secondary explosion in the van destroyed valuable evidence.

As for John St. Claire, mementos of the banking executive would be hanging around long after the incident.

"I've been at this business nearly two of your lifetimes,"—a confounded Guy Lompello gaped at Maune—"and I never thought I'd live to see a clown blown up."

Mark rubbed a temple in a futile attempt to calm the axe-wielding maniac taking swings at the inside of his head. So far, the new day was less than he had hoped for. Much less.

Two blocks away, a computer screen went black, and a fist pumped in victory. *And "pop" goes the weasel.*

The professor was most pleased with his opening act.

CHAPTER 2

"Okay, so here's how it went down..." The baritone bellowing of Sergeant Analius Dagnar Brentsen, aka Thor, aka first-precinct unabashed drama king, echoed off the walls of the detectives' bullpen. "... And I swear on my framed three-grand winning Jackpine Jackpot lottery ticket I'm not exaggerating one i-o-t-a." A mountain of a man at six foot six, Brentsen had partnered with Sylkie Maune the previous evening.

"Me an' Sergeant Maune were responding to a 459. I was about to try the back door of the house in question when I hear something behind me. I turn around, and this brute with a scraggly beard and wild hair is grinning at me with all three of his teeth. That didn't scare me so much, but he's got the barrel of a sawed-off shotgun docked with my nostrils. Before I could blink, Sylkie... Sergeant Maune, in one blinding move, grabs the barrel of his gun, knocks his feet out from under him, and clamps a foot on his neck. She says to me, 'On him!' So I flatten the guy. Then she points her gun at somebody behind me and says, 'I'm a dead shot, so decide which testicle you're more partial to, Mike or Joe, cuz one of 'em's coming off if that gun pulls up one more inch—now drop it!'

"One second, maybe two—*plink,* the sweet sound of metal on concrete. I mean, she could have been wearing a suit and cape. In fact, I do believe seeing an article of clothing flapping in the wind."

The Drama God of Thunder put both hands over his heart. "I'm in love."

"The only thing flapping, Thor, is your tongue," Mark volleyed on the way to his desk the morning after the St. Claire murder. "And don't bother to ask; she's mine."

"I want her, Truitt. I *need* her. How 'bout an even trade for Forenza? He snores on stakeouts, but he'll always spring for coffee."

"Forget it. No trade-downs."

"I'll pull rank. Lest you forget, I'm the senior investigator in this department."

Mark cast a nonchalant glance in Brentsen's direction. "I can see the headlines in tomorrow's *Star Tribune*—Veteran Cop Hits the Deck While Female Partner Apprehends Suspects."

"On second thought, I don't like buying coffee."

"That's what I figured." Truitt winked at Maune, who was staying disengaged, which, for her, was no hardship when it came to interacting with, well, just about anyone.

Sylkie Maune, Mark's new partner, had tragically lost the safety and innocence of childhood in the wake of her mother's death in the 1995 bombing of the Alfred P. Murrah Federal Building in Oklahoma City. The indelible horror spurred her on to a career in police work, and while she earned high marks for her accomplishments in getting the bad guys off the streets, it did little to resolve the loss of her mother or to pacify her demons.

"Thanks for not letting me get carried off in true Viking fashion," Sylkie sniped, her sparkling blue-gray eyes still shedding the effects of an abbreviated sleep due to the previous day's extended shift. "So are we off chasing clown killers today?"

Mark flashed a weak smile. "Clown killers, convenience-store-clerk killers—all priorities. But to answer your question, I'm sure Guy's gonna want us to jump on the St. Claire murder."

Maune raised her eyebrows. "Or as the *Pioneer Press* labeled it—The Circus Murder."

"Great. It's taken on a life."

"This is getting ugly." Guy Lompello drummed a pencil on his battered oak desk. "The feds are on this like maggots on a three-day-old roadkill."

Maune winced. "Yuk."

"Sorry. Poor analogy. But it's been, what? Twenty-four hours? I'm getting swamped for information. Upstairs wants progress reports. What can I tell them? After witnessing that…whatever that was yesterday, I don't even know what questions to ask." Guy's weathered cheeks were puffing like a blowfish. "I feel like I'm on a two-legged stool, and I can foresee the tip coming. I just don't know if it's gonna be heads or tails."

Mark was used to the lieutenant's dramatics. In a most undramatic response, he countered, "Does it make a difference?"

Lompello scowled, "Of course. If I fall forward, I have a chance of landing on my feet."

"Or your nose."

"I'm pulling for forward momentum. Anyway, Captain Kirgalis called, said a couple of FBI agents are going to stop by, want to hook into our investigation."

"Why?" Maune raised a brow.

"Why—what?" Lompello shot back.

"Why are the feds getting involved?"

"They're considering St. Claire's killing a possible case of domestic terrorism. And, of course, with the bank connection, you have the interstate-commerce thing."

"Too bad they didn't show this much interest in protecting our financial infrastructure when all the bad loans were being sold. A little late to the party, aren't they?"

Lompello cast a stern eye. "Save the editorial, Sergeant Maune. We've got a killer to catch. Let's focus on that."

Maune grimaced, looking like she had sampled Lompello's roadkill. A shallow "okay" dribbled out. Wrong response.

Guy leaned forward and rested his elbows on his desk. Mark noticed his bottom lip pulsate a slight quiver, which signaled an internal meltdown had been initiated, which signaled the old lieutenant was about to go nuclear on his young charge.

"Sergeant Maune, in case yesterday's incident didn't strike you as just a little odd, let me tell you that, in my many decades of police work, I have never, ever, experienced anything even remotely similar to what happened to that poor man. Furthermore, I am not too macho to admit I am darn scared for this city, because whoever was responsible for that treacherous act is not only heinous in the worst sense but is also strategically brilliant. Can you imagine a public execution of that magnitude while taunting us with that fake radio crap and then leaving absolutely no avenue in which to pursue the investigation? This *is* a freaking big deal, Sylkie, and I need you to focus on what your role is or I guarantee it won't be long before you won't have a role, at least not in this precinct you won't."

A deflated Sylkie Maune momentarily fidgeted in her chair, then looked Lompello in the eye, and waved a couple of mini nods at him. She bent but didn't break. Tough girl. However, she checked off a mental note to keep her opinions to herself—at least in front of the lieutenant.

Mark smiled. He had been on the receiving end of many a "teaching" moment from Guy over the years. Mark *was*, however, more than a little concerned about his new partner. Sylkie had a tendency to shoot from the lip, and because of the violent manner in which her mother had died, she carried a chip on her shoulder the size of Iceland. Mark knew unless she overcame this hurdle, it was bound to diminish, if not outright ruin her career. Though he believed Sylkie's path to an inner healing should include an expanded social life, she insisted her dog, Oscar, and her sister, who also lived in the Twin Cities, satisfied any requisite for close relationships.

The atmosphere inside Lompello's office was still rarified when two sharply dressed men filled the doorway. The older and taller dark-skinned man looked to be in his forties. Mark figured the younger Caucasian man was in his early thirties, but bless him, he owned one of those "forever young" smooth-skinned faces that complemented intense-blue eyes and coal-black hair combed to one side, save for a few strands that insisted on taking up post over his forehead. Sylkie gave the men a quick glance and then donned an uninterested look. *At least she attempted to*, Mark thought.

The older man addressed Guy, "Good morning, ah, Lieutenant Lompello? I'm Special Agent James Renner. This is Special Agent Cason Maxwell. I assume you were notified we were coming."

Lompello frowned. "What took you so long to get here?"

Introductions were passed around. Special Agent Maxwell all but froze in place when he shook hands with Sylkie. Maune mumbled a nearly imperceptible "hello."

Renner looked uncomfortable. The office was cramped, the vibes anything but melodic. "So what can you tell us about the St. Claire murder?"

Lompello pointed to two empty chairs. "Strange. That's all I can say regarding St. Claire's murder because that's all I know about St. Claire's murder. However, I'm sure your presence will shift the investigation into a higher gear."

Maxwell felt the sting. Sylkie was impressed with the lieutenant's bravado. Mark knew Guy was only protecting his turf.

As the discussion dragged on, Mark distanced himself, longing for his old partner, Jamie Littlebird. He conceded Jamie was happy in his new job working for the Bureau of Indian Affairs, but doggone it, they had been the perfect duo for the past eleven years and…

"… Is that okay with you, Mark, if we meet here for briefings each morning?" Lompello's tone was conspicuously half-hearted.

"Yeah, uh, sure. That's fine." *Not fine. I lost the best partner a cop could have when Jamie left the force. My newbie has the disposition of a barracuda. A clown—no—man was blown up in front of my eyes. And now I have to make smiley face to the feds every morning. How much better can it get?* Mark decided the word for the day would be *resilient*.

*****

Professor Kendrick Laberday gazed down at the Mississippi River drifting lazily past his office window on the Wherland-Vickers college campus. Located two bends south of downtown Saint Paul, the private college was one of the earliest institutions of higher learning to be founded in Minnesota. From the onset, Vickers distinguished itself as a top-tier college, both in the state and nation. Its prominence attracted elite educators from around the world, and among the very brightest of the bright was Ken Laberday. Regrettably, the dark forces that possessed the promising young professor crushed all the positive contributions Laberday could have made to the learning process—dark forces that confined him to a strange netherworld common to the few percent of society suffering from the syndrome clinically defined as antisocial personality disorder. In layman's terms, psychopathy or sociopathy. Darker still, Laberday mingled among an even narrower caste—that awful guild of violent psychopaths.

Ken's attention drifted to the swirling eddies of turbulence pushed along by river currents, their mission seemingly to devour the delicate ripples of water born of a lazy summer breeze. The watery skirmish, suddenly trumped by a flock of squawking Canada geese gliding in for a respite, was abruptly dismissed as dark thoughts of the dramatic erasure of John St. Claire seared through the professor's mind. The whole delicious performance demanded multiple encores. A well-conceived plan carried out to perfection.

And now I have their attention.

Included in his cruel resume of antisocial behavior was one in which Ken Laberday particularly delighted. Exploiting features that included a tall, slim frame, wavy chestnut-brown hair combed front to back, and a noble Latin nose set between high cheekbones, the professor excelled in chalking up conquests of fondled flesh with the regularity of a fitness addict's visits to the gym. Decidedly not to the world's betterment, a moment of intimacy thirty-six years previous had created this handsome monster, who delighted in preying on those so unfortunate as to drift into his cunning, sadistic world.

"… And so the question becomes: Is the path to long-term economic stability to be found in a 'hands-off' or at best 'hands-slap' policy by the federal government toward our largest financial institutions? Or do you think the government should exercise strict controls to keep the 'captains of capitalism' from crashing our economy into another meltdown? Roll that thought around and be prepared to write a short essay next time."

A hand went up. "To what 'controls' are you referring?"

Laberday assessed not the question but the student. He had felt her radar lock on him for the past several sessions. She wasn't bad looking. No wedding ring. Available? Possibly. Vulnerable? Hopefully.

"Think Glass-Steagall, Dodd-Frank. Think the role of the Federal Reserve. Think the Department of Justice—or not, in their case."

"Okay, got it," the woman nodded.

"Don't forget, people, your term papers are due next week." Laberday gathered up his notes and placed them into a folder.

"Professor Laberday?" It was the pretty brunette.

"Yes, how may I help you?"

The woman blushed, her tongue suddenly becoming pregnant. "I, ah…have some questions about my term paper. I thought, maybe, if you could give me some insight into…"

Laberday cut her off. "I have another class coming up, but if you come to my office at three-thirty, I would be happy to help you. By the way, I'm terrible with names…"

"Nora Balfour. I'll be at your office at three-thirty."

CHAPTER 3

Cason Maxwell felt kind of or sort of intimidated by the lady sitting across the table from him in the first-precinct conference room. He couldn't help but wonder how a woman that hot could laser such a cold stare. Finally, he blurted out, "So what's been gleaned from the van used in the St. Claire killing?"

Waging her own battle to click thoughts of Maxwell into the trash bin and concentrate on the murder, Sylkie shot back, "Our crime lab found the remains of a high-pressure pump that pulled fuel from the gas tank and sprayed it into the van. It delivered the intended result. Much of the van's contents were destroyed in the fire."

Renner nodded. "What do you know about the gun used to fire the bullet through the bank window?"

Truitt said, "30.06 Browning. Remotely fired. The melted remains of a camera were also found, most likely for the viewing pleasure of the mastermind behind the murder. And the audio setup was burned to a crisp."

"Safe to say the killer knows mechanics," Maxwell noted.

Lompello rocked his chair. It squeaked. Irritatingly loud. "All we really know about the van is that it was stolen from a Target parking lot three nights ago. The license plates were not a match to the van. We traced them to a Toyota pickup in Bloomington. The owner had no idea—"

Sylkie interrupted, "Which means, the suspect is very cautious."

"And the victim?" Renner probed. "What do we know about St. Claire's abduction?"

"His car was found at a stop sign two blocks from his house," Sylkie answered. "No witnesses."

"One more thing," Mark offered. "We're checking security-camera tapes within two blocks of the killing for anyone that might look the least bit suspicious."

"And I'm sure he was monitoring—and laughing at us," Lompello winced. Renner rubbed the back of his neck. "Okay, let's throw out a profile."

Mark noticed that Maxwell kept shifting his weight. He guessed either the young FBI agent had hemorrhoids or Maune's presence was making him uncomfortable.

Maxwell said, "For sure, the killer held a grudge against John St. Claire and, possibly, the Independence Republic Bank?"

Sylkie retorted, "But for what reason? Like did he lose his house to the bank?"

"I don't think it's that simple," Mark speculated. "Scores of people have lost their homes in the past few years. If they're bent on revenge, about the worst they do is trash the place to make a statement or rip out the copper to salvage a few bucks. This person is on a completely different level. Obviously we're dealing with an unstable personality who's consumed with hatred."

Maxwell added, "Whatever happened, I hope his anger is satisfied and that there won't be others."

Lompello could feel his nerves short-circuiting. "… Others?"

"Other people he perceives are responsible for his losses."

Renner looked impatient. "That's a possibility and a good reason for us to jump on this quickly." He motioned to Maxwell. "Cason and I have to meet with our supervisor."

Lompello looked equally impatient for them to leave. "Yeah, fine. We'll be sure to keep you informed on any new developments."

After the FBI agents left, Guy turned to Mark. "You holding back on anything you didn't want them to know?"

"No, not really. I'm okay with Renner and Maxwell poking around. They seem like decent guys."

"Do *you* think he'll strike again, Truitt?" Sylkie struggled to keep on task as thoughts of Maxwell kept surfacing.

"Yup. I'd say the effort required to put on that performance was designed to send a message, and it came across loud and clear. I'm guessing his success will have him salivating for more."

"I hope you're wrong," Lompello grimaced.

"So what's next?" Sylkie asked.

Mark stood. "Let's go down to the garage, see if there are any new developments with the van."

On the way to the garage, Mark made a stab at generating a friendly dialogue with his young partner. "Did I see you give that young FBI agent an extra look?" Mark teased.

Sylkie rolled her eyes. "No."

"Okay. Just askin'." *Reminder to self: don't go there again.* "Uh, Sylkie, mind if I ask you something personal?"

"Ask away, Truitt. I might answer, depending on your interpretation of 'personal.'" Up to this point, Sylkie had acknowledged Mark by his last name only. He figured it was her way to let him know she preferred an arm's length relationship. This made Mark all the more determined to establish a beachhead on her granite personality.

"Your name—Sylkie. It's so unusual. How did it come about?"

Sylkie turned her head; a hint of smile surfaced. "My birth name was Sylvia. When I was crib-size, my mother called me little Sylvie. My sister, who is two years older than me, interpreted it as Sylkie. Eventually, Sylvie withered, and Sylkie lived on. That's what my mother called me until the day she died. In honor of her memory, I legally changed my name to Sylkie."

"Nice story. Nice name."

"Yeah. My mom was quite a person..." Maune's voice trailed off.

*****

Ken Laberday yawned, pulled in a long breath of damp Mississippi River air, and watched a sailboat pull into the marina at the bottom of the hill, on which he was perched, and maneuver into a slip. Behind him, the streetlights of Red Wing popped on as an orange-red sun dipped behind the river bluff. He stiffened slightly as he observed the boat's lone occupant secure his craft.

With the boat tied to the dock, the man gripped a tote with one hand and futilely swatted at a hoard of swarming mosquitoes with the other. Attempting to outpace the pesky insects, he hurried across a parking lot, aiming for the solace of his Navigator. Ken drove alongside and asked for directions to a nearby casino.

Several miles from the marina, a dazed and confused Garrett Dover awoke on the floor of the professor's van, his hands and feet bound in duct tape.

"Who are you? What do you want?" Duel waves of panic and anger washed over him.

Laberday glanced over his shoulder. "You're wasting your energy thrashing around back there, Garrett. May as well relax and enjoy the ride. But to answer your question as to what I want? Let me put it this way: John St. Claire was my opening act, and you will be starring in my second act." Ken chuckled. "Yes, Garrett, you're going to be in my 'circus of justice.' Aren't you excited?"

Dover tugged at his restraints. "What…? You had something to do with *that*?"

"No, I *was* that."

Dover prayed he had slipped and hit his head on a dock post. This *had* to be a dream.

"You see, Garrett, I know what you did. You were in charge of your bank's bond department, through which you orchestrated the bundling of subprime home mortgage loans into low-quality bonds. Your bank held on to some of the bonds, and you sold the rest to investors, as in pension funds, insurance companies, and other invest-ment banks. When the homeowners who owned the loans began to default in droves, your bonds calved into the financial abyss."

Dover's defiant tone masked an inner dread. "No way. I sold only A-rated bonds."

"Forget it, Garrett; I know the drill. The bond-rating agencies were in your back pocket. Your so-called *A*s were nothing more than recycled *B*s. They had a 100 percent chance of failing, and when you realized they were drowning, you tried to peddle the bonds *your* bank owned. But you couldn't get rid of them all, and Independence Republic Bank ultimately took big losses. But so what? In the good times, you were paid huge bonuses for all those scummy bonds you put together. Bonds that drew in honest money only to collapse."

"I didn't do anything illegal. I followed the money, worked for my bank's fair share."

"Save your plea bargaining for a higher power—which you'll soon be facing."

Dover abandoned the head-on-post theory. This was all too real.

After a long ride, Laberday pulled into the tree-lined driveway of his country home north of the Twin Cities. The several-acre property afforded Ken the isolation he needed to tinker with custom-made props like the ones he had installed in the stolen van used in the St. Claire murder.

The success of his next act demanded additional creativeness. Satisfied his newest circus act was field-ready and having summoned Mr. Garrett Dover as the main attraction, Kendrick was ready to put his insane plan into action. He glanced at his watch. *In a little over twenty-four hours, the Twin Cities will be treated to the next installment of the circus of justice.*

Laberday pushed the remote for his garage door. A Ford F150 sat ready for duty in the spare stall. He eased the van alongside, killed the motor, retrieved a roll of duct tape from the passenger's seat, and climbed in the back. Ken knelt beside Dover, reached a hand behind Garrett's head, and grabbed a clump of his blond, surfer-boy hair.

Ken pulled him close; his hot, sour breath washed over Garrett's face; and his lips drew next to Dover's ear. "You thought you were so smart, Garrett, getting those big bonuses, living the playboy life. Your greed served you well, didn't it? Bought you all the toys you ever wanted. And what did I get? Lucky me; I got to see my hard-earned money disappear down a rabbit hole. That was *my* payoff. Well, you know what, Garrett? That's not acceptable—not acceptable at all. This time around, *you're* going down the rabbit hole." Ken ran his tongue along Dover's ear. A low, guttural laugh rumbled from his throat.

Rapid, shallow breaths passed through Dover's quivering lips. His eyes pleaded for mercy.

Ken glared at the petrified abductee. "I hear it's never too late to repent, Garrett. Think you can make a run at it in the next twenty-four hours? Let's hope so cuz that's when you'll be timing out."

After wrapping a few rounds of duct tape around Dover's mouth and eyes, Kenny stepped out of the garage and into the blackness, his dark form sheltered under a hunkering canopy of tree limbs, the branches hanging down like menacing tentacles. He took a moment to stand in the quiet of the night and relax. Impossible. Every time he thought about this whole ugly situation, his thoughts regressed to a new and deeper shade of dark.

Foremost on his mind was the failure of his business venture. It was an online school designed to help students who were having problems understanding subjects such as math, physics, and chemistry, providing practical methods of grasping basic concepts. Ken knew it would succeed because he had time-tested the material. All his savings were sunk into the project, and all of it was lost when the economy crashed. But did his bitterness stem from his failure to help students in need? Maybe. A little. Then again, as psychopaths are driven by their self-interests and delusions, Kendrick Laberday was no exception. An expert at showing feigned concern and consideration for others, Kenny was really all about Kenny. And, of course, there was the thing with his mother.

The fact he had been blindsided by others more cunning than him tormented his egocentric mind. *I should have seen the meltdown coming. I should have been the one making millions from the destruction.* His ponderings were like acid dripping on an open wound.

Ken sunk his hands into his pockets and ambled along the rutted path leading to a machine shed he used as a fabricating shop. He looked up at the night sky. An orange cuticle of new moon sliced its way to the horizon. Venus had battled its way to the zenith position and now dominated all other competing globes of light. *Just like me, alone at the top.*

Ken turned around and headed back to the garage. *Enough of this. I've got things to do before tomorrow night's performance.*

Once inside, he opened the rear access window on the F150's topper. The truck had been stolen from a shopping center and sported plates pulled from another vehicle. Separating vehicles from their rightful owners was no big deal. Actually, Ken enjoyed the adrenalin rush. He checked the hydraulics and made a few final adjustments. Yes, the topper opened ninety degrees to the side. Yes, fuel was at the ready to be pumped into the cab and box. Finally, he eyed the central component for tomorrow's circus act—the ejection seat. Tested and ready for duty. Satisfied with his handiwork, Ken locked the garage, with its guest safely secured for the night.

CHAPTER 4

Sylkie fought the moment. Not because she was alone in a car with Special Agent Cason Maxwell who had insisted on bringing along his intense-blue eyes, perfect skin, and a very muscular frame judging by the folds in his suit. No, it was because she was alone in a car with Special Agent Maxwell and felt guilty about the internal dormant volcano quivering in pre-eruption quakes. Years of effort had been strategically spent crafting a moat around her personal island of isolation, and this guy came along, plunked down a bridge, and was already halfway across. *So much for preparation and practice.*

"Is this the right exit?" Maxwell asked as they approached the Minneapolis business district.

"Yeah, then take a left at the first stoplight. The Independence Republic Bank is two blocks down. Guess you don't know your way around the city, do you?" Instantly regretting her condescending tone, Sylkie mentally placed a boot to the booty.

Cason shrugged. "I've only been in the Twin Cities a little over a month. Born and raised in Chicago. How about you, Sylkie? Are you from around here?"

Roll out the razor wire. Not going down that road. "Nope. Oklahoma City."

"Nice town. I spent a short time there when I was in training. That federal-building bombing left scars, didn't it? Devastating for a lot of people."

Tell me about it. "Pull into this parking ramp. Bank's around the corner."

There were three people Sylkie and Maxwell planned to interview in regard to the St. Claire murder. The first two employees they questioned provided no helpful information. They were winding up the third interview when a taller balding man carrying a tense look approached. He introduced himself as Tim Selman.

"When you're through here, I would like a moment." His eyes darted rapidly between Cason and Sylkie as if he was afraid they were going to arrest him for some unknown offense. Sylkie speculated what role hypertension might play in his life.

A few minutes later, Selman escorted them into his office. "I understand you're investigating the John St. Claire murder?"

"We are. I'm Sergeant Maune, Metro. Special Agent Maxwell is FBI."

"Okay. Um, I don't know if this is relevant or not, but one of our former employees might be missing."

"Go on," Cason nodded.

Selman kept fumbling with his hands like he was trying to decide what their purpose was and where he should keep them. "His name is Garrett Dover. He was the head of our bond department, left a couple years ago. Garrett was involved with some things at the bank that were, well, not illegal, but in my view, unethical. He made a lot of money for the bank by selling mortgage bonds he had bundled from individual loans. Looking back, many of the loans were of questionable integrity. As a hedge, he used the bank's money to buy insurance against some of those same bonds. He was granted very generous bonuses for his efforts. I'm talking in the millions... Well, that's what I heard. Anyway, when the industry collapsed, the bank lost money. Garrett fell out of favor and was forced out."

Sylkie regarded the unsolicited explanation a bit lengthy. "So what information do you have concerning Mr. Dover?"

Selman found pockets for his hands but then commenced to pace in jerky, bobbing steps. Irritating to say the least. "I'm about the only one from the bank who keeps in touch with him. We get together occasionally to golf, spend time on his sailboat, stuff like that. Anyway, his girlfriend called me this morning. Asked if he was with me or if I'd seen him in the last twenty-four hours." Selman quickly added, "Just so you know, I haven't seen Garrett in over a month. She said their last conversation was yesterday morning. He told her he was going sailing and might come home late. When she got up this morning, he wasn't there."

Maxwell asked, "Where does he keep his boat?"

"Red Wing Marina."

Sylkie asked, "Has she checked with the marina?"

"She did. They said his boat was in its slip and his Navigator was in the parking lot."

"Think he might be with someone?"

Selman exhaled a nervous laugh. "You mean, like a woman? Oh, I doubt it, Sergeant Maune. If you knew his girlfriend, she's ah—"

Sylkie finished the sentence, "She's everything a man could want, and then some, right?

"That's right. And then some."

Maxwell raised an eyebrow. "Everything money can buy?"

Selman nodded.

Sylkie whipped out a notebook. "Thanks for your input, Mr. Selman. We'll look into it. I'll need the girlfriend's name and address."

"I'll call Renner," Cason said as he and Sylkie stepped into the bright morning sunshine. "We'll check out the marina. We have no other leads, so I guess we should grab at anything that's connected to the bank."

"I'll hook up with Truitt. We'll pay the girlfriend a visit. I'm anxious to meet 'the perfect woman.'"

I think I might be looking at her right now, Maxwell reflected while feeling a minor blush welling up, a self-reminder of his shyness.

Sylkie took notice of the slight eruption behind his shave line and wondered what that was about.

An uncomfortably quiet ride ended with Maxwell dropping Sylkie off at precinct headquarters. She watched him drive away, along with a dollop of her estrogen along for the ride and waving at her through the rear window. Like it or not, for Sylkie Maune, the genie was out of the bottle.

*****

Ken Laberday approached downtown Minneapolis with all the confidence of a seasoned field general. Glancing in the rearview mirror, he complimented himself on his choice of disguise. For sure, the mustache and glasses made for a more intriguing (and just as handsome) face. Closing in on the target, he meticulously reviewed the details one last time. Precise timing and proper execution were critical. And as far as rewards for the impending spectacle? For the public, it would be one circus act closer and hopefully appreciated to realizing that finally someone was standing up to the financial terrorists. For Kenny, it would be another star on his superiority badge.

Rather than being hunted, I should be getting a medal, Laberday mused as he pulled into a parking ramp on Eighth Avenue. Across the street was the upscale Admiral Suites Hotel; and along with the parking ramp, it would be the centerpiece of tonight's show.

Ken backed the F150 into a slot on the fifth and top level of the ramp. He stepped out of the truck, checked a wisp of anxiety with a long pull of fresh air, and glanced at his watch. Midnight. The downtown crowd should still be partying at this hour on a Friday night. Briefcase in hand and chaos on his mind, the professor confidently set his destination for the Admiral Suites piano bar.

Music drifted toward Ken as he stepped into the bar. The entertainer, a smallish man with a full head of white hair and with a delicate face, smiled blithely as he crooned an old Dean Martin tune. He was good, sounded like Deano.

Ken spied an empty stool at the end of the bar and settled in. The hotel held a familiarity, as it had served as the playground for several of his past one-nighters. The trysts typically included a few drinks, followed by an expensive dinner at the hotel's restaurant, and ended in one of the suites. Ken's seduction routine was well rehearsed; the women were more or less forgettable. Laberday's sex life paralleled his eating habits—new menus were a must. Leftovers simply wouldn't do.

Ken played with his drink and avoided eye contact. At 12:45 a.m., he left the bar and settled into a chair in the window-lined hallway accessing the bar, restaurant, and hotel lobby. The entrance door to the lobby required a key card. It was not a problem, as the solution was staggering in his direction.

Laberday pressed his cell phone to an ear, faking a conversation. Two women wobbled by, the more unsteady of the two throwing him an "I want to lick you all over" gaze. Ken rose from his chair and followed. The woman who hadn't given him the long once-over swiped her card. The security lock clicked, and she pushed on the door. Ken grabbed the edge of the door, smiled, and motioned them through. Looking away from the direction of the front desk, he wedged in between the ladies and made small talk as they passed through the lobby. The lady who wanted to nest with the professor tried to pull him into an elevator for a ride up and probably for another ride in her room. He gently pried his arm from her grasp, blew the women a kiss, and headed for the men's restroom.

Ken settled into a stall and made a final check on the contents in his briefcase. All the parts and pieces were accounted for. He put his head back and closed his eyes. His thoughts drifted back in time to his youth—his insufferable, lonely youth.

Kendrick Laberday was an only child—his mother, a surgeon; his father, an accountant. Never allowed to have a real childhood, Kendrick's abusively dominant mother—often to the dismay of his gentile, all-too-submissive father—constantly pressured him to excel in school.

Sports? For the lame of brain. The arts? Reserved for underperformers. No matter how great the swell of accomplishments, it wasn't good enough. Trouble was, young Ken worshiped his mother and constantly sought her approval. Unfortunately, whenever Ken paraded home his latest academic achievement, a platitude would invariably be substituted for deserved praise. Her rejections left their mark.

It was 1:30 a.m. Time to make the call.

"Hennepin County Emergency Coordinator. How may I help you?"

"Good evening, emergency coordinator. I want to inform my friends in the police department that the circus is back in town with a brand-new act promising to bring heart-stopping thrills. The good seats will go fast, so tell any and all interested circus lovers to hurry to the Admiral Suites Hotel. However, I must warn you, this time, there won't be any 'clowning' around, only spectacular daredevil stunts. Better get on the horn. The show is about to begin."

The word *clown* set the 911 dispatcher in motion.

Laberday exited the men's room and rounded a corner to a bank of three elevators. He removed a smoke canister from his briefcase and set it behind a stand that supported a flower arrangement. He then depressed the elevator call button. A few moments later, the doors on the middle elevator opened. Ken stepped inside and called the fifth floor. He calmly folded his hands, closed his eyes, and rehearsed his moves.

The ride ended with the doors opening to a small lobby adorned with a generic mountain painting and two huge pots sprouting long-stemmed ferns. Ken walked across the lobby and scanned the hallway in both directions. No activity. The guests were tucked in for the night.

Ken opened his briefcase and pulled out a second smoke canister. Whistling at a whisper, he set it in front of the elevator, removed the cover, and ignited its contents. Smoke spewed from the vessel. Ken got back in the elevator and was soon on the fourth floor. He quickly set the next canister in place and ignited it. As he exited onto the third floor, fire alarms sounded. Perfect—as planned. He electronically ignited the canister he had positioned on the ground floor as well as igniting a final canister at his feet. Ken stepped into the hallway, high-fiving himself. So far, so good.

Doors flew open as half-dressed, frightened patrons tumbled into the hallway and headed for the stairwell. Ken pulled his shirt out of his pants for effect and joined the crowd.

Mark was still wiping the fog out of his eyes as he screamed down I-94. He surmised a host of vehicles would be headed in the same direction. He prayed this was a false alarm, but his prayer battled a growing sense of reality. The circus killer was smart, and this scenario presented all the trappings for an unpleasant ending. For sure, there would be a crowd and much confusion, both items in the perp's favor.

A sea of flashing red, blue, and white lights from fire trucks, squad cars, and ambulances greeted Mark as he approached the intersection of Eighth Avenue and Seventeenth Street. Police were setting up barricades, along with struggling to keep a growing crowd in check. Mark pulled his car to the curb and trotted to the hotel. Ahead, he could see people streaming out of the main entrance in various stages of dress and distress. Mark fought against a current of bodies as he made his way inside. He also fought a nagging suspicion that this was a setup, and the crowd was heading in the right direction while he was heading toward dupesville.

A dense haze and pungent odor of burning hydrocarbons engulfed Mark as he made his way across the lobby. He thought he heard his name being called through the clamor and chaos. He turned just as Sylkie grabbed his arm. A moment later, Guy Lompello panted his way over.

"What's going on?" Sylkie winced at the odor.

"What does it smell like to you?" Mark trumped her question.

"I don't know, but it's making my eyes water."

Mark stopped a firefighter rushing past them. "Truitt. Metro Police. Do you have a fire?"

"No, just a lot of smoke and some empty canisters."

Mark apologized to his ignored inner voice and grabbed Sylkie and Guy. "We need to get out front. I'm betting our circus killer is about to put on another show."

Mark's intuition was dead-on. Standing on the sidewalk, only feet away from agents Renner and Maxwell who had just made their way to the hotel, Kendrick Laberday reached in a pocket and activated a small electronic device. *Showtime.*

On the top level of the parking ramp, pneumatically operated cylinders lifted the topper on Laberday's truck box to expose Garrett Dover, who was firmly secured to an ejection seat. Another cylinder telescoped a mast with an attached speaker.

"Good evening, ladieees and gentlemen," the speaker bellowed. "Tonight we have a jaw-dropping act that is sure to excite *and* ignite your desire for the thrills and spills only *this* circus can deliver. Tonight, it is my pleasure to introduce theee...high-flying, flaming human cannonball none other thaaaan… Misterrrr Garrett Dover, former bond manager at Independence Republic Bank."

"Get your car; catch up with us in the parking ramp!" Mark hollered to Sylkie, who was at a sprint before he finished the sentence. He hailed Maxwell and Renner.

The speaker pushed on. "You see, folks, Mr. Dover is a very smart guy. He's made money from other people's financial distress. In fact, there's a term for this thievery. It's called the Mortgage Misery Index. He got the money, and you got the misery. By the way, how much bailout money have *you* received from our dear uncle? Now Garrett wants to give something back. He's volunteered to entertain you this evening by catapulting from this parking ramp in a flaming ejection seat to the top of the Admiral Hotel—what a sport!"

Sylkie pulled alongside her rides as they approached the second-level ramp. Mark flopped into the front seat. "… Too old for this." Renner tumbled in the back. Maxwell had hardly broken a sweat. They squealed up to the third level.

"Okay, folks, help me with the countdown…five…four…"

Fourth level.

"Three…two…one." Dover furiously struggled against his restraints, all too aware that his living nightmare was about to reach its climax.

"Good luck… Garrett!"

Sylkie's tires kissed the access ramp at the top level.

With the aid of a catapult and rocket combination, Dover's chair jettisoned from the truck. A moment later, chair and occupant ignited in a reddish-orange flame, at which point, gravity took over.

The speaker barked one last time. "Ooooh…looks like Garrett's not going to make it. Sorry, folks. No refunds."

Sylkie stopped the car at the top of the ramp. Mark cautioned, "Stay back; remember what happened at the bank."

A high-pressure pump fired up. A moment later, the truck exploded in a ball of flames. Firemen quickly doused the flames engulfing Dover's smoking, hot body. Kenny looked on with the rest of the crowd. Yes, the evening had gone precisely as he had envisioned. *But then, I am, after all, the great ringmaster of justice.* His plan successfully executed and ego satisfied, Ken hustled to a nearby Holiday Inn where he had made a reservation. A hot bath and a good night's sleep would be most welcome.

CHAPTER 5

Mark pondered a moment, and then it hit him. The smell in Guy's office reminded him of his old elementary school—a mixture of weathered varnish and veneer and oak flooring mixed with an added whiff of a possible long-forgotten food item stashed deep inside that battered oak desk. Lompello wasn't a sorting-and-throwing kind of guy, as evidenced in the ancient green ink blotter curled at the edges from repeated salvos of spilled coffee. It had graced the top of his desk for as long as Mark could remember.

"I met with Captain Kirgalis this morning." Guy drew a raspy breath as Mark and Sylkie settled into chairs. "The poor man is about ready to suck on a cyanide capsule. This Dover killing has put a lot of pressure on the department. Unfortunately, I couldn't come up with any news to brighten his day. I'm hoping we'll be able to glean a clue or two from the Dover murder. At any rate, we need to make some headway. Quickly. Like yesterday."

Sylkie frowned. "I gotta admit I'm confused about the killer's motives for killing these people. I plead ignorance as far as the world of high finance is concerned, and to tell you the truth, I'd rather pull hair globs out of a bathroom sink drain than get a discourse on it."

"Let me take a shot at painting a picture for you." Cason Maxwell threw Sylkie a meek smile as he and Renner stepped into Lompello's office.

"Uh, sure. Enlighten us." Sylkie feasted on Maxwell an extra moment. Lompello motioned them to sit.

"Okay, for simplicity's sake, let's pretend the bicycle trade has suddenly become lucrative and you want to cash in on it.

Unfortunately, quality bike parts are in short supply, so you buy cheap, inferior parts, paint them up, slap the bikes together, and sell the creations as high-quality bikes to unsuspecting buyers—in reality, investors. These buyers [investors] love your product so much they demand more, and the only way you can keep up with the demand is to buy any and every crappy part you can squeeze out of *your* suppliers. Of course, the bikes won't last long because the parts are inferior, but the buyers don't know that. They think they have fine, long-lasting bikes. In fact, they're certain of it because the bikes [bonds] are stamped with the quality seal of the 'National Bike Manufacturers Association.' Unfortunately, sooner than later, the bikes fail and the bike buyers [investors] are out their money."

Mark interrupted, "Hold on. How did the quality seal get on the bikes? Isn't that collusion?"

Maxwell raised an eyebrow. "You'd think so. In reality, the fictitious Manufacturers Association represents the bond-rating agencies. Their part of the story gets very murky. I don't know how it all went down, but I do know that no one is seriously looking at the way mortgage-backed bonds were rated during the subprime-mortgage era."

Sylkie was starting to catch on. "So who made money, and who didn't?"

"Back to the story. You thought the good times would never stop rolling, and so you borrowed way more money than you should have to pay for bike parts. Once your bikes started to fail, the buyers disappeared, and you're left with an inventory of crappy bike parts and no money coming in. Debt piles up, and you're soon out of business. Unless, of course, you're well-connected."

Renner jumped in. "Casey's saying that the big investment banks grossly overleveraged themselves. And this is the cruel twist: not only did the investors—that's most of us, one way or another—lose when the economy crashed, more of the people's money went out the door when it was handed to the financial institutions in order to bail them out."

Lompello's chair pitched a long, slow squeak as he tipped it back, his mind deep in thought. "Who won then?"

Casey said, "People like Dover, who raked in huge bonuses when things were going well. But even his reward was a pittance compared to the few, and I mean very few hotshots who actually studied the subprime-mortgage bond market in depth and realized it would soon collapse under its own weight. They made millions by either shorting the bonds or finding a sucker to take the other side of an insurance policy against them."

Guy felt a headache coming on. "Thanks for the lesson, but let's get to the business at hand. What have we pieced together from last night?"

Mark said, "Crime lab's sorting through the debris, but they haven't come up with much. The explosion destroyed most of the evidence. The truck was stolen and dressed with stolen license plates. The killer filed off identification numbers on the parts and pieces used to launch Dover. Sylkie and I will check the hotel registry and also look at the tape from the surveillance camera that scans the area around the registration desk. And we'll interview whoever was on duty in the hotel, piano bar, and restaurant."

"How about you guys?" Guy looked at Maxwell.

"Our supervisor wants to meet in an hour," Cason grimaced. "I didn't like the tone of his voice."

Mark scanned the airwaves for blues music as he and Sylkie drove to the Admiral Hotel. Also, he silently strategized on ways to punch through her brick-and-mortar personality.

"So what do you think of him?"

"What do I think of who?"

"Maxwell. I could sense good karma between you two."

"Oh, really? Now you're a psychic?" Sylkie dove into her bunker, only to reemerge. "Do you really think there might be?"

"Yes, and exposing a little vulnerability on your part is not sign of weakness. Give him a chance. I think he's a nice young man."

"We're almost at the hotel." Ice crystals chipped off Sylkie's words, but Mark detected a slight thawing in Ms. Polar Plunge.

"Will you at least try to keep an open mind about him?"

"Okay. Okay. I'll think about."

Mark and Sylkie exited the hotel a couple of hours later with little to show for their effort except the surveillance tape, a copy of the previous night's registry, and the bartender's remembrance of a tall, thin man with a briefcase who possibly might be a person of interest. Sylkie expressed frustration that the hotel had provided little in the way of clues.

"We need a break, Truitt. We need for him to make a mistake."

"Don't count on luck. The guy may be unstable, but he's smart."

"They all screw up eventually."

"How long did it take to catch the Unabomber?"

"The Unabomber didn't launch his victims off parking ramps."

*****

Ken Laberday was well into his morning's lecture. "And so the seventies saw the credit-card industry arise from the banks' need to establish a new source of revenue. What better way to serve the baby boomers' demand for goods and services than to provide an easy and addictive means to satisfy their financial hunger."

Ken glanced at his notes. "Of course, it goes without saying the industry has grown to the point today that a good chunk of the American consumer is monetarily chained to the banking institutions, paying them homage each month.

"All right, let's fast-forward several years and focus on the next great issue affecting the pocketbooks of many Americans—the mortgage industry.

"With the turn of the century, it was becoming harder and harder for the mortgage lenders to keep the money flowing because people that could legitimately afford to own their homes were already settled in. Essentially, the market was drying up, and those that lived off the industry had to find a way to keep the engine turning. Ultimately, they came up with a brilliant idea—entice people into homes they couldn't afford with gimmicks like the adjustable-rate mortgage, teasing them in with artificially low initial rates. When the rates reset and the homeowners couldn't afford the higher payments, the answer was…what?" Ken waited for a response.

A hand shot up. Nora Balfour. *Interesting,* Laberday thought. *She wants to be the good student, and I want to be the good "teacher."*

"Yes, go ahead."

"Refinance," Balfour offered.

"Right. And what justified the refinancing?"

"The value of homes was increasing," another student offered.

"Yes, and prompted by the mortgage lenders." Barely above a whisper to emphasize the point, Ken imparted, "Then one day, the bubble burst, and it all came tumbling down. So there you have the essence of the subprime market. Okay, that's enough for today. We'll—" Ken could not help but notice a hand waving furiously.

"Something you want to add?"

The owner of the waving hand cleared his throat. "Is this what the so-called circus-acts murders are about? Weren't the people that the killer's taken out benefitting from all this mortgage hocus-pocus?"

Before Ken could orchestrate an answer, another student spoke up, "You mean the guy the papers have labeled the ringmaster? He's all over the Internet. I read a post this morning on Facebook: 'Where the feds wimp out on crime, ringmaster wipes out the criminals.'"

Kendrick Laberday suddenly felt giddy. He could barely contain himself. How he would have loved to openly bask in the glow of his triumph!

"Settle down now," Ken admonished. "We all know order cannot be maintained in a society where a vigilante mentality prevails. The rule of law must always carry the day." The repulsive discourse stuck to Ken's tongue like uncooked oatmeal.

"Don't forget the test this Friday on chapters 11 and 12."

The classroom emptied with the exception of Nora Balfour. Lingering, she slowly gathered her books and papers.

"So what do you think about today's lecture?" Ken tested. "I surely didn't mean to start a discussion about this circus killer…or whatever they call him."

Nora blushed. "Well, it was kind of a natural connection. And you know how people are drawn to dramatic events."

"Am I to interpret 'dramatic events' as being preferred to the boring subject of economics?" Ken feigned a concerned look.

"Oh, no. I didn't mean it *that* way. I just meant—"

Laberday jokingly cut her off. "I was teasing. I know what you meant. I've been following the story. Evidently, someone's on a crusade targeting high rollers in the finance world." The professor maneuvered a step closer. "Ms. Balfour..."

"Nora."

"Nora. I was just about to have a bite to eat. Would you care to join me? I know a little restaurant off campus with a very good lunch menu."

"Well...why, yes. I would love to." Nora couldn't believe her ears. This was way too good. She choked back her excitement, measuring her words carefully so as not to ruin the moment.

The couple enjoyed a chatty lunch. Ken was the perfect gentleman, charming and witty, all the while sizing Nora up in a concubinary sort of way. Nora, on the other hand, was as giddy as a high-school freshman on her first date. They parted with Norah feeling warm and gushy, while Ken was plotting his next pump-and-dump relationship.

CHAPTER 6

Mark counted the mile markers and pondered the more pleasant side of life as he sped north on US Highway 53, which would take him to the unique and beautiful Arrowhead country of Minnesota, where he could freely ponder the more pleasant side of life. The side opposite the dark failures of the human condition he encountered on a daily basis. The side opposite the hellish netherworld where this circus-acts killer plotted his deadly schemes. The place where Mark knew someday he would have to go retrieve him. But not today. Today he was hooking up with his ex-partner Jamie Littlebird to retrieve lake trout in Minnesota's holy grail of outdoor experiences—the Boundary Waters Canoe Area.

A stab of anticipation gripped Mark as he cruised through the historic Iron Range, where low-grade ore is transformed into the iron-rich pellets that feed the great steel mills of America, which, in turn, spit out the alloyed metal products that forge the cars and buildings and bridges and railroads and countless other things that make our country strong. Left behind for future generations to ponder are the mountains of waste rock keeping sentinel over gigantic scars in the ground, many now submerged under a watery grave and in the depths of which the ghosts of past generations of miners endlessly chip away at the red rock.

Mark continued over the Laurentian Divide, north of which all waters flow into Hudson Bay. Once over the divide, he left Highway 53 and headed northeast. Before long, he was embracing his best friend in a long overdue bear hug.

After a flurry of catching-up talk, Mark warmed the stew his wife, Liz, had sent along. Liz's stew was one of Jamie's favorites, and he savored every bite. There was homemade apple pie for dessert. The offering was Liz Truitt's way of saying, "I miss your smile as much as Mark does."

After the dishes were cleaned and put away, the two friends finalized their plans for the next day's assault on Trout Lake, a short portage north of Jamie's home on Lake Vermilion, where they would test their skills at finding the elusive lake trout. Although Mark was interested in Littlebird's take on the circus murders, tonight's agenda was all about fishing.

The new day dawned clear and calm. Typical morning dampness permeated the air, holding fast the smell of lake. Not a good smell, not a bad smell, just a lake smell. In the distance, the remnants of an early-morning fog were retreating against a strengthening sun. A pair of mallards squawked at Mark and Jamie from a patch of pike reeds as the men loaded their gear into Jamie's boat. In the distance, a boat motored across a stretch of open water and disappeared behind one of the 365 islands that checkerboard the lake.

The mallards sounded a final disapproval as Jamie fired up his twenty-horse Merc. A pleasant ride over the smooth root-beer-colored water ended at a sand beach. From there, an ATV would transport the men over a 160-rod portage to the south end of the deep-water beauty. Soon the two friends were back in their boat. Twenty minutes later, the boat's bow kissed a huge slab of grayish-pink granite rock rising from the lake.

"Looks like quite a drop-off." Mark peered into the translucent water as he hopped out, lifting the bow onto the rock.

Jamie nodded. "It gets deep real fast, and this time of year, the deeper, the better for trout."

After unloading the boat, the men threaded long hooks through small ciscoes, a trout favorite. Mark then held the rods in the air while Jamie grasped their business ends with one hand and maneuvered the motor tiller with the other. He backed the boat out into the lake until he reached a spot over the desired depth and dropped the baited hooks. Soon he was back on shore.

By the time Jamie secured the boat to an overhanging cedar tree, Mark had their rods resting on forked sticks. Now it was up to the trout to provide the action. Hopefully, the fish would hear the call to duty.

The morning sun nosed over the tops of Norway pines, birches, and jack pines, its warmth finding the backs of the fishermen. Heated air aroused the appetites of black flies, which sortied in on human flesh for their first meal of the day. Socks over pants cuffs along with bug spray deflected most of the annoyance. Mark considered it a small price to pay for an otherwise perfect outing. He took a swig of coffee and stretched out. High above, popcorn cumulous clouds sailed beneath a background of blue, not the volatile kind that bring storms but the fleecy, harmless sort. Mark lazily swatted at a fly and let his eyes get heavy. All he wanted from the moment was take in the perfect day.

Suddenly, he sat up. *Almost forgot.* Mark dug into his backpack, checked his watch, and then pulled out a portable radio. He set it on the rock and tuned into WELY, the end-of-the-road radio station. Before long, rousing verses of "In Heaven There Is No Beer" danced over the lake. Yes, it was the Saturday morning polka show, guaranteed to draw in even the most flat-footed fish or, at the very least, put the icing on the perfect morning for Mark. For Jamie—not so much. To him, polka music was akin to 190-proof Everclear; a little was a lot. However, not wanting to sail a black cloud over the otherwise ideal setting, he sucked it up and hummed along with "Roll Out the Barrel" and even lopped off a few foot moves with "The Chicken Dance." But when "Grab Your Balls and Let's Go Bowling" blew out of the speaker, he'd had enough!

"Want to talk about your circus killer?" Jamie broke the spell.

"Huh?" Mark pushed up his bill cap. "Oh…sure." He turned off the radio. "I have a question or two about the case I'd like to run by you."

A much-relieved Jamie said, "Ask away."

Mark sat up, shut off the radio, and rested his elbows on his knees. "The perp seems to be darn near invisible. I mean, he puts on a show worthy of the Cirque du Soleil, minus the killing, of course, and then vanishes. How do we flush him out?"

Littlebird thought for a moment and then pointed to the far shore. "See the shoreline across the bay, all those boulders exposed?"

Mark winked. "Uh, are you about to lay one those nature-to-real-life analogies on me?"

Jamie threw an authoritative look and cracked a smile. "Of course, it's what I do. When we get good rains, the rocks are hidden below the waterline. It takes a lot of water to accomplish that. When we get a dry spell, the rocks reappear. Your killer has to be dishing out a lot of capital to pull off these elaborate schemes. Sooner or later, he'll use it up, make a mistake, expose himself."

"Like the rocks."

"If he continues these public executions, he's bound to leave clues." Jamie smiled, pulled his cap over his eyes, and lay back.

"Ah, I wouldn't get too comfortable if I were you," Mark advised.

"Why not?"

"Cuz your rod tip's waving at you."

Jamie jumped up. Sure enough, the rod was bouncing, and line was peeling off the reel. Littlebird stayed put. Mark knew Jamie wouldn't touch the rod until the line stopped playing out. After a few moments, the line went limp. "He's swallowing it," Jamie said as he carefully picked up the rod. Suddenly the line took off, this time, more aggressively. Jamie pulled back hard on his rod and set the hook.

Several minutes later, Mark dipped their landing net into the lake and retrieved a six-pound lake trout.

"And that's what it's all about," Jamie winked.

"If every day could be like this," Mark fantasized.

"Then it wouldn't be like this cuz it would lose its uniqueness," Littlebird countered.

"Always the philosopher."

Three additional trout and several hours later, the two friends were backing their boat into Lake Vermilion. All too soon, Mark would reluctantly say goodbye to his friend and return home with fresh lake-trout fillets and a new fishing tale.

*****

A break between summer sessions gave Ken Laberday the opportunity to fulfill the next step in his increasingly insane plan to make an example of those he deemed responsible for bringing the United States, along with himself, to its financial knees. Laberday chose Middletown, New York, to execute his newest circus-of-justice performance for two reasons: One, the new location was meant to keep law enforcement off balance. Secondly, the city was highlighted, as it was the present address of his next victim.

Ken spent a full day scouring the city and surrounding countryside. He found irony in the fact that Middletown was little more than a stone's throw from New York City, where much of the great desecration to the economy had found its roots. He hoped the close proximity of his next act would serve notice that the ringmaster was "a-coming."

Wheeling past one of Middletown's premier landmarks, the First Congregational Church, with its tall elegant spire, Ken unemotionally reflected on the serene image it projected. *Too bad life isn't really like that. If it were, I wouldn't have to be here.*

The professor ultimately zeroed in on the home of one Morris Lavonia. Ken parked his car a half block from Lavonia's house and waited. Before long, Morris stepped onto the sidewalk, shih tzu in tow. *Well, well, Mr. Lavonia, the former head of Forrester and Gould, it's nice to meet you.*

Morris Lavonia was indeed the now-retired head of one of the premier bond-rating agencies on Wall Street, with whose blessing (or ignorance) worthless mortgage bonds were upgraded, many all the way to the highest rating of triple A. Unscrupulous traders then peddled the toxic bonds to unsuspecting investors.

Lavonia ambled his way to a park, every so often stopping to chat or allow his dog to process scents from tree trunks and lampposts. Ken pulled into a parking area as Lavonia and pet nonchalantly strolled the asphalt paths along the park's perimeter. Finally, Morris stepped into the parking lot.

"Mr. Lavonia?" Ken called as he pulled alongside.

Lavonia frowned. "Who are you?"

"Mr. Lavonia, I'm Agent Jess Martin with the US Securities and Exchange Commission. I would like to have a word with you." Ken flashed a fake ID.

"What's this about?"

"This is about you, Mr. Lavonia. I suggest you get in the car so we can talk."

Beads of perspiration surfaced on Morris's forehead.

"Mr. Lavonia, we have reason to believe your life may be in danger. Please, get in the car."

Morris looked around and wiped his brow. Hesitantly, he scooped up his dog and settled into the passenger's seat. He measured up Laberday. Ken stared him down. Lavonia sensed a wave of evil engulfing him. "This doesn't have anything to do with those circus killings, does it?"

"This has everything to do with justice of the people, by the people, and for the people, Mr. Lavonia. You have a lot to answer for." The dark excitement in Ken's brain was releasing endorphins sheathed with daggers of revenge and hate. The intenseness of his black menacing disks drove Morris to press hard against the door. The dog puked out a pathetic whimper.

"You're really not with the Securities and Exchange Commission, are you?" Morris queried, fearing the answer.

Ken ignored the question. "What kind of alchemy does it take to make gold out of lead, Morris?"

"What do you mean?"

"You know exactly what I mean." Ken whisked out a knife, pushing its point against Lavonia's neck. The shih tzu growled.

"Look, I swear I didn't know the extent of the incompetence of my underlings."

"Not the right answer, Morris." A trickle of blood channeled onto the knife.

"Okay, Okay—stop. They...said they'd take their business elsewhere. They promised there was solid ground under the bonds. The...business is very competitive, you understand."

"That's what I thought." Ken adopted a melodic tone and stroked the back of Lavonia's head. "Oh, Morris, you should have been so lucky that I truly was from the SEC. Unfortunately it's only me and my solitary quest for truth and justice."

"What do you want?"

"What do I want?" Ken tugged on Lavonia's chin so he could look him in the eye. "I want all of you, Morris."

"Wha—?"

That was all Lavonia could spit out before Ken put him to sleep. Looking around to be sure no one was watching, he unceremoniously tossed the crying canine out the window.

The professor had bagged his quarry. A few details remained. Schedules needed to be checked, as preciseness was crucial. Also, physical props had to be set up and fine-tuned. There was but one day left to prepare for what promised to be a most spectacular event featuring a magician and horses. Lots and lots of horses.

CHAPTER 7

"Morning, guys. Where's Renner?" Mark asked as he pulled coffee from the community pot into a cup begging for a wash and rinse.

"Filling out paperwork on a recent case," Cason shot his answer in Mark's direction as he shot a glance in Sylkie's direction. "The trial date's approaching, and the DA needs to gather in the loose ends. He'll probably be tied up for a few days."

"Any new information to share?" Guy Lompello growled a general inquiry as he sauntered out of his office.

"Good morning to you too," Sylkie dryly answered. "Well, we checked out the guests staying at the Admiral Suites the night of the murder. Mostly dead ends. However, the bartender vaguely recalled a taller, thin guy possibly carrying briefcase that came in around midnight and left about an hour later. He couldn't provide a good description on facial features."

"Okay...and?"

"Truitt and I tracked down two women who showed up on the surveillance camera at the registration desk around one a.m. They had made an ice run, forgot their key cards in their room, and needed to be let in. They admitted to being somewhat sloshed, but one of the ladies 'kind of' remembers a guy coming through the hotel entrance door with them. Her description of him remotely matched the bartender's. However, they differed in that she was sure he had a mustache but the bartender couldn't swear to it. We went through the entire hotel registry, matched names with faces. Zero matches for the tall, thin guy."

"Did you get sketches with and without facial additives?"

"Yup, although the face-only sketch looks pretty generic." Mark handed Guy a folder.

Mark rubbed his chin. "Whoever this guy is, all we can really be sure of is the tall and thin part. He may be just another face in the crowd, but then again, we have so little to go on." Mark turned to Maxwell. "If you're free Cason, how about you go with Sylkie and pass the sketch around at the bank, the marina, and Admiral Hotel." Mark hoped Maxwell would bite on the proposition.

"Sounds good. I've got nothing else going." Maxwell looked at Sylkie as if waiting for her approval. Sylkie said nothing, but a nuance of color appeared on her cheeks.

Mark quickly added, "I'll be working on a profile."

Guy threw Mark a studied look as Sylkie and Cason disappeared from the office. "If I didn't know you better, I'd say you're playing cupid with those two young people."

Mark sipped his coffee and smiled.

After a morning of flashing person-of-interest sketches around the Independence Republic Bank and the Admiral Suites Hotel, Sylkie and Cason broke for lunch.

"Hmm, think I'll have a BLT," Casey muttered.

Sylkie was still scanning her menu when their waitress came for their orders. Casey was convinced she was using it as a shield. Finally, she looked up. "Chicken salad, please."

The server booked the orders and trotted off. "Chicken salad. Looks like you stick with the more healthy side of eating. Good for you, Sylkie. I, ah, wish I had that kind of willpower. Know what I mean?" Immediately regretting his rambling, Casey commissioned the tongue posse for a hanging.

Sylkie stared at Maxwell for a moment and said nothing. Then her eyes smiled. "You're blushing!"

Sure enough, a noticeable redness had pooled over Casey's cheeks, deepening the deep-blue color of his eyes along with accentuating his shave line.

Visualizing the words *miserable* and *fool* mambo their way across his field of vision, Casey petitioned the "god of all cowardly males" to grant his request to duck under the table and pretend to tie his shoelaces for the next hour. Thankfully, the sensible part of him opted out of that option, and he decided it was time to come clean.

"Okay, so now you know; I'm shy and I really don't know what to say to you. But I want to say the right thing."

"Why?"

"Why, what?"

"Why do you care what you say to me?" Sylkie was beginning to get a real strange feeling in the pit of her stomach, like there were butterflies this man across the table had somehow sprinkled with fairy dust and were tickling her insides with their fluttering wings, even those parts of her insides she refused to acknowledge. Sylkie suddenly felt herself levitating over her wall of isolation and seeking the embrace of another human being. And she liked the feeling.

"I care what I say to you"—Cason forced himself to look into Sylkie's eyes—"because I, well… I want you to like me." For the next several minutes, the couple maneuvered a clumsy conversation, the effort as out of step as two dance partners, one waltzing and the other flashing the "Macarena." Mercifully, their server was prompt in bringing their orders, the distraction allowing Casey to will his stomach out of his throat and back into its place of residence.

Consuming their lunch was a blur for the most part. Neither Sylkie nor Casey could care less what they were eating. Casey's pulsating cheeks slowly returned to normal. Stepping into rare atmosphere, Sylkie began tearing down her wall, brick by brick. The rest of the day went well.

*****

Middletown, New York. Saturday, 10:15 p.m.

Ken checked his watch. Time to gather the audience.

"You have reached the Middletown Police Department. How may I help you?"

"Ah, yes. I'm calling to inform you that the circus is in town. Not ringling—the circus of justice."

"What? Who is this?"

"Some call me the ringmaster. Now if by chance you've seen replays of my sensational one-act circus performances in Minnesota, you're going to love what I have in store for your lovely community this evening. I'm counting on you to broadcast to one and all to come see my show." Laberday's disguised voice descended to a darker tone. "For all who want to view the festivities, gather at the bridge on East Hamptonburg Road. Hurry now, I will not delay for stragglers." *Circus* and *Minnesota* set the dispatcher in motion.

For insurance, Ken also called the local FM station with the same message. He hoped for a good turnout. After all, he had put a lot of effort into this performance, and it would be a shame not to have a sizeable audience.

With the "set" ready and the call made, Ken headed back to Middletown as police cars, ambulances, and fire trucks along with a growing number of curiosity seekers raced to the East Hamptonburg Bridge. He smiled as he passed them from the opposite direction. Unfortunately, Kendrick would not be able to participate in their excitement. That would be far too risky. Tonight's success depended entirely on his preparation and the precise arrival of the "horses."

Laberday drove into town and pulled onto a side street. He set his computer in his lap and opened a program. Two flashing green lights dominated the screen. The lights represented two sensors placed one thousand feet apart on the Norfolk Southern Railway tracks. He knew from the railway's schedule a train was aiming for Middletown with cars to set out for the Middletown and New Jersey Railroad.

Propelling the burden were two General Electric Dash 9-40C diesel engines capable of generating a total of eight thousand horsepower. These were Ken's "horses." When the train destroyed the first sensor, the light would go out. When the second sensor rolled over, his program would calculate the train's speed. Knowing the location of the second sensor and the train's speed, Ken could pinpoint the time when all those horses would make their dramatic contribution to his show.

East Hamptonburg Road Bridge, 10:42 p.m.

Sheriff's Deputy Francis "Red" Wilson stood on the middle of the bridge, irritatingly swamped in a rising tide of chaos, courtesy of assorted emergency personnel and curious citizens. A tap on his shoulder brought him face-to-face with Middletown police officer Carey Black.

"What's going on?" Wilson almost had to shout to be heard. "I heard something about a circus. I sure hope it don't have nothin' to do with those murders in Minneapolis."

"You got me," Black answered. "All I know is, we got a call at the station saying a circus act is supposed to happen around here. Or something like that."

"Or something like that" was about to haunt the onlookers for the rest of their lives.

The sound of distant pulsating train engines could now be heard from the bridge. Somewhere in the darkness, a loudspeaker bellowed. "Welcome, one and all. Children to the rear, please. This may get a little heady. Thank you for coming out tonight for the latest installment of the circus of justice. Tonight we are featuring Morris the Magician. And a fine magician he is. In his previous life, Morris fine-tuned the art of turning worthless mortgage-backed bonds into beautiful butterflies of profit-bearing securities. Of course, it was all done with mirrors, and in the end, Morris faded. However, unlike the ill fortunes of many investors and mortgage holders, Morris escaped with a tidy severance, allowing him to live the good life in your wonderful community."

One hundred yards from the bridge, a circle of flames suddenly burst to life. In the center of the circle, a dark object was barely visible between the rail tracks.

Beyond the flames, throbbing engines announced the train's imminent arrival. The crowd pushed for a closer look. Foreseeing disaster, Deputy Wilson cued his mobile radio and screamed into it. "Dispatch, call the Norfolk Southern and tell them to stop their train heading for Middletown—AND DO IT NOW!"

The loudspeaker barked again. "Ladieees and gentlemen, please gather 'round and watch a repentant Morris defy death by standing in front of a moving train and, at the last minute, disappear—only to reappear as the train passes."

With that announcement, Morris Lavonia, securely strapped to a board that was hinged to a railroad tie on one end and the other end fastened to an air-operated cylinder, popped up to a sixty-degree angle as pressure from a portable air tank activated the device.

At the same time, Jerry Purcell, hoghead on lead engine no. 9823, received a frantic call to stop his train. Moments later, Purcell stared in disbelief as he rounded a curve. Flames were shooting onto the tracks ahead, illuminating a figure propped up between the rails. Unfortunately for all involved, stopping 5,800 tons of burden traveling at forty-nine miles per hour in the span of several hundred yards with a conventional braking system is a physical impossibility on this planet. Mass, weight, whatever. It gets ugly in a hurry if you're Morris Lavonia.

The helpless engineer utilized his only option: he "shot the works"—railroad jargon for applying maximum air to his braking system. The crowd raced toward the circle of flames. The lead engine, its headlights flashing desperately, barreled toward them. Screeching brakes filled the air with the sound of a thousand fingernails scratching on chalkboards. Sparks dispensed from the friction of steel wheels jamming on rails imitated sparklers guiding the audience to the "center ring."

Deputy Wilson and Officer Black ran along with the crowd, motioning them to get out of the way, as they could foresee a tragedy quickly turning into a disaster. As for Morris, any fictitious magical powers the ringmaster had sarcastically empowered him with were about to make their exit. Engineer Purcell futilely lay on the train's whistle. The shrill pitch pierced Lavonia like needle-nosed darts, topping out his panic and signaling it was time to self-perform a last rites ceremony.

The first image of engine 9823 Morris Lavonia horrifyingly witnessed beyond the flashing headlights was its car knuckle, winding up to sucker punch his midsection. It was to be Morris's farewell performance. However, in his passing, Morris, or what was left of him, participated in one final extraordinary human experience. He was "stretched out" for a mile before engines 9823 and 9535 ground to a halt.

A final sensor, crushed as the train did its destruction, activated the sound system one last time. "Sorry folks, it looks like Morris wasn't as prepared as he should have been. But please remember, we're a work in progress." With that postscript, the sound system was consumed in an acid bath.

Ken Laberday, smugly confident that all had gone well, set course for New York City and then on to a new destination where he would map the details for executing his most dramatic and heinous deed yet.

CHAPTER 8

Nora Balfour opened her eyes and returned the stare of the glowing numbers on her alarm clock. It was 6:13 a.m. She raised her head and listened for sounds of her children, Margo and Danny. All was quiet. Only the distant hum of a neighbor's air conditioner whirlpooled in her ears.

Nora rolled over, grabbed the pillow on the other side of the bed, pulled it close, and wrapped her arms around it. She tried to slip back into sleep, but her restless mind would not suppress an unwelcome rehash of her divorce to Aaron—handsome, bright-eyed, and immaculately kempt Aaron. Their marriage had coursed a cascade of failed expectations. First was the parade of unfulfilled promises, followed by endless excuses. Then pitiful accusations were designed to transfer guilt, their doomed relationship ultimately capped off by rejection. Nora had put her own ambitions on hold and worked hard to put Aaron through college. He was smooth and readily landed a high-profile job. Even in the recession, he talked his way onward and upward—the tall, good-looking-guy-with-no-substance kind of onward and upward.

Inevitably, Aaron found a soul mate in a coworker who artfully stroked his overly inflated ego. They could keep neither their eyes nor their hands off each other. Aaron claimed he was blindsided by a mutual attraction he was powerless to stop. He insisted he got physically sick about what was happening and hoped Nora would understand, even hinted at procuring her blessing.

For her part, Nora would have preferred to castrate the creep and feed the amputated parts to turkey vultures. As if breaking up their little family wasn't bad enough, Aaron conjured up more excuses than grains of sand on a Florida beach why he couldn't keep up with his child-support payments. Nora was rightly convinced that his money took a detour in order to satisfy the whims of a very needy girlfriend. At any rate, Nora was forced to make ends meet by taking a part-time job in a convalescent care facility. Balancing the demands of a job, college, and two small children comprised a feat near beyond measure; her only respite was the occasional late-night vodka gimlet. It was no wonder Nora fantasized a fine prince galloping in with a fairly-tale romance to replace her crushing burden.

Nora closed her eyes and buried her head in the pillow. Enough of the negative. Aaron was gone, out of her life for good. Time to focus on the positive, which, for Nora, came in the apparition of Professor Kendrick Laberday. She squeezed the pillow harder, fantasizing the bundle of feathers and linen was her new knight in shining armor. Of course, it made no sense that a successful academic like Ken would take notice of a relative nobody when there were so many attractive catches right on campus. Surely his fortunes with the opposite sex could easily be found in higher circles. *Then again…well, then again…* Nora squeezed the air out of the pillow. *Why not me?*

Tears welled up behind her closed eyelids, soon breaching the dam and meandering onto the pillowcase. These were good tears—tears of hope and happiness. *Yes, why not me?* Nora stroked her pillow and lavished it with her tears. She willed herself to believe Kendrick Laberday was God's belated offering for his egregious neglect of her well-being. Slowly, Nora relaxed. A soothing calmness washed over her, sending her back into the sleep mode. Sleep—a state of absent consciousness, a universe where time doesn't participate. A place to experience sweet dreams, futile pursuits, or—nothing.

The sound of little voices brought an abrupt end to all three alternatives. There were tummies to be satisfied, clothes to be washed, and worst of all, a bank statement deeper than the Mariana Trench to be reckoned with. A tactical maneuver would postpone the bank statement to the last item of the day to be dealt with after the children had been tucked in and a first line of defense in the form of a vodka gimlet was consumed.

Nora helped her children dress and then paraded them to the kitchen table. She was about to answer Danny's question as to why Oscar lives in a garbage can when her cell phone rang. It was her sister, Sylkie Maune.

"Hey, how's my favorite sis this morning?"

Nora laughed. "Favorite, and only."

Sylkie leaned against her desk. Since their parents' deaths, Nora had been Sylkie's rock, her stabilizing influence. That all changed with the cowardly departure of Aaron. Sylkie's "rock" had sadly melted into a puddle of despair. Now Sylkie felt it was her duty to put "Humpty Dumpty" back together again.

"So how's the new man in your life?" Sylkie asked cheerily as possible.

"Don't know. He's out of town for a few days. Said he would call when he gets back. I'm not holding my breath."

"But you do want him to call, right? I mean last time we talked, you sounded pretty excited."

"Well, yeah, but truthfully, Sylk, he's way above my league. If he calls me, fine, but I'm not expecting it." Nora was all but biting the phone.

Sylkie picked up on the charade. "Hope it works out. How about lunch tomorrow?" Before Nora could entertain an answer, Sylkie cut her off. "Oops, gotta go; the boss is waving at me. Call ya later."

*****

Guy Lompello rocked back and forth in his chair, each thrust producing an irritating squeak.

"They make a lubricant for that," Mark deadpanned as he and Sylkie made themselves comfortable. The jab sailed over the lieutenant as he concentrated on a sheet of paper taking up space on his desk blotter. Mark imagined twelve fathoms of pressure on the poor man to make some headway in the circus-murders case.

Guy refocused his attention to his two investigators. "Let's talk about the murder in New York State Saturday night. You've seen the report. The incident has our circus murderer's signature all over it. The bureau sent Renner and Maxwell out there to confirm the connection." Guy paused and took a deep breath. "I just don't understand this world anymore. The lines defining crimes and criminals used to be clear-cut. Nowadays you got strange people knocking off solid citizens in bizarre ways. And for what reason?" He quickly waved himself off. "Sorry for the rant." He grabbed the paper off his desk and handed it to Mark. "This showed up at the Minneapolis *Star Tribune* this morning."

> There once was a crook named Morris
> Who begged not to shake hands with the florist
> But his ethics were bad
> So his outcome was sad
> And now poor Morris is porous
> Apologies to all who missed the show, but don't frown. We strive for only happy faces at the circus of justice. The next act promises to be bigger and better!

Sylkie glared at the paper. "Who is this person? *What* is this person?"

Feeling her vexation, Mark imagined a gnome cranking on tie-down straps circling his stomach. "This also means he's got no boundaries."

Lompello flexed his white bushy eyebrows. "It probably also means our circle of associates is about to get a bit more crowded."

Mark said, "And just when I was starting to feel comfortable with our 'little family.'"

Sylkie cast a dour look. Her exasperation with the lack of progress in the circus-murders case was as annoying as a hangnail. "All we're doing is shadowboxing."

Mark said, "Well, we're going to do our best to change that. We need to dig this guy out of whatever hole he crawls into between performances."

"And how do we do that?" Sylkie warily countered.

"What cops spend 90 percent of their time doing, unromantic, mundane police work."

"I'm…listening."

Mark ignored her wariness. "Prepare for extended computer time. We're going to match foreclosures and bankruptcies with people in the area who have a criminal history, particularly a violent criminal history."

"*Extended* sounds like the key word here. I want a comfortable chair."

"We'll start with the metro area and work our way out."

"And a cushion."

Lompello studied Sylkie. She definitely had a salty disposition. He concluded past scars must have cut deep into her persona. However, like Mark, he was not about to give up on her. "Sylkie, I want your input on the New York murder. You think it's tied to our homicides?"

"I don't have any reason not to believe that. My guess is the killer at least partially used the New York murder to keep us off balance. He may be thinking if we have to dilute our search, his odds of not being caught get better."

Mark appreciated the fact that Guy asked Sylkie for her opinion. He was letting her know her voice counted.

Mark said, "All right, let's get at it. I think we should start by looking over bankruptcy and foreclosure records for the past three years. Try to connect some dots."

"Let me find my eye drops." Sylkie frowned, her thoughts involuntarily transferring to a pop-up of Cason Maxwell. She wondered how long he'd be in New York State.

*****

Ken Laberday lay back in his recliner, staring at his drink, a triple shot of scotch on the rocks. The alcohol fueled an ego already threatening to smother a good portion of the Twin Cities. He closed his eyes to a panorama of visualizations competing for the brassiest image of grandeur. After all, had not he become the premier (and sole) avenger for the corporate crimes that triggered the Great Recession? Was he not gaining, by the day, a growing legion of admirers who championed his cause?

Fools! People letting themselves get bludgeoned fifty different ways by shysters who have only selfish motives. They deserve what they get. Now it's up to me to swoop in and right the ship. Ken laughed out loud. *And, of course, I'm happy to oblige them. The question is, how can I best profit from their misery?* As always, it was all about Kenny.

Laberday pined for a way to promote his crusade against those who had one-upped him. He fantasized for the day he would cash in and recoup his losses, maybe even see a profit. Ken knew somehow there was money to be gleaned from this, though he wasn't sure from which direction it would come. After all, the whole campaign would be for naught if his wave of success did not eventually carry him off to the good life. The trick was how to plant the seeds without arousing suspicion. There *had* to be a way.

But yes, of course, there is! It's right under my nose! Ken chastised himself for not having thought of it before—his classroom. He would utilize his influence to subtly turn the sympathies of his students in the direction of the great ringmaster. Were not the campuses of colleges and universities incubators for change and for cataloging the old and birthing the new? *I will simply stoke the fire and then stand back and watch the movement grow.* It was a blueprint time-tested and brilliantly exploited by some of the great leaders of the past.

Laberday whisked up his glass with enough force to heave a volley of drink onto his wrist and shirtsleeve. No matter, a mission of utmost importance had just been conceived, and minor irritations were of no consequence. More pointedly, the effects of the Glenlivet had dulled the professor's senses.

Ken poured another, the frosty cubes happily bobbing in a sea of booze. Fresh drink; fresh thoughts. *Ah yes, sweet Nora.* The thought of Nora Balfour triggered a basic need that was overdue to be satisfied. Sexual gratification had never been a problem, and Ken could not foresee any obstacles concerning the conquering, manipulating, and aborting of his most recent conquest. He would woo her, roll her around in bed till boredom dictated a new venue, and then return the poor wench back to her banal existence.

To be sure, what Ken loved most about pursuing the opposite sex was exploiting the power of his charisma. To see and then feel the heartbreak when he terminated a relationship ignited the ultimate climax. The carefully chosen words dripping with venom that caused his discarded lover to question her self-worth gifted him a higher orgasm of dominance. And more times than not, it did end that way with Ken brushing her off like a piece of lint. What Ken refused to let surface was that his passion for degrading the women in his life was rooted in his long-past tumultuous relationship with his mother.

*****

"So do you think it was him?" Sylkie asked, stabbing her fork into a plate of orange chicken salad.

"Yes, I do." Casey poured more ketchup on his burger.

"How do you know?"

Maune and Maxwell were discussing the Middletown murder over lunch. They had sorely missed each other's company the past few days, though neither would openly admit to it. Sylkie because… well, she was Sylkie, and Cason because, A, he didn't want to appear wimpy in front of Sylkie's assertive personality and, B, he was just plain too timid to say it because, A, he was somewhat intimidated by Sylkie's assertive personality.

"The physical similarities…air hydraulics, sound system, precise timing, execution. It's his signature all right."

"So *was* Lavonia being investigated for collusion to commit fraud as far as his bond-rating agency was concerned? In a roundabout way, that's what the killer accused him of."

"There was nothing being pursued on our end, and the New York State Attorney General's Office has no open investigations."

Sylkie pushed her plate away. "Okay, so what does our killer know or think he knows that our justice system may be missing?"

Casey cocked his head. "Am I detecting a wisp of cynicism?"

"Course not." Sylkie peered at Maxwell. Something strange was happening. His gorgeous face was converting into a red beacon before her eyes. Tiny beads of water were forming on his forehead. *Is he having a seizure?*

"Would…you like to go out for dinner?"

"… Okay."

And so a date was arranged. A triumph of boldness for Cason; a journey into the unknown for Sylkie. She couldn't help thinking if Casey ever attempted a kiss. She hoped they would be close to a fully staffed emergency room.

CHAPTER 9

Mark stood at the end of his dock on Roundstone Lake, a two-hour drive north of the Twin Cities, engulfed by the serenity of a sparkling summer morning. Soothing sunbeams pierced his tanned skin, massaging muscles left sore from an early-morning workout. He pondered the inescapable conclusion that his exercise regimen increasingly leaned toward squeezing out more pain than pleasure—a reminder that time does inexorably march on. However, he refused to let his body continue its journey into his second half-century gracefully. *Weight—sorta under control. Muscle tone—good. Posture—straight. Minor hypertension, but they make pills for that. Occasionally (?) a beer or two more than necessary, but who's counting?*

Glancing down into the green-tinged water, Mark spied a couple of bluegills holding their position in the shade provided by dock planking. Below them, a lone perch raced into deeper water, chasing whatever it is perch chase. Mark kicked at a splotch of sand on the boards. A shower of fine grains exploded into the water, drawing the bluegills' interest. The fish took a sniff and returned to their holding pattern. The perch didn't show.

Mark's thoughts weren't on fish, however. The lake setting regurgitated a terrifying nightmare he'd had several weeks before, featuring the vicious murderer Tom Moore, who, in Mark's mind, surpassed even the raw evilness of the circus killer. Moore killed for the sake of the act. No reason required. The fact that Moore was alive and well in the federal supermax prison in Florence, Colorado, didn't bring Mark much comfort. Mark and Jamie Littlebird had slapped the cuffs on him, ending a crime spree by Moore that stretched over four states and highlighted with the tragic deaths of twelve innocent people. Needless to say, all parties concerned were quite relieved the day Tom Moore was carted off to prison. He didn't go quietly. Moore swore he would get revenge on Truitt, Littlebird, and their families. Mark reasoned that the threat was possibly the basis for his unsettling dream in which Moore had attacked Mark's family at their cabin. At any rate, Mark hoped the supermax prison was truly "super."

"Deep in thought, I see. Aren't you going fishing?" Liz Truitt took a seat beside her husband and offered up a dish of fresh pineapple. Liz's light auburn hair glistened in the bright sunlight. Sunglasses sheltered steel-gray pretty eyes.

Mark hesitated. Fruit wasn't high on his food chain. "Maybe tonight. The guy at the bait shop said the fish have been the most active in the evening." Mark looked at the pineapple, sighed, and reluctantly snatched a slice.

Ever the crusader for any number of noble causes, not the least of which included coaxing her husband to eat more fruit, Liz Truitt thrived on a call to duty. Her common-sense approach and strong moral character were the result of a nurturing family whose daily activities centered on the demands of maintaining a prosperous dairy farm. At a young age, Liz was exposed to the practical side of life, including the responsibilities that came with milking ninety-seven Holsteins twice a day, along with caring for a host of other barnyard animals suitable for a George Orwell novel. Although he often teased, he wouldn't trade his wife for even "ten good plow horses" in reference to her rural upbringing. Mark silently prayed being spared a recitation or two on such weighty subjects as the precarious state of the world's dwindling resources amid rising populations.

"So what are you thinking about?"

Mark had no intention of regurgitating his dream. "Aw, these circus killings… I don't want to bore you."

"Bore me."

"Okay, but consider yourself warned. Sylkie and I have been scouring bankruptcy and foreclosure records and have done several interviews. So far, we've come up empty. The guy's so clever… He leaves nothing to pick at."

"He'll make a mistake sooner or later. They always do."

"That's pretty much what Jamie said."

"See, I'm starting to think like a cop."

"Whoa, there! One cop per family please." Mark brushed a hand on Liz's cheek and drew her in close. After a few quiet, intimate moments, Mark gently released his grip. "You know, on second thought, maybe I will go fishing."

"Take the pineapple with you."

*****

The weekend went by at typical warp speed. All too soon, Mark was pulling up a chair next to Sylkie, who was at her desk, staring intently at a computer screen.

"You look refreshed." Sylkie peered over reading glasses.

Mark noticed something different about his partner. She looked refreshed as well. He hoped it might have something to do with Cason Maxwell. "Yeah, it was nice to get away for a couple of days. Unfortunately, I couldn't put a lid on thinking about our case."

After a couple of hours scanning records, the investigators decided to stretch their legs. They hiked to a coffee shop far enough from precinct headquarters to earn donuts with their coffee. Mark sensed Sylkie had something on her mind, but he didn't want to press. He didn't have to. They got their snacks and sat at an outside table.

"Um, Truitt, what do you think about guys who are really shy? Is that like a sign of like insecurity or something?"

Mark hoped Sylkie's question had the words *Cason* and *Maxwell* imbedded in it. "Oh, I don't think being shy necessarily means a person lacks self-confidence, Sylkie. It's a natural thing for some people to be shy, especially when they're stepping into new territory. Think about the opposite for a moment. Why are some people obnoxious? It's a personality trait. The difference is, obnoxious can be controlled; shyness is more involuntary until the person finds their comfort zone."

"Maxwell asked me out. I honestly thought he was going to die on the spot. I've never seen anyone that nervous."

"What was your answer?"

"I said yes."

"Good answer."

*****

Ken Laberday rubbed his hands together. This was the first day of the new summer session. Most of the students had been in his first session, Nora Balfour among them.

"Good morning, all." Ken smiled brightly at his class. "I hope the break has given you the opportunity to prepare for a new adventure because we are about to scrutinize several of the more technical elements of economics. Now how many of you have a good understanding of collateralized debt obligations?"

Ken breezed through the lecture. As he put the finishing touches on his final thoughts, his eyes locked with Nora's, the unspoken signal for her to hold back. Mission accomplished, as Nora waited until the last student had shuffled out.

"So how was your mini-vacation?" Ken probed.

"Oh, nothing spectacular; stayed close to home, did things with the ki-kids." Nora suddenly realized she hadn't mentioned her children.

Ugh, kids. "How many children do you have?"

"Two; Margo is six, Danny's four."

How nauseous. "That's great. I hope to have children of my own someday."

Nora took a deep breath. *He likes children, thank goodness!*

Ken wrapped his hands around hers. "Nora, I hope I'm not being too forward, but I would very much like to spend an evening with you." Everything that made Kendrick Laberday the vicious predator he was—particularly those deep, smoky black eyes—conspired to nearly draw Nora into a trance.

"I…would like that."

As usual, for Ken Laberday, it was so easy.

The classroom lecture and date arrangement with Nora had been the easier part of the day for Ken. At the moment, he was in his machine shed, scanning the next challenge. Parked in front of him was a stolen Hummer H1, the copycat military model. Its boxy shape highlighted with dark tinted windows and painted a midnight-black color suggested an ominous presence. *Inspirational in its own right,* Laberday reflected. Ken had gutted the inside and was rebuilding it to accommodate his special application. Parts and pieces yet to be installed were sequentially arranged in the empty stall next to the vehicle. Assembly was not a problem. The problem was that two essential elements had not yet been procured.

Until now, Kendrick had flown solo. For this next act, an assistant would be required. Just as the magician has an assistant lie in the box as he "saws" it in two, Ken needed an accomplice. He also needed a "saw."

Stretching out on the Hummer's back seat, which had been removed from the vehicle and pushed against a wall, Ken took stock of his inner sanctum, the barely visible machine shed at the back of his property. The building sported a gabled roof in the center and two shed roofs on each side that stuck out like wings. The white paint on the siding was retreating like a melting glacier, exposing large patches of weathered gray. Legions of bull thistles and bramblebushes interspersed with three-foot tall ryegrass and wild oats guarded the building on three sides.

A light over Ken's workbench cast a ghostly glow. The concrete floor was cracked and uneven. Spills from countless oil changes dotted its surface. The corners of the lone window were layered with dusty cobwebs. The sill sported a Coke can from the fifties. A loft above the back half of the shed provided sanctuary for unknown animals that pattered their way across the floor. But above all, the signature mark of this structure that sheltered the evil inventions of this evil man was the pungent smell of oil-soaked, damp wood, the two elements combining to waft the smell of "old." The odor permeated every part of the building and was overwhelmed only when a grinder was put to metal, a cutting torch ignited, or a strong-smelling adhesive applied. Ken laughed to himself. *Here I am, the "chief justice" of justice in this country, and I sit in squalor. Someday…*

Refocusing on the present dilemma, Ken continued to wrack his brain for an answer. Finally, the word *military* surfaced. *Of course! Why didn't I think of this before? I may be able to lock down both items with one stroke.* Feeling he was on to something, Ken turned off the light and locked the shed.

The route to his house followed a crude roadway consisting of two tire tracks separated by a wall of ryegrass and ending at the back of his garage. Ken stopped to admire a colorful flower bed running the length of the garage, an uncommon expression of sensitivity. The bed hosted a combination of yellow and orange daylilies, the purity of white bearded irises, and a variety of annually planted gladiolus, their spectrum of colors competing for dominance. After honoring their beauty with a prolonged stare, he followed a sidewalk that bordered an immaculately kept yard and that led to his house.

Settling into his study, Ken fired up his computer. He searched for militia groups in Minnesota and came up with a list including Front Guard, headquartered in Minneapolis. A scan of their website introduced him to their monthly newsletter. Ken discovered that along with other paranoid philosophies they embraced, Front Guard was deeply concerned with a looming economic collapse, its seeds of destruction nurtured by the "socialist" policies of the present administration. *Perfect! A subject on which I can capitalize in my search for an accomplice.*

Ken continued to scan the newsletter. The last page featured advertisements from around the country, calling for "Americans of patriotic conscience" to join any number of listed organizations. *Yes, the perfect venue to recruit my accomplice and find my "saw."* Busy fingers worked the keyboard.

CHAPTER 10

"I'll have the veal Parmesan." Sylkie smiled and handed the menu to the waitress. She was pleased with Casey's choice of restaurants. The ambiance was comfortable, not too intimate. Increasingly, Sylkie found herself enamored with the man sitting across the table. Her personal standards required the onset of anything more than a casual relationship be keenly measured, but those pesky butterflies were flapping their wings at near-warp speed, causing her insides to crave Casey's body close and even closer.

"Sylkie, are you okay?" Casey was looking at her intently. "You look a little flushed."

Sylkie cleared her throat. "I'm fine. Just warm."

"Is your wine satisfactory?"

"It's good, Cason, although I'm not much of a wine drinker. That's probably why I feel warm. I'm sure this glass will last the evening."

Maxwell had to make a conscious effort not to stare. Sylkie looked stunning. The white blouse and beige skirt revealed a woman with simple but focused tastes. They also aligned perfectly with her sleek figure. Her ponytail had given way to a more formal presentation, featuring hair with stylish lines and slightly curved at the shoulders. Just the right amount of makeup sent the message she was serious but not petitioning.

"Just Casey."

"Excuse me?"

"My friends call me Casey."

"Okay, Casey. So are we friends now?"

"I'd like to be. And you?"

Sylkie held out her wine glass. "Casey…meet Sylkie."

*****

Several miles away, Ken and Nora dined at a fancy supper club overlooking a golf course. The location was strategic as it was not far from his country home, which also meant it was not far from the bedroom he had every intention of ending the evening with his dinner guest.

Laberday sized up his date with mild satisfaction. Nora's toffee-colored hair, which blended nicely with her hazel eyes, was cut in a pixie style and framed a cute roundish face that tonight hosted a generous amount of makeup. His sole asterisk was that she slightly challenged the boundaries of the black dress she was wearing. If Nora's dress was a bit snug, her budget was even tighter, dictating prudence over fashion.

Overall, not bad, Kenny thought to himself. *She'll do for now.* "So, Nora"—Ken took a sip of his brandy Manhattan—"tell me about your family. I know you have two children."

"I do." Nora nervously whisked a fair gulp of her Seven Hills merlot, praying the alcohol molecules would stroke frayed nerves. For Nora, sharing an evening at an exclusive club with a handsome, charming man was as likely as a duck with clipped wings completing a pilgrimage across the Gobi Desert. However, Nora was determined to give it her best shot. *There was so much upside,* she thought. "The total balance of my family other than my children consists of my sister who is five years younger than I and much more of a success story. You probably wouldn't be interested in the details of how that came to be." Another generous portion disappeared from Nora's glass, prompting Ken to signal their waiter.

"On the contrary, Nora. Continue."

"I, ah, spent my post-high school years working to put my husband, excuse me, my ex-husband through college. It worked for him, but not so good for me. He left for greener pastures. I, on the other hand, have the two shining lights of my life. However, since I passed on my opportunity for an education, I don't have the skills to adequately support them; thus, my attempt at getting a degree. I only hope it'll be worth the effort. I know it's a tough job market."

Frustration and desperation equal vulnerability. Good. Come to Daddy. "You're smart, Nora. You'll do fine." Ken set his elbows on the table, folded his hands, and rested his chin on them. "So tell me about your sister."

Nora took a measured sip from her refreshed glass of wine. "I can't say enough good things about my sister, Sylkie... That's her name. After my parents' untimely deaths—my mom in the Oklahoma City bombing and my dad passing away not long after—Sylkie decided to dedicate her life to law enforcement. She followed through, got her degree. Now she's an investigator for the Minneapolis Metro Police Department."

Laberday's elbows nearly slipped off the table. He immediately processed the options. Option A directed him to terminate the relationship and stay as far removed from the police as possible. Option B told him to cultivate the relationship to his advantage. Option B won the day. "Wow, that's commendable. She had a goal and realized it. Now she's in a position to challenge the evil forces of society."

Nora fingered the stem of her glass, conducting a self-appraisal and concluding that abstinence from the red liquid would be advisable at this point. "Well, yes, and no."

"What do you mean?"

"Yes, it's good she has a career, but she can't come to terms with the way our mother died. She's chasing demons that won't die no matter how many criminals she arrests."

Laberday paused, once again signaling the waiter. "I'm not sure I know what you mean."

"Endlessly chasing bad people is not going to bring my sister peace of mind. I believe healing can be achieved only through forgiveness. It took a long time, but I eventually reached that point with my parents' deaths. Now I'm struggling with my ex-husband's infidelity and abandonment, although I have to admit, in his case, I'm still thinking daggers, not daisies."

Thanks, but I'll stick to sweet justice. "Your sister sounds very interesting. I'd like to meet her."

"Believe it or not, at this very moment, she's having dinner with an FBI agent."

"A casual acquaintance or serious prospect?"

"She seems interested, unusual for her. She lets very few people into her life."

"How did they meet?"

"I guess because of those so-called circus killings."

How much better can this get! "Yes, yes. Quite a deal. I can't imagine anyone with a mind like that. Shall we order?"

*****

"I hope you enjoyed the evening as much as I did, Sylkie." Maxwell prayed for a pleasant conclusion to the evening as he drove Sylkie home.

Enjoy? That portrayal was woefully inadequate. *How about a man in a million made me feel the warmth of being human for the first time in years?* Sylkie faced the window so Casey wouldn't see the glistening in her eyes. Silently, Sylkie covered his hand with hers. She held on tight. Maxwell had his answer.

Not much conversation was exchanged for the remainder of the ride to Sylkie's condo. As she unlocked her door, Casey made some small talk, thanking her for the evening. Obviously nervous and because Sylkie could be unpredictable, he wasn't sure of a proper exit strategy. Above all, he didn't want to ruin the mood of the past few hours. His procrastination forced Sylkie to provide the answer. She turned, reached up, and kissed him. Casey returned the gesture. Realizing what had just happened, they stood motionless for an instant, searching each other.

"I... I guess I better be going," Casey managed.

Sylkie touched a hand to his warm cheek. "Good night."

Sylkie had contemplated a meltdown from Casey should they share a kiss. The man did just fine. Sylkie, on the other hand, would have pegged the needle on a blood-pressure monitor.

*****

Between the merlot and Ken's apparent acceptance of her, Nora shooed away her anxiety and was thoroughly enjoying the evening.

"Did you two save some room for one of our signature desserts?" the waitress smiled.

"None for me, thank you," Nora waved her off. "I've already had way more calories than my quota allows."

"I think we're ready for the check." Ken kept his eyes on Nora.

On the way out of the restaurant, Ken enticed Nora with an extension to the evening. "If it's not too late, could I interest you in a dollop of vanilla ice cream drizzled with Baileys? It's a lighter dessert than anything they serve here and is sure to put you in the right state for a good night's sleep. Of course, it means you will have to come to my house where I will indulge you with a most uninteresting tour of memorabilia featuring my past accomplishments, which brazenly adorn the walls of my study." Ken failed to mention the soft leather couch that also inhabited his study, ground zero to previous conquests of the opposite sex.

"Let *me* be the judge how uninteresting you are," Nora laughed. She felt more carefree than she had since the early days of her marriage to Aaron. Prayerfully, this was her time in the sun, and she was determined to make the most of it.

Ken turned into his driveway and parked in front of the garage. A single yard light cast enough of a glow for Nora to tell the grounds were well-kept. Shadows from maple and oak trees played on the house's brick siding. Nora envisioned a daylight scene that featured a picture-perfect country setting. Not included was the machine shed, far from view.

"Make yourself comfortable." Kendrick gestured to his couch as they settled into his study. "I'll be back in a moment with dessert.

And feel free to look over my 'trophies.' I just hope they don't put you to sleep."

Nora scanned the room. Ken hadn't exaggerated. Testaments to his success in academia dwarfed every other garnishment. Degrees, awards, pictures, and even articles such as his participation on national committees for the promotion of educational standards hung from the walls like grapes. Nora felt a tiny shiver. If Ken was truly as interested in her as he seemed to be, it meant she was stepping from a life where uncertainty was the sole constant to a place where all was right with the world. Yes, this was cranking it up a few notches—no, it was vaulting it up *many* notches.

Play your cards right, Nora. You're in the big leagues now.

"So what do think of my inner sanctum of brag?" Kenny grinned, handing Nora a dish of ice cream.

"I don't think it's bragging at all. You have every right to be proud of your accomplishments."

"Well, when you have no family and have poured all your energies into your career, this pretty much becomes…well, is your family. No substitute for the real thing, of course. Hopefully, that will someday be in my future…" Ken's voice deliberately trailed off.

Nora smiled and waved a finger. "Time doesn't back up. It won't wait for you, Ken."

"Well, then, I'm not going to wait either." Laberday gently took Nora's dessert bowl and set it on the coffee table. He put a hand on her cheek and kissed her gently. They made deep eye contact. His dark, hypnotic eyes smothered her consciousness. Their lips locked a second time, each gambling their passion. Nora was slipping into submission. Ken took advantage. He went back for more. And then more.

Finally, a pinprick of resistance rose above the catacomb of Ken's grip. "Please." Nora pressed a hand on his chest. "I… I don't think I can do this."

"Wha…?" The rejection so startled Ken it was the only reaction he could muster. This had never happened to him. There was no directive in his playbook of love on how to respond to a rebuff.

He pushed away and turned his head as he felt his eyes pooling with contempt for this nobody. *But hold on—she may prove useful.*

"Nora, I'm, ah, so sorry. What did I do? I hope I haven't offended you. I... I have to admit I'm quite taken aback with you, but that's no excuse to be so forward... I'm so embarrassed."

"No, please, there's nothing to be embarrassed about. You didn't do anything wrong, Ken. It's me. I'm just having a hard time adjusting to a life that's different to what I've known for so many years. I'll be fine. I just need a little time."

"Well, then, my dear, it's time you'll have." Laberday stood and smoothed his pants. "Let us start anew, and from this moment on, you take the lead. And I guarantee, I will be the most devoted disciple you can imagine."

Atlas had just removed the world from Nora's shoulders and put it back on his own. Her fear she had blown her best chance to pull her children and herself out of the survival mode and into a secure future was allayed with Kendrick's reassuring words.

For his part, Ken mentally puked at his verbal slobbering all over this pathetic excuse of a woman. *Oh well, no matter. I'll crush her like an ant when I'm done with her.*

The ride to Nora's house was very amicable.

CHAPTER 11

Washington, DC

Clayton Rimm poked at his baked potato with all the enthusiasm of an acrophobic contemplating an assault on K2. An attorney with the Department of Justice, Rimm was having lunch with Val Docket, a partner in a high-powered Washington lobbying firm. Docket's clients, most of whom had strong ties to Wall Street, were more than a little distressed with the so-called circus killings and had commissioned him to 'impress' on the Justice Department the need to quickly resolve the case.

Both Docket and Rimm were veterans of the Washington quagmire and part of an elite crowd that cycled between government and private enterprise. Sometimes adversaries, other times comrades, their common bond was cynicism for a system that steals a person's soul.

If their careers traversed parallel universes, their physical differences in regard to the aging process was stark. For sixty-three-year-old Clayton Rimm, genetics and lifestyle conspired to create an unpleasant journey forward. Rimm's large frame was increasingly yielding to gravity due to the arthritis invading his back. His face and bear-paw hands showed enough liver spots to compete with a German shorthaired pointer. Of the two men, Rimm was the more intelligent. He was also the more indulgent.

A year junior to Rimm, Val Docket showed far fewer signs of drifting into senior hood. Thick, curly graying hair cut short and perfectly trimmed was kept at attention with dabs of pomade. Tawny-brown eyes sparkled behind long black lashes. Exploiting nature's generosity to the max, Val Docket took great pains to maintain his pretty-boy image. Of the two men, Val Docket was more cunning. Of the two men, he was exceedingly more vain.

"I'll get right to the point, Clayton." Docket pushed aside his steak sandwich. "I have clients who are upset with Justice for not pursuing these 'circus murders' with greater urgency. They want to impress upon the attorney general that it would be to *everyone's* benefit for him to spare no resources to end this thing."

Rimm got the hidden message. There was a presidential campaign on the horizon, and campaigns are expensive.

Clayton Rimm loved wine. Any well-aged wine would do, but red was his favorite. Malbec. It eased the pain. He shook his empty glass at their waiter. "Look, Val, you think *we* like what's going on? This guy has rung up three sensational public executions, and we don't have a clue as to who he is. He's even garnered his own cult following. I get it. He's opened up a lot of wounds that would best be forgotten."

Rimm nodded with approval as the waiter refilled his glass. "All I can tell you is that we have two of our best and brightest assisting the locals in Minneapolis. I got an update this morning. There is nothing new to report. Leads are scarce as snow in Singapore."

Docket thumped an index finger on the table. The watchband on his Rolex clicked in unison. "That's not good enough, Clayton. My clients are very distraught. The Lavonia murder was too close to home. They feel vulnerable."

Rimm sat back and peered through his thick lenses at Docket. He had been at this game far too long. He was hired to do the people's work, and he did. But too often, it was only for those people who could afford it—those wonderful plutocrats. As in Docket's clients.

"Be honest, Val. You're representing Wall Street whores who had their trick go sour, and now the john is getting even. They should have thought it out before they sold bonds infected with financial diseases."

Docket wasn't amused with the metaphor. "C'mon, Clayton, a few years ago, you were on this side of the table representing these same clients. It's the best game in town, and you know it." Val paused. "Then again, if it's giving you player's remorse, why do you stay in?"

"Why do any of us stay in? Maybe because of our overpowering addiction to wine, women, and just about every other material thing paraded in front of us? Sad, isn't it?"

"What's sad?"

"This town used to be about the people's business. When I stepped out of the bus terminal onto First Street forty years ago, lawmakers still had a sense of representing their constituents. Nowadays they can't focus beyond representing themselves. It's all about being connected, isn't it, Val? Getting your face on TV, your quote in the paper, your foot in the club. And for what? To take a long drink out of that ocean of money and power that has completely drowned this place?"

Docket's patience was wearing thin. "It's nice you're considering the high road to moral duty, Clayton, but right now, let's stick to the business at hand. Justice has a responsibility to protect its citizens, of which there seems to be a systems failure. There are innocent Americans who are in harm's way. Whoever is wreaking this havoc *has* to be stopped—and soon." Val leaned over the table and emphasized his point in a coarse voice barely above a whisper, "There... must...be...no...more...killing!"

Rimm swilled a gulp of wine and peered at Docket through glassy eyes. "I wonder what it feels like to own a government. Yeah, okay, I'll pass it on to Quinn Montague. He heads up the criminal division at Justice. Another recycler. Worked for Upton Law Partners couple years back. Ran interference for some Wall Street big hitters after the savings and loan crisis in the nineties. Impressive work. No indictments, no convictions for his clients." Rimm laughed an alcohol laugh. "Irony of ironies, now he's an enforcer for the other side."

Val was satisfied. Clayton was still a player. Letting go was so, so hard. However, curiosity made him dive in one more time.

"So, Clayton, if and when you do decide to leave Shangri-La, what then?"

Rimm fingered the bill. "I'm going to search the mountains of West Virginia until I find a parcel of land on a river. Every morning,

I'm going to sit on the riverbank and mentally toss one self-serving act I've puked up over the years into the water. It'll take a while, but eventually I'll wipe the slate clean. Then I just might jump in myself. If I bob back up, I'll consider myself baptized."

"And if you don't?"

"Well, I guess I'll be one more selfish act floating into hell."

"Man, you need to talk to a shrink."

"I'll get the check."

*****

Ken Laberday glanced in both directions before crossing the street, not so much for traffic as for the possibility of unwelcome company. His destination was a mailbox he had rented under an assumed name. Ken couldn't shake the fear of being under surveillance, but by whom and for what reason were circled with question marks and driven by a growing paranoia that originated with Nora's revelation about her sister being a cop. Ken was seriously beginning to doubt the wisdom of dating someone whose sibling was hunting him.

Once inside the building, his anxiety mushroomed. What if an undercover cop had their eyes trained on the mailbox? Reminding himself of the mission at hand reset his psychopathic brain to its normal no-fear mode. Ken inserted a key and opened the door. Three envelopes were waiting, three responses to his inquiry in the Front Guard newsletter for "a patriot to assist with a mission demonstrating a show of loyalty for our great country. Pay to be commensurate with ability and success of the venture. Only those applicants valuing the core ideals of our founding fathers need apply. Send inquiries to PO box…" He grabbed the letters and closed the door.

Glancing frequently through the rearview mirror on his way home, Ken's confidence returned. Before long, he was again floating on a cloud of calm assurance, adjusting his thoughts to the comfortable illusion of superiority.

The cops are so far behind I'll be lapping them if I'm not careful. He made a mental note not to outsmart himself. *Try to think on their level, whatever that is.* In fact, the thought of Nora's sister being a cop now tantalized him. *I will parade under their noses, and they will know me not.*

Glancing in the rearview mirror one last time, Ken pulled into his driveway. Soon he was at his desk, tearing open the first letter. It was anything but inspiring. The smudges alone were a forensic scientist's dream. It went downhill from there.

> I want to defend my contry from the commie govurnmint in poer. Then will get the manoratys. Call me at...

On to the second letter.

> In the realm of time and space, God created but one superior race. That entity has struggled against all odds to retain its status as premier among Homo sapiens. I believe our descendants—those who emigrated from Europe (only) are the offspring of the gods of our past. We are called to defend the honor of those true heroes of legend: Apollo, Poseidon, Odin, Zeus, etc. For an interview, call me at...

Not exactly heartening. Fearing he had tapped into the wacko community, Ken unenthusiastically sliced open the last letter.

> May be interested in your offer. I can be reached at...after four p.m.

Ken breathed a sigh of relief. He looked at his watch: 4:31. He dialed the number on a prepaid cell phone.

"Hello?"

Was that a female voice? No way. Another strikeout. O for three.

"Hello?"

Then again, I'm short on options. "Yes, um, I received your letter of inquiry from the ad I posted in the Front Guard newsletter."

"So what's this job about, and what's it pay?"

Straight forward. I like that. "First things first. What we're looking at is a very serious venture. Nerves of steel required. Once in, there is no turning back. The successful applicant will be well rewarded."

"Like I said, what's the job about, and what does it pay?"

"I don't want to discuss details over the phone. We need to meet face-to-face. Tell me a place and a time. Also, I need your name."

"Why?"

"Pardon me?"

"My name. You tell me *your* name; I'll tell you mine."

"Look, I need to check you out, make sure you're not a cop."

"How do I know *you're* not a cop?"

Touché. "You don't. All I can tell you is that I'm not playing games. Either you give me your name or I'll go on to the next applicant."

No response. Then she said, "Rose... Rose Cherotte. There's a country bar and restaurant—Good Pickins it's called—on Highway 12 a couple miles west of Waverly. Think you can find it?"

"I'll find it. Anytime after tomorrow is good."

"Meet me there Saturday at five-thirty. The bartender will point me out."

"Okay. Five-thirty it is."

Ken liked what he'd heard from Ms. Rosy Rose Cherotte. Her no-nonsense personality was definitely a positive. If his plan played out as intended, the Saturday meeting would not be necessary.

*****

The knife blade split the air inches from Sylkie's face, catching her off guard. She brushed back, tripping over a container box in the dark alley. Regaining her balance, she heard a *thwump* and a moan on the other side of a dumpster several feet away. She caught up with Mark as he was snapping cuffs on knife man, who was lying facedown on the asphalt. Mark stood and locked eyes with his young charge.

"Sylkie, someday your enthusiasm's gonna get you killed. You should have waited for me."

Thunder echoed off the walls of the surrounding buildings, signaling an approaching storm. Lightning lit up the alley. Abruptly, scattered salvos of raindrops pinged against garbage-canister covers. The two investigators stood face-to-face. Maune had fire in her eyes; she didn't appreciate being admonished. Regardless, Mark decided this was the time, right now, to clear the air.

The rain escalated into a downpour. "Bet you never said that to Littlebird. You seem to forget, Mark, I'm your partner, not your kid." This was the first time Sylkie had called Truitt by his first name, confirming she was as serious as him to having it out once and for all.

"Littlebird would have waited for me before blindly chasing a dangerous criminal into a dark alley. That's what partners do. They watch each other's backs."

"Hey, I'm getting wet down here," the cuffed knife wielder groaned.

"Shut up," Truitt admonished.

"Thanks for your concern, but it's overblown. You know what I think, Mark? I think you can't get over losing Littlebird. And maybe you're even having a 'woman-replacement problem.'"

Mark had to admit Sylkie was a little bit on the money. He did miss Jamie, and getting used to a new partner, female or otherwise, was a struggle. But that wasn't his motivation for their confrontation. His concern for Sylkie's well-being was first and foremost.

"You're right, Sylkie; change isn't easy. But know that I'm not at all wary of your abilities as a cop. What I am worried about is your anger inside. I see it every time we make a collar. You act as if every suspect had a part in your mother's death. And that may ultimately be your downfall—your overriding need for revenge. It could get you killed. You have to let it go."

Mark placed his hands on her shoulders. "Please, understand I care about you, and I care about your future. But you won't find success, not in your career, not with Maxwell, not anywhere, unless you cast out your demons."

"Hey, can you guys continue the soap opera someplace else? I'm drenched."

"We'll be with you in a moment." Truitt waved dismissively.

Rivulets of water rolled down Sylkie's face, but the moisture in her eyes was not rain-induced. She thought of her inner circle. She couldn't deny her newfound love for gentle and kind Cason Maxwell had pried open long-buried emotions. And at every opportunity, her beautiful sister, Nora, tenderly preached forgiveness. Now Mark had struck the fatal blow. In that stormy moment, Sylkie Maune finally faced the truth—love suppressed by hatred is love lost, and the soul withers.

Sylkie didn't say anything. She didn't have to; Mark saw it in her eyes. Her demons had received their marching orders.

Billy Wickers was a career criminal who had been fingered by an informant as one of two robbers responsible for the murder of two innocent people in the convenience-store robbery Mark had been investigating. In a secretly taped conversation, Wickers bragged to the informant about his involvement. An additional stroke of bad luck for Wickers caught him executing a drug exchange just as Mark and Sylkie were about to pounce. On top of that, Wickers now had the added charge of attempted assault with a deadly weapon.

Wickers rested his elbows on the table in the interrogation room. Giving away his IQ, he gave Maune a tongue wave as she and Mark pulled up chairs opposite him. Billy vowed never to go back to prison, thus the knife swipe at Maune. Ratting out his accomplice could reduce his sentence, but that option was akin to falling on a grenade, given the gang to whom he pledged allegiance.

Mark held a cold stare on Wickers. "Life really takes some strange turns, doesn't it, Billy? An hour ago, you were stuffing money in your pocket, on top of the world. Now look at you, the picture of dejection. Fortunately, we're here to help. All you have to do is tell us who your partner was in the Little Super Convenience Store robbery, and we can bring a bit of sunshine into your miserable life. Give me a name, Billy. Or would you prefer your friend go free while you rot in a cell, maybe for the rest of your life? The choice is yours."

Wickers leaned into the table. "Screw you!"

"Sorry, Billy, you got it backwards. On top of a very incriminating audiotape, we've got you for possession of a controlled substance, sale of a controlled substance, attempted assault with a deadly weapon. Want to change your mind?"

Wickers turned away and stared at the floor.

Sylkie set her hands on the table. "Billy, the surveillance camera reveals the shooter to be the taller of the two masked assailants. You're about five foot eight, so odds are, the shooter was the other guy. Who was your accomplice, Billy?"

"You're poking the wrong guy. I didn't rob no convenience store."

"Your own confession on tape says you did."

Wickers said nothing.

Mark and Sylkie looked at each other. They were deep into their extended shift, and Wickers wasn't cooperating. Time to call it a day.

*****

Casey Maxwell was waiting for Sylkie as she left the interrogation room.

"Another long day, huh?"

"The department's short. Vacations."

"How about a late-night dinner at a nice restaurant?"

"How about pizza at my apartment? I just want to put my feet up and relax."

"That was my second choice."

Mark gave a mental thumbs-up as he watched the couple walk down the hall.

Though tonight wasn't a date per se, Sylkie and Cason had spent several evenings together. Though each was still in the circling stage, neither could deny something special was happening.

"So is your sister still seeing that college professor?" Casey asked, working on his third wedge of pizza.

"Oh yeah, they've been out on a few dates. I think she's getting serious. I hope he is. Said she would like for the four of us to go out dinner sometime soon."

"That sounds like fun, although I hope he isn't as one dimensional as some of my former college teachers, or it'll be long night."

"I don't think so," Sylkie retorted, eying Cason mischievously. "The way Nora talks about him, he sounds like a pretty classy guy. I think the two of you will get along unless you're the jealous type that likes to play the alpha male."

"I swear I don't have a jealous bone in my body." *As long as no one else has his sights set on you.* Casey readily admitted to himself he was completely taken over with this woman. Even wrapping her lips around the last bite of pizza sent tremors through him. For the first time in his life, Cason Maxwell truly understood what it meant to be in love. *But is she?*

"Oh, by the way, Sylkie, rumor has it we're going to get help with the circus murders. Seems there's been some arm twisting at the bureau to bring about a quick closure."

"Is that unusual?"

"Very much so. I'd say there are well-connected people feeling the heat."

"Well-connected as in Wall Street to Washington?" Sylkie raised an eyebrow.

"Very perspective of you, Sergeant Maune."

"More pizza?"

"No, thanks. I couldn't eat another bite."

Sylkie gathered their empty soda bottles and tossed them in the garbage. Then she took the pizza leftovers and aimed for the refrigerator. She opened the door and leaned over to find them a berth. Casey's eyes followed her.

"It's getting late. I know you have another long day ahead of you tomorrow. I…guess I better be going."

Sylkie closed the refrigerator door, turned, and threw Casey a very stern look.

A confused Casey wondered out loud, "Something wrong?"

Sylkie didn't answer. She walked over to Casey, grabbed his neck with both hands, pulled him close, and initiated a particularly serious orbicularis oris muscle contraction or, put another way, puckered up her lips and planted a long hot pizza-flavored kiss.

"You're not going anywhere, Mr. FBI man."

Ah, those talks in the rain.

CHAPTER 12

Ken followed the coordinates he had set on his GPS until the address for Rose Cherotte's property came into view. The route had taken him west of the Twin Cities, deep into Minnesota farming country. Turning onto a dirt road that paralleled her eighty-acre farm afforded him a bead on Cherotte's house, a quarter mile away. Ken turned his car into a field entrance and climbed out. Damp evening air filled his nostrils with the pungent smell of recently spread manure, thankfully alternating with the more refreshing aroma of new-mown hay. A retreating sun turned silo domes into lighthouse beacons. However, the predominant feature in the pastoral setting was the endless rows of cornstalks and soybean plants rising and dipping on the hilly landscape. Ken raised a pair of field glasses and focused them on the Cherotte property.

Rose Cherotte's house was vintage, and he could see, even from this distance, it was obviously in need of extended TLC. The cedar lap siding, painted light gray, was begging for a fresh coat. Two cars occupied a driveway that separated the house from a garage that appeared to be a prime candidate for a fire-department practice burning. The driveway continued around the garage and ended alongside a barn threatening to implode. On the side of the barn opposite the driveway, a silo mimicked the Tower of Pisa but nonetheless appeared to be the most stable structure on the property.

Ken swung his field glasses back to the house in time to see a barebacked man, holding a hand over one eye and carrying a shirt in the other, burst through a back entrance, thrusting its screen door open with enough force to dislodge it from its top hinge. He launched himself off the attached porch, a pace which he maintained until he reached his car. He started the vehicle and spun it around, sandblasting the garage with gravel. Abruptly, a woman emerged through the doorway and onto the porch, cradling a shotgun. She watched as he fishtailed down the driveway, waving her a one-fingered goodbye.

Interesting, Ken thought to himself. He walked around to the front of his car, reached down, and released air from a front tire.

Fading light cast long shadows as Ken slowly crept down the driveway, hoping to draw shotgun lady's attention, whom he assumed was Rose Cherotte. He much preferred to be met outside the house as opposed to knocking on a door, knowing that the person on the other side held rights to a shotgun. Ken stopped his car short of the porch and opened his door. Cherotte stepped out of the house, shotgun in hand.

"Who are you? What do you want?" she demanded.

In spite of the fact she was pointing a gun at his head, Ken was pleasantly surprised as he gave Rose the once-over. Shapely legs stuffed into a pair of tight jeans produced a lean physical look. Well-toned arms protruded through a black tank top form-fitted over a trim, busty torso. Most prominent of all was Rose's deep-red hair, cut in a casual short style and accentuating her deep-green eyes. *A real GI Jane in the heart of Minnesota farming country.*

"I said what do you want?" Cherotte took a couple of steps closer, cradling her shotgun a little tighter.

"I…ah, I'm sorry to bother you. I have a tire that's losing air. I was hoping you might have an air compressor."

"Cut the bull. Are you a cop? If you are, I want to see an ID. If you aren't, well, that's a whole other matter." Rose readjusted the shotgun.

Ken was impressed with her style. *Okay, Red, let's see how good you are at mind games.* He crossed his arms and did his best to look unconcerned, as he was afraid a show of fear might get him killed. "All right, I'll be perfectly honest; I'm not a cop, and that's the reason I'm here. I had to check you out to be sure *you're* not a cop. If you're Rose, I'm the man you talked to yesterday about a job. You have to understand this is very important to me. I'm…"

"I don't care what's important to you," Cherotte barked. "You came onto my property uninvited and under false pretenses. Give me a reason why I shouldn't shoot you right now."

"Because I'm being honest with you. Because we have the same goals. And because I'm going to pay you a lot of money to help both of us realize those goals. If that's not what you want, Rose, either shoot me or let me drive away. You are Rose, aren't you?"

Cherotte stared at Ken and said nothing. As silent seconds ticked by, Ken entertained the thought that superior intelligence might not trump an ornery, single-minded woman holding a shotgun—correction—an ornery, *hot*, single-minded woman holding a shotgun. After a long moment, the gun began to make a slow arc downward.

"So tell me about this job, and how much it pays."

"I require your commitment to two assignments for which I will pay you ten thousand dollars."

"And those 'assignments' are?"

"First, I need you to drive a vehicle, a Hummer, to Washington DC. Secondly, I need a special type of weapon."

Cherotte said nothing and maintained a hard stare into Ken. Finally, she stepped off the porch and walked across the driveway in the direction of the garage. Laberday followed.

Rose stopped in front of a set of sagging double doors. She produced a key and poked it into a rusty padlock. A twist of the key opened the lock. Rose pulled hard against the protestations of rusty hinges to open one of the doors. Ken peered into the dimly lit building. The contents within appeared to rival the age of the structure itself. Long-outdated farm implements were strewn about haphazardly, the highlight being a 1940s vintage Ford 8N tractor. A far corner of the building featured an early seventies Ford F150 pickup in all its rusted glory. The truck had definitely seen its better days, and Ken assumed it was in its final resting place. He was wrong.

Cherotte yanked on the driver's side door. It dissented but gave in. She climbed inside, and to Ken's surprise, it started with only a few cranks. She backed it up about six feet, shut it off, and climbed out. She then grabbed a shovel and scraped away a greasy pile of hay on the floor, exposing a wood cover. She tipped the cover against a wall and stepped onto a ladder.

"C'mon down." Rose flipped a light switch and disappeared into the opening.

A slight angst gripped Ken. The thought surfaced he may be descending into an underground torture chamber to be mercilessly prodded and poked until death do he part. Could be Ms. Rosy Rose was a bone collector and about to add him to the pile. Much to his relief, one look into the hole put those fears to rest. Instead of bones or medieval torture machines was a grand selection of weapons of destruction packed into the small room. Ken gazed in wonder as he climbed down the ladder. Guns of every conceivable description lined the walls. Boxes containing ammunition, grenades, and other assorted ordnance were stacked on top of one another. Kenny wanted to ask Rose what all this was for but decided the less he knew, the better.

Instead he offered, "Impressive."

"See what you're looking for?" Cherotte extended an arm toward the cache.

Ken inspected the lot. "Nice collection but sorry, no."

"No problem. Let's go back to the house and talk business. Whatever it is you need, I can make it happen. Up you go."

Ken liked her take-charge attitude. This mission required some-one strong and someone with purpose, and so far, she did not disap-point. Rose clicked the padlock closed on the garage door and turned toward her house.

"I have to ask you," Ken inquired. "Just before I came, a guy ran out of your house, holding his eye. Are you two close? I mean, I don't want anyone else knowing about our arrangement; that is, if you do come on board."

Rose whirled around and stared angrily. "You really were spying on me, weren't you?"

Something told Laberday there would be no relationship with this woman unless he let her into his world. A fool she was not.

"Look, this mission is my life. I have to succeed at all costs, and in order to do that, I have to have the right person beside me. Are you that right person, Rose? Oh, and by the way, my name is Ken."

Cherotte turned off the lasers. "Do you have a last name?"

Ken had to stand his ground and let her know he was in charge. "I do, and you will know it in good time. That is, if we can make a connection."

Rose hinted at a smile. "Let's talk business."

"Good. But what about the guy who ran out of here?"

"Thought he could bully me into a club and drag relationship. He was wrong."

It was well past dark when Kenny stepped off the back porch. His disheveled appearance was in stark contrast to his personal standards of vanity, and he was sore from head to toe. Never in his life had he experienced anything like it. For sure, this Rose Cherotte was quite a woman. She said it was her version of kung fu sex. And he liked it. He liked it a lot.

On the way home, Ken reflected on his good fortune of pairing up with a strong-willed, like-minded confidant. And as a bonus, one who had brought him upstairs, taking him to places he had never been. His unstable mind interpreted this budding partnership as nothing less than fate. For sure, the upcoming circus act was off to a dandy start.

Those caressing thoughts crashed with a dull thud as a mental picture of Nora Balfour popped into his mind. After his escapade with Rose, continuing a fling with Nora would be akin to attending a small-town carnival after you've been to the state fair. He would have dumped her like a pan of dirty dishwater except for the fact she still might be helpful as his ear to the police. However, after the next "act" was completed and he was satisfied his trail was cold, it would be goodbye to Nora the Insignificant.

*****

Nora peered at her reflection in the bathroom mirror and decided it was time to have *the* conversation. No more excuses; no more delays. So far, her evenings with Ken had ended at her door-step. But tonight was going to be different. Tonight she would step out from behind her barricade of fear. Tonight she was going *all in*.

The decision hadn't come easily. So much of her life had been filled with turmoil, heartbreak, and abandonment. Of course, there were also the bright spots; Danny, Margo, and of course, Sylkie. She held close to those islands of strength as the thought of being hurt again made her paranoid about fostering a relationship with anyone outside her tight-knit circle. Now, finally, Nora had summoned the confidence to face her fears and bravely push away the dark clouds of uncertainty and despair and replace them with a bright sun of opti-mism shining on a wonderful new world filled with love, security, and commitment. And she liked the feeling. She liked it a lot.

CHAPTER 13

Mark and Sylkie weren't the least bit impressed with what they were hearing from Jim Renner. There were new kids on the block, and Renner and Cason wanted to prepare the team for what was destined to be something less than a love-in.

"So if I understand this right"—Lompello glared at Renner—"the FBI is pulling rank. Why?"

Renner hesitated. "Because your department is not getting satisfactory results in the circus-murders case. And evidently someone in DC feels that Maxwell and I require adult supervision."

"Says who?" Sylkie shot back.

"Says someone high enough at Justice that has an interest in the case." Renner threw up his hands. "Don't ask me; I'm a minor leaguer in an insignificant Midwestern outpost. Ask our new overlords when they get here."

Mark took offense. "Insignificant by whose interpretation?"

Renner apologized. "Sorry. I didn't mean that. I'm as frustrated as you are with the 'help' being forced on us."

Casey interjected. "It's not like we're dragging our feet."

Renner added, "Which makes the bureau's decision even more perplexing, considering who they're sending to 'rescue' us."

Sylkie shot a puzzled look. "What do you mean?"

Casey scowled, "Oh, you'll see."

Mark said, "Anyway, this *insignificant* Midwesterner has a fresh bit of information, but I may as well wait for our new friends so I don't have to say it twice."

Renner was about to cast a little more insight regarding the incoming additions to their family when a burly Caucasian man filled the doorway. "Morning. Frank Koralsky; this is Tony Chen." Koralsky jerked a thumb at the oriental-looking man standing behind him. "I take it you know why we're here." Koralsky wasted no time getting to the point. "From now on, Lieutenant, any information your department comes across in the circus-killings case will be immediately relayed to me."

Guy stuck out an obligatory palm, but his face wasn't welcoming. "Glad to have you but let me give you a little advice. Don't try and bulldoze your way around. We'll cooperate, but don't treat the locals like we're an underclass."

Koralsky retorted, "Yeah, fine, as long as you don't hold anything back. Remember, this is our case now."

"Speaking of which..." Mark reluctantly spit out the words, "Our crime lab found matching samples of dirt on the inside of the rear bumpers on both the van and pickup used in the circus murders. Destroyed as those vehicles were, thankfully a small amount of evidence survived."

"So make the connection," Koralsky barked.

Truitt wasn't liking Koralsky's attitude already. "Both samples of dirt are common to a subsoil order known as Alfisols. It's a light-gray loam and clayey mixture found in approximately half of the state, including parts of the Twin Cities metro area. The significance is that we can narrow our search for clues as to where the vehicles were modified."

"That's assuming the work was done in Minnesota," Renner surmised.

"No, I'm saying it narrows down the possibilities *for* Minnesota. Of course, we're also looking at matches in surrounding states."

Agent Chen added, "It's possible the killer did his modifying on a property he didn't own."

Mark responded, "Yes, possible, but we have little else to go on right now, and it shouldn't be too hard to work up a program that will overlay home foreclosures and business failures with people who inhabit properties with this type of soil."

Koralsky wasn't buying in. "Truitt, what I'm hearing you say is, you're paring the possibilities down from a needle in a haystack to a needle in half a haystack. Good luck with that." Koralsky motioned to Renner and Maxwell. "Let's go."

Casey opened the first inning of an extra-inning headache.

*****

Ken watched the batter take a third strike, trying his best not to look bored. His lack of enthusiasm had nothing to do with the game. Target Field is a great place to watch baseball. The afternoon was sunny and warm, and the Twins were ahead. The source for his dour mood was sitting next to him. Every time he glanced at Nora, his thoughts gravitated to Rose Cherotte. He visualized that hard, sexy body binding him into submission, and now it was as if he was paying the penalty for that erotic escapade by being forced to pretend he was enjoying himself. He contemplated dismissing Nora even this night but decided to keep her in play awhile longer. Admittedly, the tease of a good-girl-bad-girl love triangle was an amusing distraction from the intense demands of bringing corporate criminals to justice. And he wanted to keep the cop connection active a bit longer. At any rate, his goals didn't include a long-term relationship with either woman. At some point, he would wipe the slate clean.

After the game, Ken and Nora walked the few blocks to an upscale restaurant where he had made dinner reservations. Along the way, Nora grabbed his hand and pulled close. She felt his body stiffen.

"Something wrong, Ken?"

Nora's voice twanged Ken's lusty thoughts back from the white farmhouse in the Minnesota countryside to his present dull entrapment. Ever the chameleon, Ken capped his feelings and squeezed Nora's hand.

"Wrong?" he chuckled. "How could anything be wrong when I'm with you? It's just that...oh, here we are."

The couple followed their hostess to a table in the far corner of the room. Drinks were ordered and delivered. Not completely pacified by Ken's sudden mood change, Nora nervously asked, "Okay… so do you want to share your thoughts?" She was rethinking her expectations for a beautiful climax to the evening.

Of course, he would share his thoughts. And of course, it would be a lie. "Well, if you must know—and I apologize for seeming distant—it's just that I can't shake a very discouraging faculty meeting yesterday."

"Is it private information or something you can talk about?"

"Private? Well, yes…and no. The entire meeting was punctuated with negatives about today's college scene. The high costs, smothering loans, poor placement. Our president quoted a lot of figures I won't bore you with, but in a nutshell, higher education demands too many bucks for the bang. It's losing its value, and unless we can get better participation in important curriculums like math and science, the future doesn't look bright."

"Does that mean I'm wasting my time trying to better myself?"

Ken laughed and grabbed her hand. "My dear, I promise to protect you and guide you to the best of my ability." Exhibiting classic tactics of the psychopath—play on the quarry's sympathy and lavish them with charm—Kenny was back in the driver's seat.

"I'll hold you to that." Nora felt her body relax. Yes, she was ready to give it all to her love. "Now onto a more pleasant subject, I'm anxious for you to meet my sister and her friend. I thought we could have dinner with them sometime soon."

"By all means, but let's do it by the end of the week. My schedule gets busy after that."

Following a starry-eyed dinner for Nora and a forced march for Ken, they drove back to his house, where she had left her car. "Thank you for the lovely afternoon and evening, Nora." Laberday put his arms around her. "I guess I'll see you at the end of the week."

"I, ah…have a sitter lined up for the night, so if you wanted to invite a girl in…"

Of course, he would. But he wouldn't like it a lot.

*****

98

"Sylkie, take a look at this." Mark waved a sheet of paper at his partner while he gulped the morning's second cup of coffee.

Sylkie strolled over and adjusted her reading glasses. After a long minute, she said, "So have you ever come across this Elliot Cantes guy?"

"Nope. His name doesn't ring a bell. But does the report on his activities give you any goose bumps?"

Sylkie nodded. "Oh, yeah. Arrested on two occasions for domestic abuse. House foreclosed on in 2008 *and* his mortgage was with the Independence Republic Bank. Issued a speeding ticket on Interstate 84 a few miles from Middletown, New York, one day before the Morris Lavonia murder. Just a couple of coincidences here."

"One more thing."

"What's that?"

"His current address is a rental property near Forest Lake, and guess what soil type is common to that area?"

"Maybe a match for the dirt found on the bumpers of the truck and van?"

"Bingo."

Sylkie snapped her fingers. "Aha. *El principal sospechoso.*"

"Huh?"

"The prime suspect."

"We'll see."

"So what now? You gonna share this with Koralsky and company?"

"Have to, but I'm going to make the call to Maxwell."

Sylkie frowned. "Shouldn't you be talking to Koralsky? He made it clear he's in charge of the investigation."

"That's why I'm calling Maxwell."

Within the hour, four FBI agents were standing on the other side of Mark's desk. "So what's this important information you dug up, Truitt?" Koralsky growled.

"I have a person of interest you may want to look at." Mark briefed the agents on what he had discovered about the recent activities of one Elliot Cantes.

Koralsky motioned to Chen. "Let's bring Mr. Cantes in for a chat."

Mark offered directions.

Koralsky cast a hard eye at Mark. "Next time you have information to pass along, Truitt, I would appreciate a call from you directly."

Mark smiled. "Uh huh, sure. I can do that."

*****

Elliot Cantes sat in the police interrogation room, rubbing his trembling hands together. Looking very Mediterranean with olive skin and tightly curled black hair, Cantes appeared both dazed and scared. Koralsky and Chen stared menacingly at him. Renner and Maxwell were standing outside the room, peering through the one-way glass. Mark joined the duo as the interrogation began.

"I see Mr. Cantes was at home," Mark said.

"Not only at home but having a coke party with two underage girls," Renner added.

"Cantes is in a whole lot of trouble even before he may be in a whole lot of trouble," Casey noted.

Koralsky pushed himself away from the wall opposite Cantes. "So, Elliot, you like to party with young girls. You've been a bad boy, and bad boys get punished. However, tell you what we're gonna do. We are going to forget about that for now because that's not why we invited you in for a chat."

Sweat was visibly wicking through Cantes's shirt, keeping pace with the beads he was wiping from his forehead.

Koralsky backed off. Tony Chen took over. "I understand you recently took a trip to New York State, Elliot. Why did you go there?"

Cantes gave Chen a puzzled look. "I... I was visiting my cousin, why?"

"Where does your cousin live?"

"Poughkeepsie."

"Will your cousin verify you were visiting?"

"Sure, why not?"

"You got a speeding ticket near Middletown. Where were you headed?"

"I was on my way back home."

"Did you stay at a motel or use a credit card on your trip back?"

"I got no credit. I use cash. I slept at rest areas. What's this about, anyway?"

Chen checked off to Koralsky. "You lost your house in 2008. What happened, Elliot?"

"What do you mean, 'what happened'? The crooks stole it from me just like they did from lots of other people. They tell you this, they tell you that, but the fine print says something else. Once they get your hard-earned money, they invest it in dirty deals. What a gig." Cantes wagged a finger at the agents. "Those are the people you should be going after. They're the ones ruining the country."

Koralsky and Chen looked at each other. Chen pursued. "You're mad at the Independence Republic Bank, aren't you, Elliot? You were also mad at John St. Claire because he was the head of the bank that took your house."

"John...who?"

Koralsky leaned in close to Cantes. "Are you at all familiar with the circus killer, Elliot? You know, the guy that blows people up; catapults them out of trucks; stands them up in front of trains. Do you know that guy, Elliot? I think you do. I think you know him real well, Elliot, because maybe you are the circus killer... Are you the circus killer, Elliot?"

"What? You're pinning that on me? You're crazy. I want a lawyer, and I want him now!" Cantes folded his arms, signaling he was through talking.

"What do you think?" Casey turned to Mark.

"I think he can arrange a coke party with two underage girls."

Renner said, "We'll see what else he might have arranged after we dig into his background."

"Good luck."

CHAPTER 14

The naked man propped himself up on an elbow, initiating tsunami-sized rolls of splotchy neglect to splay onto the bedsheet. Definitely a sight to make for sore eyes. His attention telescoped on the woman forty-four years his junior, who, at the moment, was slipping nylons over legs long and tapered like inverted telephone poles. She had been in his service for the past year, the most recent in a long line of female companions providing pleasure for seventy-two-year-old Samuel Davis Peck, distinguished senator from the great state of Mississippi and chairman of the Senate Committee on Banking, Housing, and Urban Affairs. Peck had represented his state in Congress longer than half his constituents had been alive. And during those years, he never passed on an opportunity to represent himself.

Peck's career was born out of his association with Dixie Mafia, not the real Mafia, but a loosely defined criminal gang based in Biloxi, Mississippi, whose heyday stretched from the early 1960s to the late 1980s. Though many of his confederates were eventually obliged to take up new careers, such as license-plate manufacturing, Slitherin' Sam skillfully sidestepped (bought off) any and all legal attempts at linking him to criminal activities. With equal deftness, the wily senator maintained his popularity among his constituents by elevating the pork-barrel concept to nosebleed altitude.

The woman finished dressing, snatched up her purse, and sauntered over to Peck. She leaned down and lightly tapped her lips on his. "See you next week, lover boy."

"Stay out of trouble, dawlin'. Now y'all remember to bottle up your lovin' and save it for Sammy. Never know, the ole groin may be a-shakin' an' a-bakin' 'fore the week's up."

"Sam, you are one perverted old man. But that's the way I love you, baby."

Yeah, right. What you love is the money, the apartment, the car, and whatever else you can wriggle out of me. But so what? My life is every man's fantasy. And Peck had the means to keep the good times rolling. He was the very definition of the abuse of position and power. His palms were so greased even air slipped off them, which was the reason thoughts of his mistress quickly evaporated in light of the problem at hand.

Peck rolled out of bed and scratched his enormous belly, much of which hung over his groin like a glob of whale fat. He sauntered into the bathroom, reached down, and pulled open a door on the vanity. There were towels, toilet-bowl cleaner, mouthwash, and a bottle of Southern Comfort. The senator half-mused how efficient the toilet-bowl cleaner laced with Southern Comfort might be. No doubt, it could go a long way toward permanently solving *the* problem.

Shaking off the macabre thought, he opted for the Southern Comfort, minus any sides. The intoxicating liquid "waterfalled" down his gullet, initiating a strong desire for an encore. He opted for a half-ration for the second round, as Val Docket would be there any minute for their meeting—a meeting that promised to be uncomfortable but necessary. So necessary.

The doorbell interrupted Peck's breakfast of toast washed down with the other half-ration of Southern Comfort.

"Morning, Sam. What's up? Your voice sounded a bit tense."

Peck politely nodded an affirmative to that. "C'mon in, Val, set yourself down. You want a drink?"

"A little early. Thanks anyway."

"Not me. Not today." Peck strutted to the kitchen and dumped the remaining half-ration into his glass, but who was counting?

"You at all familiar with that young senator, ah, Sheridan, from New Mexico? He's sitting on the Senate Ethics Committee."

Docket said, "No. Why?"

"Seems the boy wants to move up in the world, and evidently he's decided the fast track is to bring trouble upon old civil servants. I hear through the grapevine he's pushin' for a criminal investigation that's going to target its venomous fangs directly at me. I also hear there's a lot of rats coming out of the cellar ready and willin' to sell out old Sam. The water's risin', and they don't want to get wet. You know what that means, don't you, Val?"

Docket suddenly didn't feel so well. *Think fraud. Think illegal campaign contributions. Think obstruction of justice.* Docket fantasized the necessity to invent new terminology for some of the shady dealings Peck had authored. And worst of all? Val Docket himself would not escape scrutiny. There was no halo over *his* head.

Docket was trapped, and he knew it. "So what are you proposing, Sam?"

"Well, I can't personally do nothin' about it. I'm compromised. It's what I want you to do, Val."

"You're going to drag me into this?" Docket protested.

"You're already in it, son. You know that. You think you're going to sit on the sidelines while I get carved up for catfish bait? Ain't gonna happen. You got bones buried in your backyard, too, and you just never know when an old dog might come along and dig up a few."

Peck unsteadily drifted back to the kitchen for a further half-round of the spiced whiskey.

Docket could barely take a breath. Peck wasn't just a snapshot of the Washington machine but he *was* the Washington machine—well-oiled and finely calibrated. Docket was but a minor gear. Nonetheless he was a part of the machine, and that bit of truth could easily get him jammed up along with the rest of the parts.

"Okay. Okay, Sam. I'll start pulling together the best legal defense team Washington has to offer, just in case this thing gets legs. In the meantime, give me a message to pass along. You know, just to be sure all involved understand the gravity of the situation."

Peck massaged his forehead. "Ever see a feral house cat caught in a leg trap, Val?"

"No, why?"

"Ain't nothin' more vicious. They hiss and claw and bare their teeth at anything or anyone that gets close. More dangerous than an animal that's natural to the wild. Know why they do that, Val?"

"I don't."

"Cuz they're scared. A wild animal's equipped with an inbred survival mode. They'll plot and figure. Maybe even chew off the leg that's caught in order to get free. A feral cat's most likely had a lick of the good life. They don't know how to react in the cold, cruel outside world. It turns them mean. Real mean."

"I see."

"Know what scares me about being incarcerated, Val?"

"What's that, Sam?"

"No female companionship. I cain't fathom that. I'd ruther be drug bare-balled, belly down, and backwards through a legion of bull thistles than go without my women."

"Sounds brutal."

"You know what else bothers me, Val?"

Docket didn't like where this was heading. "What else bothers you, Sam?"

"I love to play cards—five hundred rummy, poker, hearts, whatever. I have visions of nobody to play cards with. So you tell all concerned—you know whom I mean—I'm very adept at giving card lessons. Need I say more?"

Docket got the message. "Think I'll take that drink now. Do you have any BJ Holladay?"

*****

Nora leaned back in her patio chair and stared up at wispy cirrus clouds sweeping across a steel-blue sky. She willed them into musical notes that strummed out Dusty Springfield's "The Look of Love"—the perfect ode to her night with Ken Laberday. The liaison had been profoundly more than she had hoped for, exquisitely more than she had hoped for, and rapturously more than she had hoped for. It had been sensuous and beautiful. Nora loved this man with all her heart and soul. Finally, she could share her love for Ken openly with her sister, for now she was sure their relationship was real, pure, and honest. And finally, she could shake the dark scabs of her past and venture forward unafraid with her two beautiful children into a new world filled with love, caring, and comfort. Nora was all but convinced that her scary, turbulent world had finally drifted full circle into calm, secure waters.

May the circle not be broken, Nora smiled to herself.

*****

Ken felt a surge of anticipation as he dialed Rose Cherotte's number. He couldn't wait to see her again—mostly for reasons other than business. Yes, he wanted to begin Rose's induction into the sordid plan for his next circus act. And yes, he was anxious to find out if she had made a connection for his specialized weapons' need. But he had to admit, above all, he was anxious to once again journey into Rose's high-energy, profane world of forbidden desires. He ran his tongue across his lips in anticipation.

"Hello?"

"Rose? This is Ken. I, ah, thought if you were free sometime today, I could come to your house and go over some logistics with you."

"Sure. Why don't you come later in the afternoon, say around five? Mind stopping for fast food? Anything is good. Oh, by the way, I found what you're looking for."

"Five it is. I'll bring some fine dining." Ken snapped the cover on his phone. What a breath of fresh air this would be from his forced arousal with that nit, Nora. The only way he got through it was to pretend he was with Rose. Tonight there would be no pretending. Tonight he would rendezvous with a *real* woman. Things were definitely looking up. Ken felt confident he was coming full circle with his plans. *May the circle not be broken.*

Ken sat across the table from Rose, digging into a carton of Chinese cuisine and doing his best to pretend he was not staring at her while he was staring at her. He was all but convinced Ms. Rosy Rose was genuine but felt compelled to go the extra mile just in case.

"What brought you to join Front Guard?"

Cherotte pitched a forkful of rice back into her carton. "My father, my love for this country, my fear of losing my freedom. From as early as I can remember, my dad drilled into me how we, the people, have to standfast against an ever-encroaching federal government. He said, little by little, they nip at our freedom until they have so much control we can't fight back. His favorite quote was, 'First they take your guns, then they tax you into poverty, then they take your rights—and if you protest, they'll come and take *you*.' Well, they're not taking me. Not without a fight!"

"Do you really think your guns and your rights are in jeopardy? I mean, there are more citizens carrying now than there ever have been."

"That's only because the states have fought to keep gun laws intact. And individual rights? Let me tell you a story about that: I worked hard to get a good education. I graduated with a business degree and applied for a management job. The company I interviewed with was an equal opportunity employer. Said they hadn't filled their quota. Guess who didn't get the job even though she was way more qualified? Yeah—me. Where were my rights? I'll tell you where they were. They were being violated by federal-government mandates." Cherotte's cheeks were trending toward the color of her hair.

No further convincing required. "I do believe we're a match, Rose. Maybe not for exactly the same reasons, but our goals are compatible. With you and me working together, I believe we can make a statement in Washington DC in a most dramatic way. It will be dangerous, but I promise it'll be worth the risk."

Rose folded her arms and all but snorted at Ken. "Not so fast. I still don't know who you are. Until we get that little item clarified, it's a no-go on my part."

Ken's icy blacks honed in on Cherotte's pale blues. The test of wills began. He conceded to himself she would settle for nothing less than an open and honest partnership. However, he couldn't allow her spunk and A-type personality get the upper hand.

And so, the stare-down commenced. Rose teased with her lips; Ken didn't flinch. He also didn't blink, not once, a common characteristic among psychopaths. After an uncomfortably long silence, Rose's glare retreated in quantum strokes. No woman had taken a long dip into those eyes and not drowned.

Having won the test of wills, Ken revealed himself and his plan to Rose. "Your training begins tomorrow. There's no time to waste. Also, we need to get the showpiece of our mission secured."

"You'll have it in two days."

"Perfect. You can help me install it. Okay, so here's the plan in a nutshell…"

Rose nodded her approval. "I think it will work. I really do." She stood and headed for the stairs. "Now if we're done with business, come on up. I have a new whip I want to try out."

Ken nearly ran her over.

CHAPTER 15

It wasn't looking good for the home team. Casey was circling the final pegs on the cribbage board while Mark was all fifteen holes back. A final but futile late surge fell short with Mark graciously conceding defeat by passing out a fresh round of ale. The two men sat back and gazed through screens on the front porch of Mark's cabin onto the glassy surface of Roundstone Lake. Hot, humid summer air drifted around them, tempered only by a fan struggling to keep up.

"This is my first summer in Minnesota," Casey yawned, settling deeper into the wicker rocker. "It's a beautiful state, but is it normally this hot this time of year?"

"No, and not for so long. Fortunately we're blessed with the perfect way to cool off." Mark nodded toward the lake.

Liz and Sylkie were standing in ankle-deep water, admiring a late-afternoon view of the lake.

"I'm so glad you and Casey could come for the day," Liz smiled. "You know, Mark thinks a lot of that young man."

Sylkie agreed. "Don't I know! Mark was playing cupid practically from the day he met Casey. In fact—" Sylkie's cell phone interrupted the conversation.

"Hi, sis. Are you busy?" Nora chirped. "I thought we could go out and get a bite to eat. I'm dying to talk to you."

"Oh, sorry, Nora. Can't do it today. Casey and I are at Mark and Liz Truitt's cabin. We won't be back till later tonight."

"Oh, Okay. That's fine. Um, would you and Casey be available to go out for dinner with Ken and me next Tuesday? I'm anxious for you to meet him."

"I'll ask Casey, but I think Tuesday is good. See you then."

"My sister Nora," Sylkie smiled at Liz as she set her phone on the dock. "She has a new man in her life. Sounds so happy, and I'm happy for her. I just hope this guy will be able to heal her wounds."

Sylkie didn't notice Casey stealthily approaching from behind. He grabbed her hand and pulled her into the lake. A moment later, Mark and Liz were admiring the young couple enjoying themselves in the refreshing water.

Liz shot an approving smile. "They seem very happy. Isn't young love great?"

Mark raised an eyebrow. "Not any better than old love." He grabbed Liz's hand and pulled her in.

*****

"I'm so glad you're finally meeting Ken," Nora grinned across the table from Sylkie and Cason. Ken held her hand tightly, his body language implying a slight shyness. As true with most psychopaths, Ken was acutely aware of the importance of first impressions.

"Believe it or not, this is my first experience sharing a dining table with members of the law-enforcement community," Ken proudly announced.

"No problem," Sylkie retorted. "We eat with forks and knives just like ordinary folks."

Nora mentally cringed, not sure how the statement was going to be interpreted. Casey adjusted his chair.

Ken stared at Sylkie. Abruptly, he reared backed and laughed. "Well, I would imagine you do. And I hope your choice of cuisine will keep your utensils busy and your stomachs satisfied."

The evening progressed within everyone's comfort zone. The food was superb; the conversation, light. Eventually, Ken felt emboldened to do a little probing.

"Nora tells me you two are assisting in those so-called circus murders. From what I've read, the killer apparently has amassed quite a following."

Casey took the bait. "I guess. The infamous antihero, right? Casey paused. "Sorry to disappoint his fan club, but we *are* going to shut down his circus."

Laberday retorted, "Uh-huh. So you have leads then?"

"Sorry, we can't openly discuss the case. Let's just say we're optimistic about getting a break in the near future."

Casey was alluding to the arrest of Elliot Cantes. Of course, Ken didn't know that, and so Casey's words were less than comforting.

Sylkie asked, "May I pick your brain for a moment, Professor?"

And wouldn't I like to pick at your body, blondie? "Most certainly. Fire away."

"As an expert in the field of economics, how do you interpret the significance of the circus killer's targets?"

Ken purposefully kept his answer vague. "Well, I mean, the whole economic downturn…it's so muddled. Just about anyone can find reason to feel threatened or cheated in some way. There are a lot of accusations about wrongdoing, but I haven't heard of any criminal indictments. Maybe this guy thinks he's fulfilling some high-minded cause."

Ken was suddenly anxious to call it an evening. The questions were hitting close to home, *and* he needed to get working on his project. He also hungered to get back to working on Rose. He loved the whip-thing.

Casey asked, "Could we recruit you in the future for your expertise if need be? Would you be open to that?"

Open to that? Does the eight ball want to find a pocket? "Of course. I'm more than willing to assist in any way possible. I'm as interested in seeing justice served on this person as those pursuing him." No one understood the true meaning of his answer.

Unseasonably cool air refreshed the couples as they stepped into the night. Nora clutched Ken's arm tightly. "Um, Sylkie, could the kids stay with you tonight? I promise I'll pick them up before you go to work," Nora pleaded in her usual disarming, sweet voice. Ken played the game, producing a thin, sly smile.

Sylkie was happy for her sister; her spark was back. "Sure, Casey can give the sitter a ride home. You two have a good evening."

"So what do you think of Professor Laberday?" Sylkie probed as they left the restaurant.

Casey took a second to answer. "He was okay, I guess. Pleasant enough. Never know, if Cantes proves to be a dead end, maybe his knowledge will prove useful, but..."

"But what?"

"I don't know. He *seemed* sincere."

Sylkie said, "I'm suspicious by nature, anyway. I mean, he's very charming, but I kind of got mixed signals. I hope I'm just misreading him, and for Nora's sake, I *really* hope there's nothing to worry about."

Casey said, "Yeah, but you're her sister. You're naturally going to be more protective. Maybe Nora thinks the same way about me."

Sylkie pinched his cheek. "Well, she'd be wrong."

"Yeah, and we should give him the benefit of the doubt, unless we find out differently. The man is probably a warm and wonderful human being."

"Better be."

*****

The days leading up to the departure for Washington, DC, passed quickly, magnifying the race to put the finishing touches on Ken's new instrument of death. Fortunately, Rose was a good student and completely on board with the plan. With her help, it was all systems go.

Along with being a perfect fit for the mission, Rose Cherotte's recruitment resulted in one more unexpected blessing. The headliner in Laberday's Washington circus act was to be Quinn Montague, head of the criminal division at the Department of Justice. Ken blamed Montague for not vigorously pursuing Wall Street predators for, at the very least, violating federal fraud statutes. The fact that no Wall Street executives had faced criminal prosecution for their roles in the crisis rolled through Ken's unhinged mind like a wall cloud, further convincing him that life is a winner-takes-all game—suitable justification for his heinous acts. He was tormented in his certainty that the game was rigged, skewered toward the big money—money that his own hands begged to cradle. Ken's choice of Montague as the sacrificial lamb was intended to send a message, and in a brilliant exposé of irony, Washington itself would administer poetic justice.

The one glitch in his plan had been securing the target. Ken feared it would be hard to get Montague alone, and time was of the essence. Fortunately, now that Rose was on board, he could devise a plan that would solve the problem. His research on Montague showed him to be divorced, and Rose was an attractive woman. She willingly volunteered to do some trolling.

The other glitch in Ken's plan was Nora. Her pesky desire to be with him these final days of preparation was an unwelcome distraction. As compensation, he had treated her to a fancy dinner as an appeasement for a feigned yearly sabbatical. He claimed this year's pilgrimage would take him to the Grand Canyon.

Finally, everything fell into place. A few finishing touches promised a most dramatic Washington, DC, introduction to the ringmaster's traveling circus.

*****

Nora happily joined along in singing a Sesame Street favorite with Margo and Danny as their car headed in the direction of Ken's house. On the seat beside her was one of his research manuscripts. She found it under the front seat earlier in the day when she had reached for a dropped toy. Exploiting the dual purpose of giving two cranky youngsters the diversion of a car ride and dropping off the manuscript, Nora eagerly anticipated surprising Ken with a quick visit.

Her route took her through the tiny hamlet of Cummins, whose premier (and only) retail establishments were a liquor store and a little father along and on the opposite side of the road, a convenience store. As she passed the liquor store, she glanced in that direction—and her world froze.

What? Nora blinked and looked again. Ken, cradling a paper bag, was opening the driver's side door on his van. A pretty red-headed woman was about to climb in the passenger's side. Nora's stomach jumped up into her throat. *It can't be!*

She turned into the convenience store's parking lot. Her mind processed a thousand logical scenarios for what she had just witnessed. A few moments later, the van passed by, its occupants smiling, animated. Nora pulled back onto the highway, hoping with all her heart and soul a simple explanation would erase the wave of dread infiltrating every cell in her body. She strained to convince herself not to believe the validity of what her eyes were seeing and what her mind was interpreting.

A few miles down the road, the van's left-tail signal light came on. The vehicle turned onto the road leading to Ken's property. Nora was shaking, hardly able to grasp the steering wheel. Her children were still singing Sesame Street songs, admonishing her to join in. Nora could hardly breathe, let alone sing.

The left-turn signal blinked once more. Nora pulled onto the side of the road and rested her head on the steering wheel. *No, no, no...don't let it be; please don't let it be!*

"Mommy, what's the matter?" Margo tensely asked.

Nora had all but forgotten her children. "N-nothing, honey. Mommy's...just a little tired." Nora pulled herself together and turned her car back onto the road. She drove past the wall of bushes and trees that blocked most of the view into Ken's yard. Looking back as she passed the property, she caught a blurred glimpse of Ken with an arm around the woman's shoulders and the woman's arm around his waist. They were walking alongside the garage in the direction of the machine shed. That image would initiate many sleepless nights.

Nora Balfour's future had just disintegrated in front of her eyes. In a quantum moment, prayers answered were transformed into prayers shattered. She and her children's bright tomorrows suddenly slipped away with the speed of the tears rolling down her cheeks. Replaying over and over the ugly scene she had just witnessed dominated her being—and impeding her acknowledgment of the approaching train's whistle.

"Mommy! Train!" Margo cried.

Nora slammed on the brakes, and her mind forced back into her body at the sound of Margo's warning. Tires screeched on the warm pavement. She frantically prayed for maximum friction between rubber and asphalt. Staring Nora in the face and approaching all too quickly were blood-colored semaphore lights flashing frantically and the meager barrier of the red-and-white striped gate, which was guillotined in the down position. Even more foreboding was the ominous sound of the Canadian National train's whistle. The car slid sideways, threatening to crash into the gate. The engine's headlights were blinking in desperation.

"Kids, get your heads down and fold your hands over them!" she screamed.

In a moment, it was over. *Clackity-clack. Clackity-clack. Clackity-clack.*

Nora registered the sound and slowly opened her eyes, vacantly watching set after set of steel wheels roll by.

"Can we go home now, Mommy?" Danny whined.

Nora took a deep breath, her maternal instincts triumphing over the horrid events of the past hour and bringing her mind to clearly focus on what was *truly* important—her children.

"Yes, we can go home now, Danny."

Going home but not going away.

Ken unlocked the door to his machine shed. Behind him, Rose cradled a bottle of port wine. The couple entered the building and set the wine bottle on a makeshift table consisting of a door scantily clad with remnants of what was once a coating of brown paint. Two wooden sawhorses supported the door. Two glasses awaiting their burden patiently stood at attention.

The wine was poured; the glasses were raised. Ken turned to their prize, the black Hummer—outfitted, polished, and ready to roll. "To success on our dangerous but necessary mission to free America from the greedy clutches of the rich and powerful."

"To sweet success," wild Rose echoed.

They drained a portion of the bottle's contents into their glasses. They gulped the glasses empty. The celebration appeared to be completed, but then Rose hung her arms around Ken's neck and glanced at the table. "Wanna try seduction on a door?"

The party wasn't quite over.

CHAPTER 16

The conference room at First Precinct headquarters radiated enough tension to swing the earth out of orbit. On one side of the long oval table sat Special Agents Koralsky, Chen, Renner, and Maxwell. On the opposite side were Captain John Kirgalis and a very out of sorts Guy Lompello, who along with Mark and Sylkie were playing host to a stable of dark thoughts.

"We've come across some interesting information concerning Elliot Cantes," Koralsky opened. "Seems like Cantes had it in for the Independence Republic Bank. So much so he fired off a threatening letter to the bank in which he declared he would get even for them 'stealing' his house. It was buried in his file and apparently forgotten."

Kirgalis pressed, "Have you talked to him about it?"

"We'll be doing that shortly."

"How about his cousin out in…where is it?" Lompello queried.

"Poughkeepsie," Maxwell answered.

"Yeah, there. Did he verify Cantes's visit and his whereabouts around the time of the Lavonia murder?"

Koralsky returned, "Well, no, we're still working on that."

Mark thought the answer somewhat evasive.

Koralsky continued. "We're going to keep digging, but I have every reason to believe we have our man. I discussed the evidence with the US attorney. He's considering an indictment."

Sylkie frowned. "The only evidence I see is circumstantial and a stretch at that."

Agent Koralsky set both palms on the table, hard. "Look, I don't really care what you can see or what you can't see. Cantes is guilty; I'm sure of it, and I'm going to prove it. End of discussion."

Kirgalis said, "I hope you're right. Just remember, use the tax-payers' money wisely."

The meeting broke up with a definite chill in the air. Not the kind generated by the air conditioning.

"So what do you think?" Sylkie looked at Mark.

"I think Cantes can arrange a coke party with two underage girls."

"Hmm."

*****

Creeping rays from an already-robust sun intruded Nora's bed-room window, licking her face and rousting her from a fitful sleep. She felt wearier now than when she had crawled into bed several hours earlier. No matter. Time to get moving. There was work to do.

She got Margo and Danny dressed, fed, and into the car in record time. She dropped them at Roundup Day Care and then pointed her car north. Nora's plan was to confront Ken before he left on his trip. He'd thrown out the excuse about making a solo pil-grimage to a different natural wonder in the country each year. He claimed it was a time for refreshment and renewal from the arduous demands of his profession.

Yeah, right. He claims his destination is the Grand Canyon. Probably more like the Grand Caymans. In fact, Nora doubted every-thing he had told her. Ken Laberday had a lot of questions to answer, and answer he would.

Nora pulled her car into Ken's driveway and parked in front of the garage. She walked briskly to the house and rang the door-bell. Her heart was in her throat, but determination was her ally. No answer. Rang it again. No answer. Knocked hard. No answer. She retreated back to the garage and peered through a side window. Ken's van was gone. *Had he, they (?) left for wherever it was that he, they (?) were going?*

Nora thought about the machine shed. The image of Ken and the woman strolling arm in arm in that direction was burned into her memory. What was back there? She walked around the garage and followed the wheel ruts. A light rain had fallen the night before, making the ruts slippery. Nora slid a couple of times on the U-shaped tracks before reaching the shed.

The machine shed was kind of a mystery in itself for Nora. She had noticed the tracks leading to it on a previous visit and asked Ken what was inside. He said it was a storage building for old unused belongings he had inherited from his family. *Great,* she thought. Being an antique buff of sorts, she was thinking hidden treasures. However, her advance on the shed was quickly reversed by Ken's hand as he gently but firmly turned her around. "It's a mess, and I'm afraid to admit there are rodents in there." The word *rodent* had quickly squelched her curiosity.

Nora tugged lamely on the padlock. It didn't budge. She walked around one side of the building and spotted a window. If she could get to it, she might be able to see what was inside. The hard part would be avoiding the platoon of cocklebur weeds protruding from a sea of ryegrass, a formidable adversary standing between her and the window. Nora remembered Ken's mention of rodents. She gently bit her lip. As the options were few, she bravely waded into the uninviting vegetation. By the time Nora reached the window, she resembled a giant cocklebur herself, covered from head to toe in the prickly little balls.

Nora cupped her hands around her eyes and pressed them to the window. Along with the window, splits in the siding admitted enough light for her to get dim view of the interior. The first thing that struck her was what she didn't see—namely anything resembling the old family belongings that Ken claimed were stored in the building. Another lie! What Nora did see included a couple of car seats, an assortment of tools, some round cylinder-shaped objects, and a door resting on sawhorses. The door supported a rug and two glasses. *His and hers,* she speculated. Nora stepped back from the window. She had seen enough. Kendrick Laberday was one big lie!

Nora slipped and slid her way back up the trail, picking cockle-burs from every part of her clothing. By the time she reached her car, Nora felt dirty, itchy, and most of all, still as much in the dark about Ken as when she came.

Even in his absence, he's tormenting me. Nora momentarily fantasized burning his house down. Instead she put her head against the steering wheel and sobbed—for a very long time.

*****

A disguised, blond Rose Cherotte took a sip of her vodka martini and set it back on the bar at Finley's Pub, a popular Washington, DC, watering hole. Her attempts to make eye contact with Quinn Montague fell short as he was engaged in a heated conversation with Val Docket, who was representing clients extremely uncomfortable with the idea of targeting icons of capitalism, namely themselves. Docket's mission was to exert pressure on Justice to utilize all resources necessary to apprehend this crazed killer. Clayton Rimm, a DOJ attorney was also at the table.

"Look, Val," Montague said. "I hear you. I'm as anxious as anyone to get this so-called circus killer off the street. My agents in Minneapolis are certain they've found the guy, but they're lacking evidence to seal the case."

Docket stayed aggressive. "What do you think, Quinn? Is the guy guilty?"

"From what my agents tell me, yeah. I'd say there's about a 90–10 chance he's our man."

"Well, then?"

Rimm echoed, "Well then, what?"

"Make it happen. Make sure there's enough evidence to get him off the street."

Montague and Rimm looked at each other. Montague said, "Come again?"

Docket scolded them with his eyes. "90–10 are pretty solid odds. Take it and run, put the case to bed. Orchestrate something to nail him."

Montague looked up and noticed Rose. "I...ah, well, there *is* one potential witness who could damage the suspect's claim as to his itinerary in upstate New York at the time the third victim was killed. A cousin, I think. Trouble is, he's an addict, not reliable. Fuzzy on his facts."

"So? Persuade him."

"What're you saying?"

"You said the guy's most likely guilty, right? And like it's the first time, the department steered a case? Do we need to review some history? How 'bout we start in Boston...?"

Rimm put up a hand. "Okay, Okay. We'll see what happens, but you know, Val, things can't *always* go your way."

Docket ignored Rimm and focused on Montague. "Oh yes, they can. And while you're working for the public good, remember, consensus is not on your side, what with this killer pulling off these executions in front of our noses. In fact, *he's* more popular than the people trying to catch him. My clients want the whole mortgage thing dead, gone, buried, and he regurgitates it with every killing."

Docket pulled out his wallet. "Okay, enough. Message given." He stood and tossed his share of the evening's tab on the table. "You guys have a good night."

Rimm shot daggers at Docket until he disappeared.

"Settle down, Clayton," Montague admonished. "I'm surprised at your show of emotion. Just Beltway business. But then, I don't have to lecture a pro, do I?"

Rimm tugged at his ear. "Yeah, I know. Elections get more expensive all the time, and Docket's clients have the means to show their patriotism in big ways. Doesn't mean I have to like it."

"Good night, Clayton." Montague motioned in the direction of the bar. Rimm got the message.

Montague sauntered over to the bar. Following a couple of drinks and some light conversation, the couple left Finley's.

*****

Casey rubbed his eyes and leaned his head back on Sylkie's couch. Normally not prone to headaches, this night, he was crushing walnuts behind his forehead.

"Try this." Sylkie handed him a pain reliever and a glass of water. She sat down and leaned her head on his shoulder. "So does your headache have anything to do with your new associates?"

"How'd you guess?" Casey sighed. "I mean, there's nobody's way but Koralsky's. His ego extends farther than the asteroid belt."

"He's really stuck on Cantes, isn't he?"

"Yup. He's close to having the US attorney hand down an indictment. Way too early in my opinion, but I have a feeling he's getting pressure from above. On the other hand, think what it would do for his career if he cracks the case."

"He must have something more on Cantes than what he unloaded on us the other day."

Cason put his arm around Sylkie and pulled her close. "That's my speculation, but he isn't sharing any possible new information. And there seems to be some mystery surrounding Cantes's cousin in Poughkeepsie. Koralsky's being tight-lipped about him, which, to me, means the guy could be pivotal. Now what were you saying about your sister? She's seemed a little distant the last couple of times you've talked to her?"

"Yeah, kind of. I asked her if anything was wrong. She said no, but even if there were, she would try to shield me. I don't think it has anything to do with Ken. He's been out of town for a few days. I hope it's not her ex, Aaron, giving her grief about the kids."

"I'm sure if it's important enough, Nora will share it with you." Casey brushed a hand along Sylkie's arm. "The pill seems to be working; my headache's getting better."

Sylkie reached over and turned off the lamp. "Well, then...?"

CHAPTER 17

12:59 p.m., Thursday. Federal Building, Minneapolis

Special Agent Franklin Koralsky masked his excitement as he scanned the noisy room overflowing with reporters and cameramen impatiently waiting for the news conference to begin. Standing behind him were Special Agents Chen and (reluctantly) Renner and Maxwell.

At one p.m., Koralsky read a prepared statement: "Good afternoon. This news conference has been called in concordance with new information concerning the ongoing investigation of the murders of John St. Claire, Garrett Dover, and Morris Lavonia. For several days, we have been interviewing a suspect whose activities parallel several aspects of the case. This morning, we obtained additional information that has resulted in the US attorney handing down an indictment against Elliot Nicholas Cantes. Mr. Cantes is currently being held in the Hennepin County Jail. That is the extent of my statement. I will now take questions."

Maxwell tuned out, digesting Koralsky's explanation of Cantes's indictment. The additional information to which Koralsky referred was courtesy of Cantes's cousin in New York. Apparently, the cousin said Cantes spent a good deal of time during his visit ranting about the corrupt financial system and how he was going to get even with "those who stole his house." Also, he confirmed Cantes and he had parted company three days before Lavonia was killed, plenty of time for Cantes to attend to the details of the murder. However, the icing on the cake was his claim that Cantes had asked him where he could find a hardware store and said he needed to buy some "special helpers," which the cousin later saw but said he didn't know what they were for. Maxwell wanted hard evidence. As far as he was concerned, all Koralsky provided was hearsay and precious little else.

*****

4:20 p.m., Thursday. Washington, DC

Rose Cherotte could see the dome of the Capitol Building several blocks away. Her field of vision quickly swelled with people ending their workday and transforming into restaurant patrons and retail-store clients. The trial run confirmed Cherotte's optimism for the success of the mission. She glanced at the passenger-side rearview mirror of the Hummer. Ken's van was one-car length behind and in the right-hand lane. A quick peek through the Plexiglas window mounted behind the front seat offered a backside view of Quinn Montague, secured to a makeshift turret and ready for combat. Rose felt a slight pitch in her stomach at the thought Montague was drugged to the point of restricting his reflexes but still mentally alert. Not only did he perceive his fate but he would also see it coming. Her initial feeling of remorse quickly resorted to anger.

So what? He's part of the corrupt federal government I'm fighting against. Screw him! Rose rehearsed *their* plan one last time. *Approach the designated intersection via the inside lane. Block one lane of traffic. Ken would pull up alongside and electronically set off smoke bombs on both ends of the Hummer to create a diversion and provide cover. Get out of the Hummer through the passenger-side door and jump into Ken's van through the rear driver's side door as he passes by. Meld with the rush of commuters exiting the city. Sweet!*

Comfortable with the plan, Rosey's thoughts turned to the master planner himself. She could not deny that Ken's overpowering persona was slowly turning her armor-plated will into sponge moss. This wasn't supposed to happen. Rose was a self-avowed loner, a survivor in a cruel and uncaring world. Use, abuse, then lose was her blueprint for comingling with the opposite sex. Now quite unexpectedly, her enamored feelings for Ken had bent that lifestyle to the point of breaking. She could totally envision a volatile but long-term relationship with this like-minded confidant. And she liked the feeling. She liked it a lot.

Little did Rose understand the smothering characteristics of Ken's psychopathic persona. This "like-minded confidant" knew exactly what buttons to push and when to push them. Unfortunately for Ms. Rosy Rose, she also failed to understand the flip side of the process—that is, the ease with which a no-longer-useful minion can be discarded.

Ken lifted his insulated mug and pulled a long sip of coffee, more of an anxiety reflex than a caffeine fix. He thoughtfully reviewed *his* plan. It was slightly different than *their* plan, in that his plan featured one performer to "fall off the high wire." Unfortunately for Rose, her demands for equal partnership coupled with her knowledge of Laberday's true identity made her a liability. Kenny would miss Ms. Rosy Rose but not for long. She had been a passing curiosity in his life, but that was about it. The time had come for Rose Cherotte to unceremoniously make her exit.

The two vehicles rounded the corner and throttled up for one last lap. Ken drained his cup. Washington, DC, was about to host the circus of justice.

The Dillon Aero M134D Gatling gun is an awesome weapon. Firing three thousand to four thousand rounds of ammunition per minute through six rotating barrels, it is guaranteed to make its presence known—especially when being introduced to an unsuspecting Washington, DC, populace as one half of the featured act in Kendrick Laberday's one-ring circus. The accompanying half of the act, Quinn Montague, was securely strapped to the makeshift gun turret, giving the impression he was firing the weapon.

The Hummer headed for its destination, ready to unleash on an unsuspecting audience the thrills, chills, and spills conjured up by the great ringmaster. Rose drove into the targeted intersection far enough to block one lane. She shoved the Hummer into park and slid over to the passenger's seat. Her exit would be a snap—jump out and climb into the van.

Rose yanked on the door handle. Nothing. She tried again. The door didn't budge. Ken pulled alongside. A wide-eyed Rose pointed to the handle and mouthed, "I can't open the door!" Ken cast an indifferent look and shrugged.

In that fleeting moment, Rose Cherotte came to grips with reality—*it had always been about him.* She slapped her palms against the window again and again while shouting curses that went unheard.

The macabre scene ended with vapor filling the cab, mercifully putting her to sleep. Subsequently, an acid mist rained down, melting away her being. Ken rounded the corner and executed a command on his computer.

A small pop discarded the Hummer's back window onto the hood of the car behind, leaving its startled occupant aghast at the scene unveiling before him. In the now-windowless opening, a speaker pumped out a calliope rendition of "In the Good Old Summertime." A section of roof slid back, allowing the gun turret and its passenger to hydraulically pass through. Secured to the rotating turret, the Gatling gun came to life, pouring near-nanosecond rounds of ammunition well over the heads of the instantly terrorized crowd and moving in an up-down motion, emulating a horse on a carousel.

In grim rhythm, turret and gun kept in cadence with the music. Empty shells bounced off the Hummer like hail. Pandemonium engulfed the scene. People dove for cover. Shards of bullet-shattered glass pelted the sidewalks.

Officer Jack Crowley of the Washington, DC, police department pushed against the tide of people, heading in the opposite direction. He fought to get close enough to the Hummer to get a decent shot at the man wielding the gun. Crowley crept along, ducking behind vehicles. Finally, he got a good line on the shooter who became vulnerable twice each rotation of the turret. Crowley took aim. *Wait, something's not right. Why is the shooter...so rigid?* Chance missed. Next half rotation, Crowley raised his weapon and fired. Quinn Montague's head jolted sideways. Blood poured from his neck. Another 180 degrees. Crowley pumped two more rounds into

Montague. Abruptly, the Gatling gun went silent, programmed to stop shooting when its operator registered zero heartbeat.

Police from all directions swarmed the Hummer. The calliope music suddenly melted way to a dire warning: "Move away from the vehicle! It is about to be destroyed! You have ten seconds. Move away—now!"

The voice gave way to a series of beeps, the eerie introduction to the grand finale. Seconds later, an explosion rocked the Hummer, breathing fire through its shattered windows and destroying valuable evidence. By the time fire crews wove their way to the scene, only a burned-out hull and two cremated bodies were left to sift through.

The curtain had closed on another circus act.

Ken labored on a problem as he waved goodbye to Washington, DC, and set course for Minnesota. Multiple replays of his circus act had planted that blasted calliope music in his brain. "In the Good Old Summertime" swam around in his head until he reached the Pennsylvania Turnpike, whereupon, with much concentration, he replaced it with Muddy Waters sloshing out "Champagne & Reefer." *Oooh, yaaah!*

CHAPTER 18

Nora maneuvered a soft landing on her couch, tightly cradling a cup of coffee. The normally pleasing smell of caffeine turned against her this morning, inciting further protest to an already-rebellious stomach. She conceded it was punishment for the excess of alcohol ingested the previous evening in a vain attempt to reconcile a world turned upside down by Kendrick Laberday. Of course, it didn't work. She knew it wouldn't. Dumb. But there was no plan B. She set the cup down and contemplated what to do about Ken. As her mind wandered, dark thoughts ratcheted to increasingly dour levels. *Yes, what I would like to do to you!*

Nora's dark thoughts were interrupted by giggles floating from her children's bedroom. Thankfully, a mercy ship of innocent squeals had broadsided her galleon of revenge. Nora put her head in her hands. *Who am I kidding? I know I could never hurt anyone.* True enough for Nora Balfour. Even in the wake of her mother's death in the Alfred Murrah Federal Building bombing, Nora eventually squeezed out a measure of forgiveness for the bomber. Deep down, Nora knew healing of the heart comes through forgiveness, not revenge. Though petite in stature, she loomed large in the big-heart department, always looking to please others, always looking to resolve conflict. After much deliberation and with her heart broken, she determined the best recourse was to confront Ken, have it out, and move on.

The mental massage seemed to calm her stomach. The coffee now smelled and looked more inviting. She took a sip and picked up the TV remote. The morning news was filled with the previous day's sensational shooting in Washington, DC. Most alarming of all was that one of the bodies found on the Hummer was identified as Quinn Montague, a high-level official in the Department of Justice. Nora tuned out a recap of what was rumored to be the latest "circus killing" as the coffee continued to warm a now-welcoming stomach.

As Nora pulled herself off the couch to retrieve a second cup, a breaking-news bulletin flashed across the screen. An anonymous letter had shown up at the Washington Post. It read as follows:

> In the evil City of Milk and Honey
> Where loyalty circles endless money
> (Listen)
> The people cried
> For an offender to die!
> Now a new morning dawns
> So bright and sunny
> Applications to perform in my next circus act are
> available either at the Department of Justice or at
> your nearest Wall Street investment bank. R.

The newscaster released a second piece of breaking news. The remains of the lone occupant in the front seat of the Hummer were determined to be that of a female.

Nora was pushed back onto the couch by an invisible hand. She gawked at the TV; her mind simultaneously darted in several directions, finally converging to one impossible conclusion. The coffee cup hit the floor, its remaining drops staining the carpet. *A woman. The remains were those of a woman.* Somehow, Nora knew. Or thought she knew. It made no sense, but yes, it did. Ken was out of town when the New York murder took place, and now supposedly he was in the Southwest. Her mind raced. *He lives here, in the Twin Cities, where the first two murders occurred. He had a woman with him the last time I saw him. Were the remains in the Hummer her remains? And then there are the lies about furniture being in the machine shed. Who really is Ken Laberday?*

Nora rubbed her sweating forehead with a sweaty hand. She second-guessed herself. *Am I losing my mind? Am I contriving a story because of what Ken did to me?* Her thoughts drifted back to her mother's death. If any of those in the Oklahoma City bomber's inner circle had come forward, 168 innocent souls would have been spared an untimely demise. Her heart pushed her not to ignore her suspicions, even if no hard proof existed. *Yes, I must do something. But what?*

"Mommy, I'm hungry. Mommy, why are you crying?" Danny was tugging on Nora's arm. Nora rubbed a pajama sleeve across her eyes. "Mommy's fine, honey. Hey, let's get you guys some breakfast. How 'bout pancakes?"

An action plan would have to be put on hold for now, but one thing Nora had already decided: Sylkie was not to know of her suspicions. With all her other problems, the last thing she needed was for her best friend to think she had fallen off the reality shelf.

*****

Mark and Sylkie stared at the message sent to the Washington Post. Boiling and ready for bear, Sylkie glared at her partner. This was taunting, pure, and simple—*Here I am. Catch me if you can, stupid cops!*

Mark stared back but for a different reason. Being human, more pointedly being man-human, Mark was admiring how good Sylkie looked this morning.

"So what do you think?"

Mark refocused. "I, um, think I can hardly wait for Renner and Casey to get here. Those boys got some splainin' to do."

Sylkie felt a little defensive on Casey's part. "Yeah, but the Cantes deal... I mean, that was all Koralsky and Chen."

"That don't make no...never mind, Sylkie. They were part of the team."

"That don't make no...what?"

"No, never mind. Festus used to say that to Marshall Dillon— you know, *Gunsmoke?*"

"I've seen a few reruns."

A few moments later, Jim Renner and Casey Maxwell shuffled in, grim-faced and avoiding eye contact.

"Morning. Where are your compadres?" Mark asked, tongue-in-cheek.

Renner looked at his watch. "Well, right now, I would guess they're about thirty-five thousand feet above Ohio."

Casey added, "And probably hoping high traffic volume will keep the plane circling Reagan National for a long, long time."

"Cuz they're going to have some splainin' to do?" Sylkie threw a wink.

"Bring it on," Renner sighed.

Mark saw no reason to draw blood. "If it wasn't such a serious matter, I might take a few self-indulgent pokes, but I...we know *you* guys didn't screw this up."

Maxwell said, "I can think of a better expletive than 'screw up.'"

Renner added, "And we're *not* falling on our light sabers. Even if it affects our future with the bureau."

Sylkie threw a puzzled look. "What do you mean?"

Casey explained, "The easy answer is that Koralsky was looking to enhance his future. But from the little quips he threw at us, we think he was getting pressed to come up with a face and a name. Rumor has it there are a lot of influential people who feel they have a target on their back."

Sylkie rebutted, "Yeah, well, there are a lot less influential people trying to keep their homes who feel that they have a target on their back."

Mark asked, "What about Cantes? Obviously he couldn't have been involved in the DC murder when he was in jail here."

Renner said, "I've been told he stays put till we hear differently. If and when we release him, he'll be turned over to you for the drugs and the underage thing."

Sylkie pressed, "What about the cousin's claim that Cantes threatened to get even with those he felt were responsible for him losing his house. And what about the 'special helpers' story?"

Casey raised an eyebrow. "Koralsky was more than a little vague about the interview with the cousin. We know he's an addict so maybe…a little coaching, you know? As far as the 'special helpers,' Cantes had an answer for that. He also had an explanation for the missing time between leaving his cousin's place and getting stopped by the highway patrol outside of Middletown. He claimed he had lined up a couple of sexual fantasy nights over the Internet with an escort service in New York City. He bragged about it. Said the 'special helpers' he purchased at the hardware store were nylon rope, a length of chain, and a box of disposable gloves. He also bought a roll of duct tape because it was on sale. It happened to be the same brand used to wrap Lavonia around the plank between the tracks."

"Disposable gloves?" Sylkie blinked.

Casey blushed. "You got me."

Mark said, "Was Cantes holding any of those items?"

Renner said, "Just the chain. He said it was too pricey to leave behind."

Sylkie asked, "What about the duct tape?"

"Cantes said he used some of the tape to bind together a Styrofoam cooler he had dropped at a rest stop in Indiana. Said he forgot the tape on a picnic bench."

Mark said, "And then Koralsky filled in the spaces."

Casey asked, "So where does the team go from here?"

Mark answered, "Unless something dramatic is unearthed in Washington, its back to foreclosures and bankruptcies."

Sylkie winced. "Ugh."

*****

The following morning, 5:45 a.m.

Ken turned into his driveway and activated the garage-door opener. The sun had not yet pulled up the shade on another day. He drove into the garage and hit the remote. The door cleaved down, leaving him in quiet darkness. It had been a long trip, and though he was physically spent, he allowed a few moments to revel in his latest victory. It was a splendid event for sure, and Ken was confident he had successfully covered his tracks. But just in case, he mentally reviewed the details one last time.

The sun's first rays pierced the garage windows as he completed a mental rerun of the Washington episode. Finding no holes to be plugged, Ken relaxed, more than ready for a long restful sleep. He opened the back of his van, removed a bag of tools, and headed for the machine shed.

Early morning dew bathed the assortment of weeds and grasses growing alongside the bare, rutted tracks leading to the shed in sparkling droplets of water. The fresh, sweet aromas coaxed from the plants by the moisture filtered through Ken's nostrils to sensory receptors in his brain, injecting a fresh shot of energy, not enough to emulate a "Julie Andrews dancing through a field of flowers" type of moment but an acknowledgment that life was good, that he was on top of his game, and most importantly, that he was free to begin a new campaign. Yes, Kendrick Laberday was quite pleased with every aspect of his insane life, until...

Until he spotted the footprint. Ken knelt down and inspected it closely. It was smallish, pointed in the toe. A woman's print. *Nora's print. It has to be!* Ken walked slowly along the path. The gathering sunlight zeroed in on additional tracks.

Reaching the shed, Ken examined the padlock that secured the sliding double doors. No signs of tampering. He walked to the side of the shed harboring the lone window. A narrow canyon parting the foliage pointed to an intruder. He noticed a string of red lint clinging to a cocklebur. No question, someone, Nora, had been snooping. *But why? What was she looking for? What had piqued her curiosity?*

Ken disgustedly disposed of his tool bag and stomped back to the garage. The beautiful summer morn now harbored storm clouds of trouble. The perfect crime suddenly was in danger of being compromised by some nosy little nymph, and now he was going to have to deal with her. Ken noticed a car driving by suspiciously slow as he reached the garage. Instinctively he ducked behind the building. Then he reminded himself not to let his imagination run wild. When the car passed, he went into the garage, removed a few items from the van, and quickly walked to the house, entering by the back door.

Ken set his computer case and clothes bag on the kitchen counter and headed for the study. The air inside the house was cool, damp, and uninviting—the perfect complement to his dark mood. He entered his study and aimed for the liquor cabinet. He turned over a glass and pitched in a couple of ice cubes that he retrieved from a mini-refrigerator. The cubes wagged a protest, crackling and clinking as they hit the glass. He then drained a generous round of the great equalizer, Chivas Regal. The cubes shouted out a renewed objection. Ken gulped the contents, refilled the glass, and dejectedly slumped into the chair behind his father's oak desk.

For the first time since he had given birth to his circus-of-justice crusade, Kendrick Laberday felt a loss of control, which had been initiated not from without but from someone he had let into his inner circle. *I did this to myself. I didn't follow my cardinal rule—never allow anyone to linger in my private world.* Though the scotch was now manning the controls, there was something deeper, much deeper, driving his thoughts.

Ken hesitated for a small eternity, then slowly, painfully, pushed back the curtain on a long-suppressed world. He reached down, opened a drawer, and removed an empty folder meant to hide what was beneath it. Then he removed what was beneath it and placed it on the desk.

The framed picture of Kendrick Laberday's mother hadn't seen daylight in over fourteen years. He stared at the picture and stroked its frame. A beauty she was, his mother. Chestnut-brown hair dropped past her shoulders. Deep, secretive coal-black eyes and mile-long lashes floated in symmetry with a slightly oval face. Golden tanned skin was delicately stretched over high cheekbones. Her seductive, perfectly aligned snow-white teeth teased behind full, inviting lips. Yes, Ken was his mother's son both in appearance and in the coldness of their beings. Her beautiful, emotionless face was stern as always, reaching into him, admonishing her son without saying a word. Ken leaned back and closed his eyes. A stream of booze floated his overly tired brain back to the day that would forever define their relationship.

The scene unfolding before young Kendrick was so mesmerizing all he could do was stare. Rows of goose bumps on his scrawny arms stood at attention like terra-cotta soldiers. Never in his life had he witnessed anything like it. Performers dressed in flamboyant costumes proudly displayed both skill and attire as they delicately balanced atop a parade of elephants, with tail linked to snout. Next to come were clowns and knife throwers and lion tamers and human cannonballs—it was truly a dream come true. A dream made all the more delicious because his mother was sitting alongside him.

Yes, it was really his mother, lavishing a day of undivided attention on her boy. Sort of, but not to dissect, as it was a prayer answered. Unusual? Stronger—unheard of. Why? Because excluding this day's outing, her otherwise rare spurts of attention served only to correct, no, humiliate Kendrick in the harshest terms each time he failed to live up to her impossible standards. Kendrick's bottom lip often ached from being vise gripped by clenched teeth, his sole defense to still the quivering that shook loose acid tears welled up by her frequent reprimands. His mother scolded that crying was a sign of weakness, and she would have none of that from her little man.

But today was different. Today her cruel rebukes were tucked away in a memory box and banished to an outer orbit. That his mother consented to lay aside her surgeon's tools for a day and spend precious time with her only child was a miracle in itself. Kendrick subjectively brushed away his mother's true motivation behind their outing—the result of a vicious argument between her and his more gentile and caring father, who had finally mustered the courage to confront his domineering wife and demand she give her son some long-overdue attention.

It mattered little to Kendrick that his attempts at conversation were squelched with mumbled responses or that his mother allowed the food vendors to pass without flagging down so much as a box of Cracker Jack. All that mattered was that they were together. Kendrick reached over and grabbed her hand. She stiffened but didn't pull away. He considered it an affirmation of acceptance.

The final act of the matinee performance featured high-wire acrobats. Kendrick watched with delight as scantily clad performers flashing sequin-covered costumes swung back and forth through the air as if grav-

ity had granted them a pass for the day—fit ladies taking turns in midair leaps of faith, then reaching for the secure grip of a fellow performer.

Suddenly, his delight turned to horror as a high flyer's fingertips fell short of awaiting hands. Down she plummeted toward the life-saving safety net. But wait! What's this? The ropes securing the net twanged and snapped as the acrobat sunk deep into its webbing. Kendrick gasped as performer and net smacked the cement floor with a sickening thud. Blood dripped from the lifeless woman's mouth. People screamed and turned to the exits. Kendrick's mother grabbed his hand, yanked him out of his seat, and fell in with the retreating crowd.

The ride home was strange. Kendrick tried to sort out the horrific scene he had just witnessed. "Mama, why was there blood coming from the lady's mouth? Is she badly hurt? She's not dead, is she?"

A traffic snarl jamming the exit route granted a momentary eye-to-eye encounter. Kendrick's mother latched his chin between her thumb and index finger and pulled his face close—a teaching moment. Her smoky black eyes stared into their mirror image. "Things happen," she said. "You're going to see a lot of ugliness in your life. Man up, son, or the world will devour you."

Ken vividly recalled staring out the window on the ride home, chewing on his mother's words and pondering why he hadn't felt more empathy for the fallen acrobat. But mostly, he remembered that his yearning for a simple warm hug to temper the horrid scene of the fallen performer was instead replaced with a stern warning of self-preservation. That sterile bond between mother and son would remain intact until the day she abandoned him. *So much for motherly instincts. But then you did prepare me for the world, didn't you, Mother?*

And about those "teaching" moments? Add to that list the numerous times his mother schooled him on friendships, especially those of the opposite sex. "They will trip you up, shutter your ambitions," she cautioned. *A tutorial disregarded. But I will make it right.*

And make it right he would. Kendrick Laberday was, after all, his mother's son. The details would be worked out after much-deserved sleep. Ken felt liberated. Who needed God on their side? Kendrick had his mother. His twisted mind felt no empathy toward his new nemesis, Nora Balfour, only justification for his own survival.

Ken relaxed. The march of alcohol molecules continued to stream toward his brain, stroking the organ into semiconsciousness. After the long drive and recent turmoil, sleep would be an invited guest. Nora would be dealt with in due time.

Ken felt the presence before he saw it. Was he dreaming? He opened his eyes. No, he wasn't dreaming. There were two men standing on the other side of the desk. A man with Hispanic features along with a white-skinned man. They were wearing dress suits.

"Who...what? How did you get in here?"

The Hispanic man answered in a gravelly voice. "The same way you did, Laberday, through your back door. It was unlocked."

Ken was suddenly wide-awake. "Who are you? What do you want?"

The Caucasian man said, "Let's just say I'm Mr. One, and my friend here is Mr. Other. Feel free to address either one of us. As to what we want? That's going to take a little explaining."

Mr. Other said, "Yes, it's going to take some explaining." And he sat on Laberday's conquest couch.

A normal person in this situation would surely feel the powerful emotion of fear. Not so with Kendrick Laberday. His sociopathic wiring instead calmly processed the options. He waited for either Mr. One or Mr. Other to make the next move.

One picked up the picture on Ken's desk. "Beautiful woman. I can see a resemblance. Your mother?"

Ken said nothing. He reached over, took the picture, and put it back in the drawer.

Other said, "We know you killed Montague, Laberday. And most likely St. Claire, Dover, and Lavonia."

Accepting the accusation without the slightest expression of surprise, Ken responded, "How?"

One said, "You were given up by a tourist."

"Really."

"A tourist was taking a picture of his wife when your Hummer stopped behind her in the intersection. He kept snapping pictures when all the excitement started. Let's just say he offered them up and we got ahold of them. Guess what else we saw when we blew up the picture of his wife and the Hummer? A van with Minnesota license plates registered in your name. A van that looks exactly like the one sitting in your garage. Your head was turned toward the Hummer. There was woman in the Hummer looking at you."

Other said, "Your call, Laberday. Do you want us to turn you over to the FBI, or do you want to listen to the rest of our story?"

My second mistake. I switched plates on the Hummer but not the van. Damn! "Are you going to arrest me?"

Other said, "To the contrary, we're here to make you a deal. A man of your talent is much too valuable to incarcerate."

Ken couldn't believe his ears. *Do I really have a following?* Not quite.

One said, "We have a little problem that needs to be resolved. If you help us, we'll help you."

Like...yeah. "What do you want me to do?"

"Before I go into the details, do you have any loose ends you need taken care of? Once we set the project in motion, we don't want any skeletons popping up."

"Well, I can think of one..."

CHAPTER 19

Nora stabbed the snooze button on her alarm clock. *Goodbye, world.* Her cell phone had other ideas.

"Morning, sis. Hope I didn't call too early."

"Not at all. I...ah, was about to get the munchkins in the bathtub. Then it's off to day care. I need to spend some serious time at the library."

"Can you get them scrubbed up and ready to go in an hour? Casey and I begged a day off, and we want to take them to the zoo. Then I thought they could have a sleepover with Aunt Sylkie tonight."

Sylkie was truly a knightess in shining armor. "The children will be clean, fed, dressed, and ready for duty in one hour."

Time zipped by, but Nora had the kids shiny and full when her doorbell rang. Margo and Danny ran to their aunt and were quickly swept into Sylkie's arms. Their giggles turned to stares when they noticed the strange man standing behind Sylkie.

"Kids, this is Casey. He is a very nice man, and he will be coming with us to the zoo today. Can you say hi to Casey?"

"Hi," Margo meekly offered, dry-washing her hands. Danny buried his head in Sylkie's shoulder. The absence of a man in his life had taken its toll.

Sylkie winked at Nora. "I guess we better get going. C'mon guys, it's off to the zoo. And I promise Casey will protect you from the polar bears."

Nora watched her children pile into Casey's car, fighting back tears as she momentarily miraged herself and Ken, replacing her sister and Casey.

Regaining her composure, she admonished, "You guys be good now. Listen to your Aunt Sylkie."

As Casey backed the car out of the driveway, Nora waved goodbye.

*****

Ken pinched himself to be sure what his eyes were vouching for wasn't the outcome of sleep deprivation mixed with a generous amount of Chivas Regal.

A few short hours ago, he had faced two uninvited, ominous visitors. Now he was driving north from Cedar City, Utah, where he had disembarked a private jet and climbed into a van similar to his and onto which he had attached his license plates. Since he let it be known he planned to vacation at the Grand Canyon, he was set down near there. The orders were clear. He was to make his way back to Minnesota, leaving a trail of receipts along the way in case his whereabouts were questioned. Messrs. One and Other would clear up loose ends at home, paving the way for a new circus act.

Of course, the execution of this act was to be exclusively for One and Other's benefit and the reason Ken was enjoying the sights of southern Utah. Other made it clear that certain people would just as soon see *him* become the victim of a circus act. However, One assured his safety if he would buy into their proposal. They said they needed a performance that would clearly reflect his imprint. It wasn't hard for Ken to deduce his safety would be guaranteed until the job was done, whereupon they would wipe the slate clean with his body.

Ken contemplated his options as he exited I-15 and swung onto I-70. Grand Junction, Colorado, lay four hours to the east. His choices could be counted on two fingers. He could cut and run but, A, he had no place to run. Or he could choose option B, which would fulfill his mission but with a twist not contemplated by One or Other—a twist that would preserve the ringmaster's dignity and hopefully insulate him from their clutches. It wasn't much of a choice.

All in all, Kenny counted his blessings. Though he had been discovered, he was still free and confident his superior intelligence would keep him that way.

*****

Nora paced back and forth in her kitchen, pondering what to do about her fear that Ken was the circus killer. She had no evidence. Not one little piece, only his lies along with the voice inside telling her there was something wrong, very wrong, with this man.

Finally, Nora decided on a plan. Though she had never met Mark Truitt, Sylkie had nothing but good words to say about him. *I'll call him. Hopefully, he can keep a confidence…and he won't think I'm crazy.* The last thing Nora wanted was for Sylkie to find out what she was up to, just in case her mind had taken a detour to Fantasy Land.

She called the number for the First Precinct and asked for Sergeant Truitt. Mark's extension rang four times, followed by a message prompt. Nora stated her message and hung up.

Nora's call puzzled Mark. She had asked to meet with him at Sizzler's Bar and Grill, located in the far western Twin Cities hamlet of Corcoran, at nine that evening. She didn't say why, but he could sense tension in her voice. Mark hadn't met Nora, though Sylkie mentioned her quite often. *Why does she want to talk to me? And about what?* Mark had an unsettling feeling. He assumed it must have something to do with Sylkie, as she was the common connection. Could it involve Cason Maxwell? Mark hoped it wasn't a jealousy thing now that Casey was an active part of Sylkie's life.

Mark walked into Sizzler's at 8:45 p.m. Two groups of patrons were enjoying a late dinner, one table enjoying their evening with noticeably more gusto. The cop in him wondered who in the group was the designated driver. Several customers hunkered at the bar. The male guests alternated between watching the Twins trying to hammer out a win and watching the blond bartender or, more precisely, watching her tank top, whose fabric was hanging on by a thread(s) in a Herculean attempt to contain everything stuffed into it. Mark slid onto an empty stool and watched the game.

The bartender set down a fresh Bud Light in front of a patron and sidled over to Mark. She solicited his order in a tone and accompanying body language that one might interpret to have meaning beyond taking a drink order. Mark was not, by any means, an unattractive man and was not unaccustomed to being hit on. However, it was obvious that she was pandering for tips.

Mark eyed the chorus line of bottles behind the bartender, all pleading to be relieved of their contents. Jack on the Rocks was the most vocal.

"I'll have a ginger ale, please."

The bartender shot Mark a questioning look at his low-octane request.

Mark glanced at his watch as he toyed with a second round. It was 9:20, but Nora hadn't showed. Maybe she changed her mind. Maybe something more important came up. Guessing wouldn't get him any answers. Dialing her number might. Dispatch returned his request with a cell number. Mark punched it into his phone. The fourth ring elicited a response.

A voice on the other end said, "Who am I speaking to, please?"

"Ms. Balfour? This is Mark Truitt. Are you on your way to Sizzler's?"

"Sir, this is Trooper Shirley Kiick, Minnesota Highway Patrol. Would you repeat your name for me and your relationship to Nora Balfour?"

Mark stared at his phone. "This is Sergeant Mark Truitt, Minneapolis Metro. I have an appointment with Nora Balfour at… well, we're supposed to be meeting right now."

"I'm sorry, Sergeant Truitt. Ms. Balfour will not be making the appointment. She was killed in a one car rollover a short time ago."

Trooper Kiick explained she was removing personal items from Nora's car when the cell phone rang. She briefed Mark on the accident, ending the conversation with, "And I detected a strong presence of alcohol on Ms. Balfour."

Mark asked for directions.

On his way to the scene, Mark wrestled with himself whether to call Sylkie. Would she be mad if he delayed notifying her? Probably. But Nora's mysterious phone call plus the alcohol diagnosis rattled him, and he wanted to get a good visual before he jumped to any conclusions. He strongly sensed something amiss.

"What's your take on the accident?" Mark asked Trooper Kiick as ambulance lights flashed past them. Mark was a good hand's width above average height, and every bit of his frame was needed to make level eye contact with Trooper Kiick. Her posture and gait as well as vernacular strongly suggested a military background. Kiick gave him a likely scenario of how the accident unfolded, followed by the two of them retracing the path of the vehicle in its final moments.

Nora's car had approached a bridge on County Highway 37 from the east. It then swerved into the eastbound lane as it approached the bridge, sideswiping a guardrail on the south side of the bridge. The car returned to the westbound lane. But Nora apparently overcompensated, and the car plummeted over a steep embankment. Nora's body was found in the car, her neck broken. The extent of the damage indicated the vehicle was not traveling at a high rate of speed.

"She probably would be alive had she been wearing her seat belt. Another statistic and film shot for our school education program," Trooper Kiick impassively offered. Mark detected coldness in her voice. He couldn't blame her. She had probably seen more than her share of gruesome accidents. Maybe it was her way of separating herself from trauma. As it was pitch-dark, closer inspection of the accident scene would have to wait till morning. Mark told Trooper Kiick he would inform the next of kin, as she was a personal friend. Kiick looked relieved and thanked him, revealing a more sensitive side.

Mark settled into his car and took a deep breath. He stared at his cell phone as he gathered his thoughts. He needed to make two calls before he broke the news to Sylkie. The first was to Casey—yes, he was at Sylkie's condo. Mark told him he was on his way there. He provided no details.

The second call Mark made was to his wife, Liz. There could be no better person to befriend Sylkie in this time of grief than Liz, with her motherly instincts and compassionate heart.

CHAPTER 20

Mark parked in front of Sylkie's condo and stared at her door. On the other side, a happy young couple was preparing to take on the world. That world was to become very, very ugly. Though he had done this countless times as a part of his job, Mark had yet to discover a "best" way to break this kind of news.

"Mark...hi. Come in."

The burdened look on Mark's face betrayed him.

"What's wrong?" Sylkie felt alarm bells going off.

Mark pulled a driver's license from his pocket and showed it to Sylkie. "Is this your sister's picture?"

"Y-yeah. Why?" Suddenly Sylkie's knees struggled to keep her legs vertical.

"Sylkie, I'm so sorry. Nora died in a car accident tonight."

Sylkie stared numbly at Mark, his words appearing to have shot right through her, not registering. Then they did. Sylkie tilted backward in slow motion. Casey caught her.

"How...why?"

Mark put his arms around her. "We'll help you through this, Sylkie. I'll explain what I know about the accident." Sylkie started to shake. Mark said, "Don't try to be brave. Let the tears come."

Sylkie obeyed, not that she could help herself. Casey held her tight. She dug her head into his shoulder.

"Tell me what happened," Sylkie finally groaned, drying her cheeks. "Tell me all you know."

"What I do know is that your sister was found alone in her car. It had rolled down an embankment."

"That's it?" Sylkie squinted at Mark through bloodshot eyes.

Mark hesitated. For the life of him, he didn't want to step into this arena. The rest of the story was going to be a hard pill for Sylkie to swallow, and she had already had more than enough grief this night.

"Well? What is it, Mark? What aren't you telling me?"

"The state trooper on the scene detected a strong presence of alcohol on Nora. She found a half-empty bottle of vodka under the driver's seat."

"No...no way. That's not Nora. No way, Mark!"

"There's more. Nora left a message on my office phone earlier in the day. She wanted to meet with me. She told me where, but not why. Evidently, she was on her way because the accident was five miles from the bar and grill where we were supposed to meet."

Sylkie looked incredulous. "This...ah, no. It doesn't make any sense. Why would she call you? And about what? She doesn't...didn't even know you. There's something wrong here."

A knock on the door broke the tension. Mark was much relieved to see Liz arrive. Before long, she stepped from the kitchen with a freshly brewed pot of coffee and four cups. As no one was going to sleep this night, the group elected to pound down caffeine and sift through the details of Nora's death.

Mark speculated on the possibilities for motive. "Let's say some-one wanted to do Nora harm. Who was she close to?"

Sylkie contemplated the question. "Nora worked part-time at a convalescent care center. She talked about having a few friends among her coworkers, but I can think of no one in particular she was close to, like on a social basis. Also, she was attending college, work-ing on a business degree. She never talked about any fellow students. So I guess, other than me, her world consisted of her ex-husband, Aaron, and the new man in her life, Professor Kendrick Laberday."

"What about her ex? What was their relationship like?"

"Strained, at best," Sylkie spit out. "Aaron is a jerk. The divorce totally crashed her world. He left her with two young children and little else. She was always fighting to get child-support payments out of him. He claimed the divorce gutted him financially, but we perceive his new girlfriend as very needy. You know, easily bored, rarely satisfied."

Mark stroked his chin. "Let's go a step further. Would Aaron gain financially from your sister's death? Think life insurance policy, that kind of thing."

"I don't know. I'll have to dig."

"Does he live in the area?"

"Yeah, Woodbury."

"If you want to wait to contact him until morning, I'll respect that. Otherwise, Brentsen's on duty tonight. I'll have him pay your ex-brother-in-law a visit."

Sylkie, though broken, was determined. "Have Brentsen go. I don't have the stomach to face him tomorrow, or ever. It's hard, you know—they're his kids." Sylkie covered her face and leaned into Casey.

After a strained silence, Mark said, "Tell me about Professor Laberday."

Sylkie regrouped. "Kendrick Laberday. He teaches economics at Wherland-Vickers College. My sister was taking one of his classes. They started dating. It wasn't long before she fell head over heels for him."

"I assume you've met him."

"Casey and I have met him once. He's very charming, quite good-looking. But we thought perhaps a little hard to read."

Casey added, "He was a real gentleman to Nora. Seemed to enjoy being with her. I caught him eying Nora with admiration once or twice the evening we had dinner with them. He referred to her as his college sweetheart. They looked like a good fit."

"Do you want to contact him tonight or let it go? Your call, Sylkie."

"He's supposedly on a trip to the Grand Canyon."

Mark said, "Well, then, if he is out of the state, it should erase any suspicion in his direction."

"Do it."

Mark procured a cell phone number for Kendrick Laberday and keyed it into his phone.

"Uh, hello?" a sleepy voice murmured on the other end.

"Professor Kendrick Laberday?"

"Ah…yes, this is he speaking."

"Professor Laberday, this is Sergeant Mark Truitt, Minneapolis Metro Police Department. Would you please state your location?"

"What? Is this a crank call? Because if it is—"

Mark interrupted, "Professor Laberday, I assure you it isn't. I'm sorry to have to inform you that Nora Balfour was killed in a car accident earlier this evening. Though it may sound a little unusual, I need to verify your whereabouts."

"Oooh…no, no, no. Not Nora. Please say it's not her. I loved her so much. I'll… I'm in Grand Junction, Colorado. I'll leave immediately for Minnesota."

"That's not necessary, Professor. Her family's in good hands. Again, I'd like your specific location."

"Well, sure, but I don't understand. I'm at the Comfort Inn, second floor, room 211."

"Please stay put. I am going to have the local police verify your location, then you can do what you feel is best."

"Do you want me to meet them in the lobby? I'd be happy to do that. It would save them the inconvenience of coming up to my room."

"That's not necessary. They'll find you."

"This is terrible. Please give Sylkie my most heartfelt condolences."

"I will, Professor. Good night."

"So what did he say?" Sylkie asked.

"He wants to convey how sorry he is. He seemed very upset."

Casey said, "I think we can scratch him off as a suspect. Maybe a little awkward around people he doesn't know too well, but harmless."

Ken sat on the edge of his bed, thinking about Truitt's call. *Why are the police questioning my whereabouts? That cop said Nora died in an accident. Oh well, no matter, I have the perfect alibi—I'm two thousand miles away.*

Of course, Ken knew Nora's death wasn't an accident. She was the "loose end" he had offered up to One and Other. He wondered which assassin did her in—Mr. One or Mr. Other. Or maybe both. *Who cares? The cops will never have a clue.*

As for Nora? Because Ken's brain was not wired for the emotion of sympathy, it was easy to write her off. *Good riddance to the twit. What a dreary wretch. I can envision her considerably more enticing sister and her cop friends slobbering all over themselves in their sorrow. They should look on the bright side. At least now her sticky little kids won't have to be brought up by such an uninteresting mother.* And Kenny? He had a sudden urge to search for a new bed partner.

*****

Cascading raindrops deluged Val Docket's windshield. Inside the car, Docket rubbed a finger along his steering wheel. Clayton Rimm stared into the downpour. The inclement weather paralleled their moods. There was big trouble brewing in the nation's capital.

"So in a nutshell,"—Docket blew out a long breath—"Sam Peck is more than willing to sell out anyone and everyone for so much as a day's less time in jail."

Rimm curled a lip. "There's more shady deals attached to that man than barnacles on an ocean freighter. If he told all, there would be so many job openings in Washington the national unemployment rate would go up a full percentage point."

"Not to mention a building boom in detention centers."

Rimm probed for a clearer picture. "This, ah, Senator Sheridan you claim that's leaning on Peck, what are his motives?"

"I suppose to get his name in print, his face in front of the camera. How do I know? Why can't these young bucks keep their mouths shut and get along? The system is working just fine. I mean, they ought to know the highest bidder fuels the machine. If this guy wants to get ahead, he better learn the rules… Geez, Clayton, now I'm starting to sound like you."

"I'll ask the question another way. What's Sheridan trying to pin on Sam?"

Docket gripped the wheel with both hands. "Among other things, he claims he's got proof Sam took bribe money to use his influence to shoot holes in the Dodd-Frank Wall Street Reform Act."

"How?"

"Writing bills to create loopholes, blocking funding from the regulators who are charged with carrying out the law, providing guidance for lawsuits against specific portions of the bill. Of course, taking those actions inside the system isn't illegal. Taking money under the table in exchange for those services is."

"Hmm. So what happens next?"

"I'm putting together a top-notch team of defense lawyers. But understand, Clayton, I'm not asking anything from Justice. I'm just saying the more vigorously your side pursues allegations against our client, the more embarrassing it might turn out. I don't have to remind you about some of the recent SEC litigation against targeted Wall Street institutions. Our Slick Willies made your government boys and girls look like congressional aides in training."

Rimm's voice notched up. "Val, are you hinting that I should spread the word to back off?"

Docket chuckled. "Now, now, Clayton, you know me better than that. What I'm saying is that Sam Peck is going to have some big guns doing their best to keep the damage to a minimum. Right now, what this country doesn't need is a hot scandal from its elected leaders."

The rain stopped. Rimm pushed his door open and threw Docket a parting shot. "I see; look at the bigger picture, right? Country first? Best to sweep a few minor indiscretions under the rug and get on with the people's business. If I didn't know you better, Val, I'd say your 'hear no evil, see no evil' position might have a personal commentary. Are you afraid of the possibility of *your* name surfacing?"

"Clayton?"

"Yeah?"

"You know the river that runs through the land you're thinking of buying? The one you're looking at to cleanse yourself in?"

"What about it?"

"I may want to hold your hand when you jump."

"Goodnight, Val."

CHAPTER 21

Photons of sunlight pierced the stained-glass windows, a simple gesture from a faraway source seeking to brighten the somber atmosphere inside the little country church—the attempt falling short as those close to Nora Balfour weighed the pews with heavy hearts. Because Sylkie considered the box burial a perverse pagan tradition beneficial primarily for the profit of the mortuary profession, she insisted her sister's passing be celebrated with a simple memorial service—the sole physical remembrance to be Nora's sweet face set in a black frame and positioned on a linen-covered table in front of the altar rail. Flower arrangements were placed on each side of her picture.

Mark and Liz Truitt sat in the third row from the front. Mark took notice of those around him. In the first row and directly in front of him, the broad shoulders of Cason Maxwell stood out. Sylkie sat beside him, their arms intertwined, her head slightly bent. Alongside were Margo and Danny, who had been ushered in with their father, Aaron, but snuggled against Sylkie like baby ducks in a storm.

Aaron Balfour, looking very uncomfortable, shot frequent glances at the ever-widening gap between him and his children. Filling out the row was Aaron's new love, Brooke Pope. Mark noted that her body language fairly shouted at wanting out of this dreadful inconvenience.

Relatives from Oklahoma and Kansas, an extension of whom sat alongside Mark and Liz, filled the second row. There was one person on the opposite end of Mark's row that did interest him, Nora's special friend, Kendrick Laberday. He was staring at Nora's picture and appearing very distraught. More than once, he pulled out a handkerchief and dabbed at his nose.

The service was brief. A few kind words about Nora were spoken; a homily was given. The soloist ended the ceremony with "Amazing Grace." The congregation filed outside.

"Are these balloons going up to heaven to be with Mommy, Auntie Sylkie?" Margo innocently asked as she cut loose a volley of white balloons into a blue cloudless sky.

Sylkie started to answer, but the words stuck in her throat. Casey crouched down to eye level with Margo. "Yes, they are, honey. And because your mommy's up there and we are down here, your auntie Sylkie and your daddy are going to help her by taking real good care of you and Danny."

Margo dug her head into Casey's chest. "I don't want my daddy to help her. I want to be with Auntie Sylkie—and *you*." Sylkie reached down, picked the little girl up, and whispered something in her ear.

Aaron Balfour heard the exchange and threw a frown toward Casey. Aaron's girlfriend, Brooke, rolled her eyes and tugged him in the opposite direction.

The mourners filed into the church basement for coffee and sandwiches. It was a Lutheran church, so green and red Jell-O was served. Mark made a point to sit at the same table as the professor. He introduced Liz and himself to Ken Laberday.

"A terrible thing. I can't come to grips with it yet," a forlorn-looking Laberday uttered.

"I feel so sorry for her children. It's so very fortunate they have Sylkie," Liz said, fully understanding why Nora had fallen for this man.

Ken wiped a drop of moisture from the corner of his eye. "Do you know what makes me feel the worst?"

"What's that?" Mark sized up the professor as Ken was sizing up Mark.

"I should have insisted that Nora and the children accompany me on my trip. If I had, this terrible accident wouldn't have happened. I feel almost, well, responsible. It's just that, once a year, I take off by myself for a sabbatical to one of our country's great natural wonders. It kind of rejuvenates me for another round of teaching."

Mark was about to ask a question when Sylkie approached. Ken immediately stood and wrapped his arms around her. Sylkie returned the hug. "Sylkie, I am so, so sorry. I loved Nora more than she knew. I have a void that will be impossible to fill, as I'm sure you do also. If there is anything you need, please don't hesitate to call upon me."

Ken turned to Mark and Liz. "It's been nice meeting you, even under these circumstances. It's good for me to know that Sylkie has such wonderful friends. Now if you will excuse me..."

After Laberday had disappeared up the stairwell, Mark turned to Liz and Sylkie. "So what do think of him?"

Liz, obviously taken in by his charm and looks, responded, "I think Nora had found her man."

Sylkie said, "I can't find fault with him."

Mark said, "Hmm."

Ken whisked out of the church parking lot. *Glad that's over. What a bunch of soppy simpletons.*

*****

A ghostly cloak of morning fog had dissipated to the point where Mark and Sylkie could retrace the final moments of Nora Balfour's fatal ride. Both investigators strongly suspected foul play.

"Let's start where Nora first appeared to have lost control of her car," Mark said. "The amount of damage to the guardrail and Nora's car suggests she was not moving very fast. After hitting the guardrail, it appears Nora overcompensated when she swerved back into the right lane. The car continued to drift to the right until it went over the embankment."

Sylkie said, "What do you mean it 'appears' Nora overcompensated?"

"Let's finish our walk-through."

They walked to where the tire tracks disappeared over the edge of the road. The embankment dropped sharply—thirty to forty feet—then leveled off. Farther on, thick patches of alder brush blanketed a small stream. Wild raspberry bushes thornily guarded most of the slope, absent only where Nora's car had tumbled through. Swarms of hungry mosquitos circled the investigators.

Mark turned to Sylkie, who was swatting at the pesky little insects. "You sure this isn't too hard for you?"

"I won't be at peace till I know the truth."

"Okay. The autopsy report states the cause of death was the result of a broken neck. Nora was not strapped in when Trooper Kiick found her. There was a deep bruise near her left temple, and her neck was broken. So it can be deduced that she hit her head hard enough at some point after she lost control of her car—that is, before the airbags deployed—to break her neck. Sound feasible to you?"

Sylkie shook her head. "No. Because Nora would never, ever be in a car without her seat belt strapped on any more than she would drink and drive."

"I was hoping you'd say that."

"Why?"

"The crime lab isn't making any plausible matches for what may have caused the bruise on her temple. There's also another item that has me scratching my head."

"And that is?"

"The driver's seat was extended to nearly its entire span of travel. Your sister was, what? Maybe five four? And oh yeah, the driver's side window was open."

Sylkie frowned. "That casts more mystery on the alcohol found in her system. More reason to believe that somebody did this to her. Not much of a consolation prize, but...what did you say? The window was open? What's that about?"

Mark said, "I'll explain in a bit. But first, there's another piece of the puzzle I want to confirm. We need to go see Giles."

The crumpled mass that had been Nora Balfour's car sat alone in one end of the Hennepin County crime-lab garage. Standing next to it was Giles Halifax, head of the forensic garage section. Towering over everyone at an astounding seven foot one and as wide as a soda straw, Giles stood out for reasons other than his physical stature.

Blessed with an intuitive nature, a high intelligence, and a vivid imagination, Halifax was absolutely a perfect match for his chosen career.

"What have you got for us?" Mark looked up at Giles.

Halifax adjusted his wire-rimmed specs. "Looks like your hunch has some legs, Truitt."

"What hunch?" Sylkie asked.

Halifax gestured. "Come around to the back of the car."

Once there, the threesome peered at the car's bumper. "Look closely," Giles pointed. "See the scuff mark here on the left-hand side?" The two investigators took a close look. Something definitely had rubbed against the bumper.

"As you can see, this bumper is jacketed in plastic. The scuff mark is peppered with tiny flecks of shiny metal. I analyzed a sample, and yeah, you guessed it—chrome. This bumper had been in contact with a chrome bumper."

Sylkie stared at the mark. "Nora's car was pushed into the guardrail, then over the embankment?"

Mark said, "You're half right. Her car *was* pushed off the road by another vehicle. However, it was being driven when it sideswiped the guardrail, but not hard enough to deploy the airbags."

"How do you know?"

"Remember I said the driver's seat was pulled back much farther than what would be a comfortable position for Nora? This was the sequence of events in my estimation: First, Nora was abducted and forced to drink alcohol. Then," Mark hesitated, reluctant to share the next part with Sylkie, "her head came into violent contact with some hard object. I believe that's when her neck fractured. Next, one of her killers, and there had to be at least two, got in her car and adjusted the driver's seat. [He] then sideswiped the car against the guardrail. [He] got out and placed Nora in the driver's seat but failed to readjust the seat."

Sylkie looked pale. "Okay, I'm with you so far. Then they pushed the car over the edge with another vehicle?"

"Not quite that simple," Halifax advised.

Mark continued, "Giles did some figuring. The angle at which the car went off the road and the distance it traveled across the embankment before it rolled over indicates it was traveling at a speed close to twenty miles per hour. If it had just been bumped over the edge, it would have made a straighter downward trajectory. Maybe wouldn't even have rolled. It was made to look like it. Nora cascaded over the edge under power."

Sylkie was confused. "But you said Nora was put back in the driver's seat while it was still on the road. Who steered the car?"

"This is why I believe it was a team effort. One person drove the vehicle that pushed Nora's car from behind. The other was alongside Nora's car on mobile transportation, possibly a skateboard or Rollerblades. This made it possible for the assailant to keep up with the car, holding onto the steering wheel through the open window until it reached the embankment."

Giles added, "And the asphalt shoulder would have allowed [him] to hang with the car till the very end without making another set of tracks. I did check for fingerprints on the car but came up empty."

Sylkie shot both men a questioning glance. "You keep saying 'him' and 'guy' when referring to the murderers. How do you know that one of them wasn't a 'her'?"

Giles shrugged. "We don't. It's all still out there."

Mark wondered what she was thinking.

Sylkie leaned against the battered vehicle. "So most likely my sister was dead before her car went over the embankment. She was murdered. Why? What did she know that got her killed? What was she going to tell you?" She wiped away tears, forcing herself to blank out a mental picture of Nora's last moments.

Mark rested her head against his shoulder and rubbed her back. She didn't resist the show of affection, as she once would have. Mark was grateful Sylkie was becoming increasingly open to both himself and Liz. And she kept Casey within close range at all times.

"We're going to answer those questions, Sylkie. Whatever it takes, we're going to answer those questions."

CHAPTER 22

Senator Samuel Peck stepped outside the Milwaukee hotel and drew in hefty gulps of cool Lake Michigan air. The fresh breeze flushed out stale remnants of the atmosphere inside, where he had spoken at a party fundraiser. Generous portions of food and drink had been provided. All in all, another indulgent evening.

Peck wobbled his way to the curb and hailed a cab. "Marquette Hotel," he ordered, slumping into the back seat. The cabby didn't answer. "Hear what I said? Marquette Hotel." No response. "What's the matter? You deaf?" Peck slurred. The cab driver punched the accelerator.

Ken Laberday turned into a truck stop off I-94, near Madison, Wisconsin. He checked his watch. One-thirty a.m. His payload would be arriving within the hour. This was indeed a strange preliminary script to one of his circus acts in that the main attraction was about to be delivered to him. Fine, but it was designed to come with a price. A very hefty price. And the "fulfillment associates" expected to be paid in full. Kendrick expected that wasn't going to happen.

Messrs. One and Other had given Ken an offer he truly couldn't refuse—either he feature Senator Peck as the main attraction in his next circus of justice or the picture of his van with its Minnesota license plates alongside the fateful Hummer would find its way to the FBI. Then, of course, there would be questions. Then, of course, he would be obliged to explain why his van was in Washington, DC, just a couple of days before Mark Truitt had reached him in Grand Junction.

The deal had not been one made in heaven. Not that Peck wasn't a good prospect for Laberday's circus. To the contrary, he had hovered over the big banks like a mother hen, removing teeth from financial regulatory bills with the skill of an orthodontist. Peck qualified not only for a top spot on Ken's pick list but had also caught the ire of a mysterious other party. Unfortunately for Ken, he was being forced to do another's bidding, and all fingers would point directly at the ringmaster. Nice package, neatly wrapped—for someone(s) other than Kendrick Laberday.

The obvious problem for the professor could be summed up with the adage, "Dead men tell no tales." Mr. Other promised Ken that if he cooperated, they would disappear like houseflies in winter. *Yeah, right. And seventy virgins are awaiting me in heaven.* Rather than looking for an out, Ken looked for an opportunity. Psychopaths don't panic; they plot. And he had a plan in mind that would save both his skin *and* Peck's. But only after the senator took a spin in the hot seat.

Ken was mentally working out details of his grand plan when a Suburban swung around behind him, then slowly backed toward the rear of his Town & Country. Ken jumped out into the misty night air. He motioned the Suburban to stop just short of his van. Laberday's new associates exited the cab. Mr. One, a brooding tall man with closely cropped blond hair and beady eyes, peered at Ken with unveiled contempt. Mr. Other—shorter, stockier, and featuring a moonscape face partially hidden behind a Hulk Hogan mustache—projected the appearance of a natural-born killer. The "delivery" men opened a rear door on the truck and pulled out a bundle loosely wrapped in a plastic tarp. They ungently tossed it into Ken's van. The bundle moved, groaned, and went still.

"When are you going to put Peck down?" One growled.

"I need at least a week to get my act set up. Also, I want to get some good press going; it'll make the act all the more dramatic. I crave the attention, you know."

Other pushed a finger into Ken's chest. "You got ten days max."

Ken stepped back. "You guys a little grouchy tonight? Must be past your bedtimes."

Other made a move toward Ken. One put an arm out to stop him. One said, "This show of yours better go off without a hitch or you're gonna see just how grouchy we can get."

Not the least bit intimidated, Ken retorted, "So this will be our last contact? I'll never see your smiling faces again?"

"That's the deal—*if* everything goes according to plan."

"Oh, it will. I promise you—it will." As he turned to leave, Ken threw a parting shot.

"By the way, nice job of taking out Nora Balfour."

The men ignored the compliment. They climbed into the Suburban and sped off.

Ken watched the truck pull onto the highway.

*****

Jim Renner tipped his chair backward and swept his hand across his forehead. "What kind of weeds do you grow in this state, Truitt? My sinuses are killing me."

Mark didn't look up from the memo he was studying. "Climate change."

"What?"

"My wife says climate change is the culprit. The warmer weather is pumping up the sneezeweeds. She's an encyclopedia on nature. Grew up on a farm."

"So what advice would she have to get the pitchforks out of my head?"

"Stop burning fossil fuels. I think she has protest signs left over from her last clean-air march. I can get you one if you like."

"Thanks, I'm good. How's Sergeant Maune doing?"

"She's having a tough time, especially since we believe her sister's death wasn't an accident."

Renner planted his chair back on the floor. "Huh?"

"Evidence at the accident scene points to Nora Balfour's death as a homicide. We're trying to figure out who and why."

"Wow. That's a plateful. Poor kid. It's a good thing Casey popped into her life when he did."

"Casey, her dog Oscar, Liz, me. And, of course, her niece and nephew. That's pretty much her circle."

"How about the children? How are they holding up?"

"Children are resilient. With good nurturing, they'll be okay. Liz has been helping out, mothering them nonstop."

"Along with saving the planet."

"Along with saving the planet."

"What about Nora's ex-husband? I mean, his relationship with the kids."

"He hasn't spent much time with them. Sylkie says keeping his girlfriend happy is a full-time job. And the woman doesn't particularly like kids."

Renner opened a folder. "On a brighter note, I've got some new information on the Washington, DC, murders. Through dental records, the body in the front seat of the Hummer has been identified as belonging to a woman by the name of Rose Cherotte. Her home address is about forty miles west of here."

Mark said, "Guy mentioned you did a search of her farm with Brentsen and Forenza."

"Yup. Nice guys. That Brentsen's quite a storyteller. Forenza didn't talk much though."

"After fifteen years of trying to compete with Brentsen, he's given up. Did you come up with anything?"

Renner said, "We found literature belonging to a local militia group that goes by the name of Front Guard. There were a couple of guns and some ammo in the house. That was about it. We took a look in the outbuildings. Didn't find much."

"I'm familiar with Front Guard. They keep themselves out of the spotlight. We've never had any problems with them."

"Brentsen, Forenza, and I paid their headquarters a visit. There were about twenty members present. Our take was that they were in the dark as to Cherotte's activities. Although once they learned she was involved in the DC event, there was a collective chest swelling. I'm sure she's already reached legend status. I think they're way more bark than bite, but we'll keep an eye on them."

"So all in all, we're still chasing a phantom."

"Yup. This ringmaster, or whatever his growing army of admirers call him, not only officiates over a circus of horrors, he's also a class magician."

Mark's cell phone rang. Casey was on the other end. He asked Mark to take a swing by Sylkie's condo. He didn't elaborate.

Sylkie and Casey sat across from each other at her kitchen table when Mark entered the room, papers and folders spread out before them.

"Take a look at this, Mark." Sylkie held out a document with an attached note. It was a life-insurance policy declaring Nora as the principal and Aaron as the beneficiary. It was purchased when they were first married.

Mark studied the policy. "Uh-huh. I see there's a double indemnity clause attached."

Sylkie said, "Yeah. In case of death—accidental *or* wrongful—the payout is twice the value. Double would be five hundred thousand."

Mark set the document back on the table. "Payable to Aaron, unless, of course, he was involved in her death."

Sylkie pointed to a sticky note. "Nora had written herself a reminder to change the beneficiaries from Aaron to Margo and Danny."

"Do you think Aaron was aware she was about to make the change?"

Sylkie's eyes grew intense. "Obviously, he would assume it would happen at some point, but if you knew my sister, well, she was a procrastinator. She was also very, very mad at Aaron. I could see her tossing it at him for revenge."

"Do you think Aaron had something to do with your sister's death for the purpose of benefitting financially?"

"All I'm saying is that he loves Brooke, and she is *very* needy."

Casey put an arm around Sylkie. "Tread carefully, Sylkie. If you get too heavy-handed with Aaron, you may never see Margo and Danny again."

Sylkie retorted, "Yeah, I'll watch myself. Aaron and I are going to meet on Saturday. There are a lot of loose ends to tie up, the life-insurance policy not the least of them."

Casey said, "Has he mentioned the policy to you?"

"Not yet."

"Have you tipped off the circumstances surrounding Nora's death?"

"He's asked no questions at all, which shows how much he cared about her. All I've told him is that there are circumstances surrounding the accident that have not yet been put to rest."

Mark said, "Okay. Here's how we'll approach this: Tell Aaron that Nora's death is being treated as a homicide. Skirt the details as best you can. Also, tell him that he cannot cash the life-insurance policy until he's been cleared as a suspect. Emphasize it's only a formality. We'll have an investigator from another precinct interview him."

Sylkie closed her eyes and took a deep breath. "I just have a feeling…but, yeah, I'll put on a good show."

*****

Ken's basement was a collection depot for discarded items from the floors above. It was musty. And it was dark, save for the puny beam of light dribbling from a seventy-five-watt bulb screwed into a porcelain socket. Beneath the dreary glow, Ken sat backward in an antique wooden chair, staring at the repulsive apparition facing him, his quarry duct-taped to an identical chair.

From head to toe, Senator Samuel Davis Peck resembled anything but a person of national prominence. Strands of thinning gray hair shot in all directions. His eyes were blindfolded; his face sprouted stubble. Dried vomit decorated his blue dress shirt and blue-and-white striped tie. Bicycle tubes of midsection excess strained against heroic shirt buttons. Most interesting to Laberday was how, in defiance of gravity, those chicken legs could keep all that inflated flesh and fat vertical.

"I need a drink," a hoarse voice scratched out. Ken put a glass of water to Peck's lips. He gulped it down. "How about something stronger?"

"Sorry, Senator, you're on the wagon. I require all of my performers to be in top form."

"Performer? What're you talking about? Just who the hee-ell are you, anyway?"

"I'll give you a hint. You've been chosen to perform in my circus of justice."

Peck's dazed mind was slow to catch on. Then he got it. "Wh-why me?"

"You have admirers, Senator. *They* chose you, not I. And I'll bet you know why."

Peck tilted his head downward and pondered Laberday's statement.

Ken let the silence hang like pre-storm air. Finally, he re-engaged the conversation.

"Your nonanswer is your answer. Someone wants you permanently silenced. But lucky for you, they tapped me to be your executioner."

Peck raised his head. "Lucky? What're y'all mean, lucky? Are you going to feed me Jack Daniels and pile on prostitutes till my heart gives out?"

Ken laughed out loud. "Sorry. That's *my* dream death. I have an even better offer—how 'bout you don't die?"

"I'm listenin'."

"Okay. First off, you're going to tell me about all the backroom deals you've made the past twenty years. I want names. Big names. Important names. Then we're going to figure out who wants you dead the most. Are you willing to do that?"

"Keep going."

"I've created a circus act in which you are going to be the main attraction. Nothing will be required of you other than you will have to 'hang around' for a while. Now here's how we bargain for minimum collateral damage to ourselves..."

After Ken threw out the plan, he got close to Peck's ear. "So you see, Senator, we are compadres; we give each other the gift of life. Do we have a deal?"

"Do I have a choice?"

"Do we have a deal?"

"Yes."

Ken separated Peck from his chair and led the blindfolded senator upstairs to a bedroom-turned-holding-cell room. He shackled the very despondent and very unwashed public servant to the bed. Ken wasn't allowing Peck the comfort of a bed out of pity. Pity is not in a psychopath's dictionary. He merely wanted to keep the senator in good-enough shape to complete the upcoming circus act.

Ken walked into his study and slid into his desk chair. He needed to review his plan and strategically put the puzzle together. All the pieces had to fit. Any leftovers could come back to haunt him.

First off, there were the two goons: One and Other. He didn't only think they were goons. He had a strong suspicion they worked for a government agency—maybe NSA, maybe CIA, or maybe DIA. Didn't matter. They were following orders for someone(s) who wanted a man, who knew too much, put down. What they didn't know was that Kenny intended to compromise their plan with a plan of his own, one that had been jump-started with a little help from his van. *Thank you, Fiat Chrysler.*

Ken had altered the camera electronics and positioning in his Town & Country's rear backup camera, transforming it into a recorder. He taped good visuals of One and Other as they heaved the tarp wrapped around Senator Peck from their truck into his van. Also, he had an audio recorder hidden in the wheel-jack storage compartment. His conversation with the two men sealed their involvement in the murder plot. The professor was a bit disappointed in that he tried to get their admission on tape to killing Nora Balfour. But it didn't really matter; he would delete that part of the tape. All in all, Ken concluded he had enough visual and audio evidence to box them up long enough to play out his final circus act.

Of course, the success of the complicated plan swirled around the blindfolded, shackled, and smelly senator flopping around on a bed upstairs. Ken had begun extracting from Peck a list of high-profile conspirators who had danced with him over the years. As for Peck? He was screwed no matter what. In his favor, he would be taking his punishment in an upright position.

Admittedly, the plan was full of sand traps and a few water hazards, but it was the only hand Ken was holding. He had no choice but to go all in.

Satisfied his strategy would achieve checkmate with his antagonists, Ken relaxed and closed his eyes. He thought of his mother. He wondered what she would think of her offspring, her product, her baby boy. She wouldn't be happy. Because he killed? Maybe. Maybe not. His mother had been a doctor, a surgeon. She was no stranger to death. Who knows what thoughts had coursed through her cold, sterile mind in the operating room?

As for Kendrick, her wrath would be wrought from his discovery as the ringmaster. Her chastising words were chiseled into his soul: "You can't achieve perfection unless you work for it. Unless you sweat for it. You're lazy, Kendrick. You'll always fail because you don't crave perfection. You settle for mediocrity. Get away from me, lazy boy." Kendrick's mother had left scratch marks on his psyche that could never be rubbed out. Too bad. Two brilliant minds. To the detriment of humanity.

CHAPTER 23

"Hello...?" Mark blinked at his alarm clock. It waved back—two a.m.

"Mark, this is Brentsen. Sorry to wake you, buddy, but I thought you might want to be in on this. We got an alert a short time ago from a patrol unit that three van trucks and a couple of pickups drove away from Front Guard headquarters. Forenza and I are following them west on Highway 12, which coincidentally heads in the general direction of Rose Cherotte's farm. I'm not the smartest guy in the world, but I am a good storyteller. So let's pretend this parade is heading to the Cherotte farm for—night exercises?"

Mark was finding his socks. "On my way. I'll alert Renner."

Brentsen added, "I put a call in for the SWAT team, just in case."

"Be careful."

"Yeah, I'll try to hold Forenza back—after I wake him up."

Mark called Renner. Renner would pick up Casey. He also alerted the Wright County Sheriff's Department. Sylkie was out of the area, as she and Liz had taken the kids for an overnight to see the animals at Liz's family farm. Mark fired off a "thank you" for that. This could get dicey, and Margo and Danny had already lost one mother.

Mark swung his car off the county highway that passed the Cherotte farm and onto the dirt road that bordered the property. He stopped behind Brensten's car on which Thor Brentsen had his elbows planted and was looking through a pair of night-vision glasses. Evan Forenza was leaning against the passenger door, sipping coffee from a travel mug.

"There's a van backed up to the garage. Guys are loading boxes and other stuff—I can't tell what—into the van." Brentsen handed the glasses to Mark.

Mark took a long look. "I can't make out what it is they're hauling out of the garage either, but I'm sure it doesn't include bringing good will to the world."

Brentsen said, "You think?"

Forenza added, "Does a glassblower suck?"

A few minutes later, Renner and Casey pulled their SUV behind Mark's car. Mark handed the binoculars to Renner.

Jim Renner peered over the cornfield that separated the lawmen from the Cherotte farm buildings. "Suspicious by any stretch of the imagination. Hold on, there's a guy carrying an armful of rifles to one of the vans."

"I'm afraid we got us a situation here," Brentsen concluded.

Mark turned to Evan Forenza. "How far away is the SWAT truck?"

Forenza checked. "Five minutes."

"Tell them to hold back. Request the Wright County Sheriff to block the highway a mile on each side of the farm. No sirens. Stay here; be our relay. The four of us will head through the cornfield toward the farm. I'm guessing it's about a quarter-mile hike. There's a fairly good breeze tonight, and the cornstalks are crispy. That should provide noise cover. When we think Front Guard's ready to pull out, I'll call you. There's no way to sneak up on them, so have SWAT barrel in as fast as the truck can gear up. We'll use the house for cover. Hopefully Front Guard will be smart and give up without a fight."

The men walked back to their vehicles. They donned protective vests and black bill caps. Brentsen declined the cap and tugged at his fedora. Mark and Brentsen loaded shotguns, a Remington and a Mossberg. Mark closed the trunk lid and walked over to Renner and Casey. They were cradling Heckler & Koch assault rifles.

"Good luck, children of the corn," Forenza saluted and headed for the highway. Mark was relieved Forenza was going to be in the rear. He had less than a year to retirement. No sense in tempting fate.

The foursome waded through the cornfield. A steady night breeze ran interference, and a full moon splashed down ghostly beams of light to guide them. Mark pushed back thoughts of his family by calling up Joe Bonamassa to massage his mind with "Midnight Blues," a fitting introduction for the coming storm.

Mark could see over the cornstalks to the garage. Front Guard militiamen were busy as ants, running in and out the building. He didn't hate these people. He only hated that their misguided allegiances could be putting him in a position to kill.

Four rows from the edge of the field, the men stopped. They watched as an empty truck backed up to the garage. Truitt heard an "almost-done" waft from the building. He gave Forenza the go-ahead.

Moments later, the growl from the SWAT truck's engine signaled its imminent approach. Men in and around the garage scrambled, and engines roared to life. The SWAT truck turned into the driveway as the convoy slapped their transmissions into gear. Good and something less than that converged in a standoff.

The lawmen stepped out of the field and headed toward the house. The convoy was trapped, the SWAT team in front of them and Mark's team at ninety degrees. The SWAT leader called out, "Come out of your vehicles, no weapons, hands in the air."

A few moments of agonizing silence ensued. Finally, doors opened, followed by hundreds of flashes of light as bullets hammered the SWAT truck. Mark felt his stomach tighten; his mouth went dry. There would be killing tonight.

Militiamen jumped from the convoy like bats leaving their cave at twilight. Several of the men started for the farmhouse, guns blazing. The four lawmen stepped out of the shadows and welcomed them with lead handshakes. An instant later, a similar response came from the convoy and from inside the garage, where some of the group had hunkered down. The SWAT truck inched forward but was blasted with a rifle-mounted grenade launcher. Then it was blasted again. The SWAT team spread out, taking advantage of the cover provided by trees lining the driveway and dotting the yard. Suddenly, the lead Front Guard truck exploded like an entire fireworks production gone awry. Good and bad alike hit the deck.

Just as quickly as the shooting stopped, it resumed. Several militiamen rushed the house. Jim Renner went down. Mark, Casey, and Thor Brentsen launched an offensive of their own. Brentsen saw one of the Front Guard members sneak around the opposite side of the house. Thor doubled back, hoping to surprise the man. He walked the length of the house but saw no one. Then he heard a noise behind him. A man jumped from a clump of bushes next to the house, rifle raised, an evil smile on his face. He had Thor Brentsen dead to rights.

Brentsen's mind jumped back to the night he and Sylkie Maune had encountered the burglary suspects. Maune had sailed in like Supergirl in the nick of time to save him. Unfortunately, Supergirl couldn't come to his rescue tonight, but maybe someone else could.

Brentsen saw a flash of light to his right. The smiling man's head suddenly went away. Bone and brains and blood splattered against the peeled siding of the farmhouse.

Evan Forenza stepped out of the cornstalks. "You're buying coffee in the morning."

One by one, Front Guard was losing its membership. The SWAT team gained ground to the point where the Front Guard trucks were surrounded. The remaining Front Guard members begrudgingly threw down their weapons and gave up. Except for one.

Mark saw him crawl out of a garage window and run down the driveway toward the barn. Mark gave chase. The man ran past the barn and skirted the silo. Mark was close behind, rounding the silo from the opposite side. The two men converged at the far side of the silo. Mark crunched his shoulder into the man's chest while his head smacked a hard kiss under the assailant's chin. The hit would have drawn a flag in the NFL. But this wasn't the NFL. The men rolled. The Front Guard man got up. Mark lunged and planted a left hook on his jaw. The man spun and fell on his belly, blood oozing from his mouth. Mark grabbed his wrists, yanked them together behind his back, and slapped on cuffs.

The takedown felt strangely invigorating. The man looked to be half Mark's age, yet he took him out like a middle linebacker. Maybe because he was pumped to the max or maybe there's a "conquer" gene in our DNA. Whatever the reason, Mark wanted more but quickly nixed the urge. He cuffed the man and pushed him down the driveway.

Red, white, and blue lights flashed everywhere, creating a near discotheque atmosphere in the Cherotte yard. Agent Renner was being whisked away in an ambulance as Mark handed off his catch to a uniform. Casey Maxwell, looking a little ragged, caught up with Mark.

"How's Renner doing?" Mark asked.

"He took a bullet in his left thigh. He's lost some blood, but he should be all right."

"What's the count on our side?"

"Two from the SWAT team killed, four injured."

"The Front Guard?"

"They're still counting."

"How about Brentsen?"

"Ask him yourself." Maxwell pointed behind Mark. Brentsen and Forenza were walking toward them.

Brentsen said, "You disappeared. Just wanted to make sure you're okay."

"I'm good. Looks like we'll have to do without Jim Renner for a while though."

Brentsen put an arm around Forenza's shoulder. "Evan and I are going to head back to town. I'm buying my buddy here the biggest breakfast he can wolf down...and all the coffee he can drink."

Forenza winked. "In case anyone asks, this time, he didn't duck."

Mark turned to Maxwell after the two had left. "What was *that* about?"

Casey smiled. "I think Sergeant Brentsen has a newfound respect for an old partner."

CHAPTER 24

A late-summer sun kept Mark comfortable as he relaxed in his Adirondack chair. The tranquil moment was enhanced by the sound of little feet bouncing off dockboards. The time had passed far too quickly since his own children, Maggie and Brian, had taken turns barreling off the end of the dock and letting go with big "whoops" as they plunged into the water.

Today Margo and Danny were repeating the process. Sylkie and Casey Maxwell were posted in the water with waiting arms, the chilling effects of the now-cool water reversed with frequent trips to the sauna. And, of course, the kids had life jackets strapped on tight—a rule the Truitts strictly adhered to. They could easily have passed for a happy family, as Margo and Danny were well into the healing process. Sylkie was having a harder time. She missed her sister terribly, and she feared for the children's future. Also, it was not going well with Aaron. They were more or less circling each other, with the kids caught in the middle. Mark felt Liz's hand on his shoulder. "Time to eat. Gather up the crew."

The adults feasted on a "cabiny" meal of pulled pork, baked beans, and late-season corn on the cob. After filling up on hot dogs and potato chips, the kids disappeared to attack the sandpile behind the cabin while the grownups retreated to the screened porch.

Mark turned to Sylkie. "How did your meeting with Aaron go? You haven't said much about it."

"Because it was disgusting, just as I expected." Sylkie shook her head. "We gathered up the important documents, which were scattered throughout the house. My sister, the great organizer. And, of course, Aaron hadn't paid much attention when they were living together, so he didn't have a clue where anything was."

"How about the insurance policy?" Mark queried.

"That's when the afternoon went south. Up until then, I tried really hard to keep it genial. Anyway, when he picked up the policy, I detected a look of relief on his face. That's when I broke the news about the continuing investigation into Nora's death."

"How did he react?"

Sylkie curled a lip. "He looked surprised, but he didn't pursue the subject. I informed him he would have to be interviewed—as a formality. That seemed to agitate him. I'm guessing he was connecting me to the interview. I mean, it's no secret between us that I basically can't stand his guts for what he did to Nora."

Mark put a leg to his rocker. "Well, unless we come across evidence from the accident scene that would prove his presence, we'll have to rely on the interview, gleaning something that would tie him to Nora's death. Otherwise, I'm afraid he'll be free to redeem the policy."

"I just hope he puts the kids before his lover, although I don't expect that to happen."

The conversation was interrupted with Danny grunting to open the screen door with one hand and holding onto a toy truck with the other. With help from Casey, the little guy was soon standing next to Sylkie. "The wheel fell off of my twuck, Mommy. Can you put it back on?"

No one said a word. Until now, it had been "Auntie Sylkie."

"Why don't you give it to Casey, honey? I'll bet he's really good at fixing toys for boys." Sylkie had been trying to get Danny to feel comfortable with Casey. So far, success had been minimal.

Liz glanced over at Mark. Tears welled up in his eyes. She could have predicted that.

Danny cautiously walked over to Casey and held the toy out to him. "Can you fix my twuck, Uncle Casey?"

A bridge had been crossed.

*****

"How's Renner doing?" Guy Lompello looked at Casey, who was sitting on the other side of his desk. Mark plunked down in the chair next to him.

"He's in stable condition. Hurting, of course. Already clacking about getting back to work."

"I wish him well." Guy played with a paper clip. "I suppose you've heard we have a United States senator missing. He was last seen in Milwaukee six nights ago."

Casey nodded. "Our office got an alert."

Mark said, "Who is it, and why has it taken this long to report him missing?"

Casey explained, "The missing senator is from Mississippi; name is Sam Peck. Congress was scheduled back in session yesterday, and he didn't show up for a committee meeting. No one can seem to find him. My briefing this morning emphasized it's not all that unusual for him to make himself scarce, especially if he's found some pretty young thing willing to do the deep dive with him. His nickname is Slitherin' Sam, if that tells you anything."

Guy smirked. "Looks like he's slithered his way into the missing person's file."

"Any information on his last visual?" Mark queried.

Casey said, "A cabby that works the area where Peck attended a fundraiser was abducted about an hour before Peck left the event. He was found the next morning tied up, unharmed, in his trunk. He said he had picked up a fare. The guy sprayed something in his face before he left the curb, knocked him out cold. He couldn't give a decent description of the man. So speculation is that cab may have been used to abduct Peck."

Guy swiveled his chair in short back and forth motions. It squeaked. "And now Senator Peck is nowhere to be found."

"Not to say there's a connection, but"—Casey brushed at his pants—"Peck was about to be investigated on a variety of charges—charges that could highlight his favoritism toward Wall Street insiders. There are no fingers being pointed, but it could…probably will involve lobbyists for some prominent firms."

Guy asked, "Is there any possibility this could tie in with our circus killer?"

Casey answered, "Peck has done a lot of favors for big banks. With his position on the Senate Banking Committee, he's been able to water down or completely stall several of the regulations the government has tried to strap on them."

Mark nodded. "And that would make him fair game for our circus killer."

"It would," Casey confirmed.

Guy speculated, "*If* the senator was abducted by our perp, he's had him for several days. I would expect if he were planning to publicly execute him, it'll be soon. And Milwaukee's not that far away, so it could happen here in familiar territory. Anyway, Mark, where are we at with the investigation?"

"Sylkie's still wading through foreclosure records. As for physical evidence? There are the dirt samples from the vehicles used in the murders. We have a lot of burned up parts and pieces that have given up little in the way of leads. And we have the Cherotte farm, which Giles and his crew are scouring as we speak."

Guy tossed the paper clip on his desk. "Okay. I guess all we can do for now is hope our killer isn't planning to bring his dark circus to town—and hope this senator is back in DC very soon, sporting a big smile and a frisky step."

*****

Casey pulled up in front of the First Precinct headquarters as Sylkie made her way out of the building. "Are you hungry?" he asked as she slid into the car.

"I might be able to push down a salad."

Casey closed a hand around hers. "Something's wrong?"

"I got a call from Jim Whitman, Fifth Precinct. He interviewed Aaron this morning."

"And?"

"We share the same opinion."

"What's that?"

"Aaron is a jerk."

"That's pretty much a unanimous opinion, with the possible exception of his girlfriend."

"Well, she's going to like him a lot more. Whitman couldn't find any reason to block him from cashing in the insurance policy." Sylkie slammed a clenched fist on the dashboard. "Why didn't my sister change that policy? It was the first thing she should have done after the divorce."

Casey tightened his grip on Sylkie's hand. "Hey, calm down. Remember, honey, Nora had a lot on her plate, balancing two kids with a job *and* going to school. Not easy."

Sylkie stared down at her knees, rethinking her outburst. "Oh, I know, I know. She was better than I ever could have been in that situation. I just feel so bad for those kids. And I'm sorry, but I can't help but think Aaron's involved in Nora's death. Maybe he is, maybe not. I just hate him because of what he did to Nora."

"Well, someone killed your sister. Whoever it was, I won't rest until her death is solved."

Sylkie leaned her head into Casey's shoulder. "Thanks. I think I'll have grilled chicken to go with the salad."

CHAPTER 25

Ken paced back and forth in his machine shed, mentally packaging his next performance. Satisfied that all the parts and pieces required for the upcoming circus act were assembled and ready to go, he reviewed his escape plan—post Senator Samuel Peck. It was far from ideal, but under the circumstances, it was the best he could come up with. Or was it? *"Look for perfection,"* as Mother would say. *"Scrape every last bit of marrow from the bone."* Then it hit him; yes, he *had* missed something—an insurance policy. He thought about Peck, who was still chained to a bed and in the latter stages of *"rottium smellium."*

I believe a small revision to our contract is in order.

Ken dragged a chair toward Peck's bed but stopped short as the senator's odor would make buck scent smell like Chanel No. 5. He crossed his legs and said nothing. Peck turned his blindfolded eyes toward Laberday; he could sense a dark aura hanging over him— sick, depressed, and scared. Peck stayed silent.

"I think I'm going to kill you," Ken finally announced.

Peck's head shot off the pillow. "What? I thought we had a deal."

"We did. I terminated it. My plan won't work. It's missing an essential ingredient."

The senator's head sunk back down. "I think *you're* missing some essential ingredients."

"I need money. For my plan to work, I need money."

Peck's voice found strength. "Is *that* what this is all about? Money? I'm gettin' shaken down for money?"

"Not at all, Senator. Everything I told you is true. And the good news is that you may still have a chance to save your skin. So let's get down to business. How much money do you have, and where is it? Don't lie to me; your life depends on it."

Peck groaned and tugged uselessly at the ropes restraining his arms and those chicken legs. "About nine million. Some in Switzerland, some in the Caymans."

"That's the best you could do for all the years at the money trough?"

"Elections are expensive. So are concubines. If *you're* so fiscally acute, why do you need money?"

"I gave my savings to a charitable cause—it's called Wall Street. Trouble is, the beneficiaries of my involuntary generosity don't have a provision where I can deduct my losses from their fat accounts, so I'm deducting *them,* one miserable crook at a time." Ken stopped himself, realizing it was more information than he needed to give away, as Peck was expected to survive the next circus act. "But enough about me, Senator. How about if I take seven million and leave you with two for seed money?"

The offer satisfied Peck's concerns about his status. If his kidnapper intended on killing him, he wouldn't have signaled any generosity. A dead man would have no use for it. A live man would. Besides, he wasn't exactly in a position to bargain. "Deal."

Ken logged into his computer. "Let's get started."

*****

Downtown Saint Paul. 8:34 p.m.—showtime

Ken hugged his van tight to the rear wall of the downtown Saint Paul warehouse. He climbed out of the cab and looked around. Beacons of light cast from offices and apartments in the surrounding buildings punched through the evening's blackness. The smell of river floated in from the Mississippi.

The professor opened the back of his van and tugged on a leg. Senator Samuel Peck's leg. Peck's physical condition was deteriorating, and it hadn't taken much drug to send him into a semiconscious state. Conversely, his body odor was off the charts. Laberday had a real penchant for cleanliness, and Peck-er, as the professor fondly referred to the now slimier than slitherin' senator, was starting to remind him of standing on a lakeshore at the height of a mayfly hatch.

Ken prodded Peck into a sitting position. Then he unlocked a nearby service door with a key he had "borrowed" from the maintenance department at Vickers, which rented a portion of the warehouse to store books and office equipment. Ken had been in the building a few times and so was familiar with the layout. The front of the building faced a bustling part of the downtown, ensuring a substantial audience for tonight's circus act. If circumstances had been different, Ken would have avoided using the building, as it had ties to the college, but time and caution were not on his side. He guided Peck into the building and taped his legs together then hustled back to the van and drove away.

Several minutes later, Ken was back in the warehouse. He cut the tape from Peck's legs and led the blindfolded man to a freight elevator. They rode to the third floor and then walked to a set of windows. Ken opened two windows that were about ten feet apart. He unzipped a tote bag and removed a remote-controlled mini-helicopter. He tied one end of a spool of four-pound test fishing line to the helicopter and flew it out one of the open windows and back in the other. Peck sat on the floor, mumbling incoherently.

"Hang in there, Senator," Kenny smirked. "Your much-needed shower is within sight."

Ken reached into the bag again and pulled out a roll of quarter-inch aluminum wire rope. He taped one end of the fishing line to the wire rope then went to the other window and pulled the fishing line and wire rope through that window. He completed the first step of his props assembly by "cable-clamping" the ends of the wire rope together, making a loop.

Ken gave the still-awakening senator a slight hair tussle. "Okay, showtime, my boy. Let's look our best—which, in your case, would be just about anybody's worst." The professor ripped Peck's shirt open to reveal three sticks of dynamite securely strapped to his chest, along with exposing his Jabba the Hutt splotchy red belly. The senator's blue-and-white tie, decorated with crusted puke, remained looped around his neck. He wriggled Peck into a full-body safety harness and then half-lifted and half-shoved the filthy mass onto a window-sill. Next, he attached a snap hook connected to the cable end of a specially altered retractable safety block to the back of Peck's harness. Finally, he attached the snap hook built into the safety block around the wire rope. Ken faced the senator's head away from him and jerked off the blindfold. He almost wished he hadn't. Peck's eye sockets were swollen and red. His eyelashes were swimming in moist yellowish ooze. The whole putrid apparition could have been titled "The Blob Meets Bacteria Man."

Okay, world, meet one of Washington's finest. Kenny gave him a shove. The senator, held tight by the harness and safety block, slid down the wire rope until gravity centered him on the loop. Laberday quickly secured a CD player, speaker, and fireworks setup to one of the windowsills. He then hurried down to the first floor via a stair-way and dashed out of the building.

Ken made his way to the front of the warehouse, joining a growing crowd of onlookers gawking at an open-shirted man—a very pathetic-looking open-shirted man with a blue-and-white puke-encrusted tie hanging loosely around his neck—flailing around in midair.

Sirens wailed to the scene, announcing the start to the great-est show—if not on earth—at least for the moment in Saint Paul, Minnesota. Ken pushed a button, setting off the fireworks. The speaker boomed to life.

"Laadieees and…gentlemen, welcome to tonight's featured attraction at the circus of justice. Folks, we have had many requests for a high-wire act. After all, what's a circus without a high-wire act? Tonight it is our pleasure to announce we have a brave soul who has volunteered to fill the void. Please give a rousing welcome for our featured performer, Senator Samuel Davis Peck. Oh, and by the way, if anyone should try to terminate the senator's performance before the scheduled ending, those little sticks tied to his rib cage will go 'boom.' So let's all relax and enjoy the show.

"We start tonight's performance with a public service announcement. To Messrs. One and Other, your full-image pictures have turned out with vivid resolution and are awaiting your review. It's only my personal opinion, but I think they make great Christmas shots. Also, your confessions have been taped. No doubt there will be numerous requests for copies, so please respond with haste."

Mark wearily shifted his car into gear. A murder-suicide late that afternoon had nixed another evening meal with Liz. With the preliminary investigation completed, Mark looked forward to a homemade pasty and a hot shower. Not to be.

A call from dispatch sent Mark speeding to the nearest I-94 exit. Soon he was driving with Talladega speed for downtown Saint Paul, a scenario being repeated by just about every available law-enforcement unit in the Twin Cities. The circus killer was once again flaunting his evilness for the entire world to see, in this case, by hanging a man from a building. Mark bet his next five fishing trips to Lake Vermilion who the victim was.

The crowd gathering on the street below Senator Peck was increasing geometrically. Restaurants and bars were quickly emptying as word of a new circus act spread. Interestingly, many of those hurrying to the scene were among a rapidly growing cult of followers who championed the ringmaster's revulsion for the status quo, even if they didn't condone his methods of punishment. The rumor that a United States senator was the flavor of the evening served to pique their curiosity.

Mark screeched to a halt at police barricades a block from the warehouse. He jogged the remaining distance, soon finding himself among the crowd hooting and catcalling at the disgusting spectacle of copious quantities of whale fat bulging from the half-naked senator, who was desperately flailing his arms and legs and looking like he had just been pulled from a vat of corn mash. The repulsive display did not beg warm and fuzzy feelings toward the featured performer.

Mark weaved through the crowd not exactly sure what he was look-ing for, but he was certain the killer was in the vicinity.

Ken saw Mark first. He purposefully angled toward Mark and stepped in front of him. Mark recognized him immediately. "Professor Laberday."

"Sergeant Truitt, I guess I shouldn't have to ask what you're doing here."

"For sure. And you?"

"My college is about a mile from here. I was on my way to get a bite to eat. It's not much fun to cook for one, you know. Say, how is Sergeant Maune doing? I've been meaning to call her. I must do that."

Mark began to move on. "It's hard, but she'll be okay. Sorry, I don't have time to chat. Nice to see you."

"Same here, Sergeant. Good luck catching your man." *Hello— you caught him, knucklehead.* Ken shrugged his shoulders and contin-ued to enjoy the show. Of one thing he was sure: if he ever did get caught, it wouldn't be by the likes of gumshoes like Truitt.

"Laadieees and gentlemen," the ringmaster continued. "You have before you a splendid example of greed versus need. The sena-tor's greed as opposed your need to live a decent life, formerly known as the American Dream."

The incendiary words prodded the crowd and poked at an already-sour opinion of the cells of power inside the Washington beltway that selfishly amassed wealth for themselves at the expense of their constituents. Jeers and taunts exploded in volume and number as the voice in the speaker played to their disgust with "politics as usual."

Ken looked on with bemusement at the sight of how individuals randomly brought together can be verbally whipped into a frothing assemblage of accusers practically begging to tear apart a supposed antagonist—people who, only moments before, knew little or noth-ing of Senator Samuel Davis Peck. Ken was convinced if a rock pile were close at hand, the senator would be getting pummeled.

"And so, folks, at your expense, the good senator has made him-self wealthy. While you have perhaps lost your house, he has three.

While you're finding a good-paying job to be elusive, he has a part-time gig that pays quite well. While you struggle to pay for decent medical insurance, he has no worries; you're paying for a good share of his. So now, without further ado, I present to you a man who is second to none in his balancing act on the Washington 'high wire of greed' by stuffing his own pockets while keeping his constituents loyal with pork, not by the barrel, but by the boatload."

The cops had broken into the warehouse, but there was little they could do. The explosives taped to Peck's chest kept them at bay. They could have snatched the unguarded speaker and CD player on the windowsill, but that would have provoked the ringmaster. Their only recourse was to watch the show and hope for the best.

The speaker vibrated one last time. "As this is to be his one and only performance, Mr. Highwire wants to show his appreciation for your support by being available for photo opportunities and auto-graphs. How 'bout a selfie with the senator to make your friends jealous—sweet!"

A "click" and a "pop" could be heard behind Peck, followed by the line on the safety block being played out. Peck descended quickly into the center of a ring of cops. The crowd pushed menacingly in, trying to get either a photo or a piece of the groggy, disheveled sen-ator. A chorus of taunts revealed the position of the crowd's collec-tive thumb of conscience, and it was definitely thumbs-down for Slitherin' Sam. As soon as Peck hit the ground, he was unhitched and escorted away.

Ken was amazed, gratified, and emboldened by the reaction of the crowd; so much so, he was tempted to jump up and down and wave his hands to get their attention. He fantasized being raised on shoulders and paraded along the street in a victory celebration as the great purveyor of justice for the masses. Maybe some of the cops would even join in. On the other hand, he was sure his "associates" were most eager to discuss their future (and his) with him. The vic-tory parade would have to wait.

Although Mark had no choice but to chalk up another one for the ringmaster, the overriding question was, Why was Peck allowed to live?

*****

Ken flopped on his "love couch," exhausted. Forewarnings of a headache rumbled in the back of his head as he relived the evening. So much planning had gone into the performance. It had gone off without a hitch, and yet somehow the victory seemed hollow, tempered to a mere flicker where there should have been a fireball of self-gratification—all because a stupid tourist had taken a picture. Oh well, nothing left to do but outflank the two morons who, by now, would be salivating to get a piece of him, the intrepid duo of Mr. One and Mr. Other. To Ken, they were more like the Bo brothers—Dumb and Bim.

He yearned for the comfort of a Grey Goose gimlet. It would degrade the storm gathering in his head down to a light drizzle. Unfortunately, Kendrick had to stay alert. He was certain the "brothers" would be paying him a visit before the night was over. In fact, he was so sure of it he posted notes on both the front and back doors:

> The door is unlocked
> Come on in
> Don't wake the children

Ken glanced at his watch. 12:22 a.m. A chilly wind had blown in and was launching leaves that were prematurely undocking from their moorings due to the prolonged drought the state was experiencing. The mother branches swayed back and forth in rhythm. Ken suddenly felt alone. Very alone. His plotting, scheming mind, dark as the night outside, almost felt the emotion of—panic.

The light sleep into which he eventually drifted was interrupted by a squeak at the front door. 3:12 a.m. A figure appeared in the hallway, soon joined by another, shorter apparition coming from the direction of the kitchen. Ken flipped the switch on a lamp. One and Other burst into the study, guns drawn.

Ken stuck out a hand, palm down. "Put away the hardware. If I had intended on violence, I'd be packaging up you geniuses for disposal as we speak."

One, the Caucasian man, marched up to Ken and pressed the barrel of his Glock to the professor's forehead. The steel felt cold. "Unless you start talking, and fast, about your 'public service announcement,' the violence is going in only one direction."

Ken stared One down with impassive eyes. "It's late. I'm tired, and we have a lot to discuss. Please put the gun away so we can get this over with."

One and Other looked at each other. Hesitantly, the guns were "re-holstered," and each took a chair. Round one—Laberday.

Ken rubbed his hands together. "Okay, here's the deal. When you delivered Peck, I had a camera and voice recorder rolling in my van. I got some great shots of you lifting a plastic bag out of your van and placing it into mine. The senator will certainly attest to being the occupant of that bag. Also, our conversation in regard to carrying out the act, along with your personal threats against me, was recorded loud and clear. There's plenty of evidence to get you two to the gallows. Also, Peck was kind enough to offer names of some very important people with whom he's dealt, let's say, on a less-than-above-board basis. Those names, along with very incriminating associated events, are scribed in letterform."

Other said, "Your face and voice were recorded too. You'd go down with us."

"I have a plan B. But hey, there's no reason for any of us to 'go down.' Let's work this out."

One said, "How about plan C, I put a bullet through you right now? What would happen to your so-called evidence?"

"Please, give me credit for being at least a little enterprising. If I die, or even if you foolishly choose to detain me, the evidence *will* be in the hands of the authorities by morning."

Other, the Hispanic man, snarled, "And what if we beat it out of you?"

Ken rolled his eyes. "Look, if you lay a hand on me in any way, shape, or form, it's gonna happen. The cops get the information. If you want to test me, go ahead, but it's at your own peril."

One gave the slightest hint of resignation. "Okay, so what's your interpretation of a 'happy ending'?"

Ken felt the noose around his neck loosen. He had won round two. "Peck is willing to fess up to criminal activity with some lesser players. Tell your handlers he won't cough up any big fish as long as this drama ends with a soft landing for Sam. Hopefully, the senator that's trying to make a name for himself at Peck's expense will be satisfied with a minor conviction. Peck only demands that his punishment be contained to a few years at a 'fine dining' correctional institution. As for me, I will soon disappear and so also will the information I possess."

Checkmate. The professor had won round three. There was no way to tell if Laberday was bluffing, but if he wasn't and certain names were exposed, Messrs. One and Other may as well volunteer to be in his next circus act because their lives would be worth about as much. Both men rose in unison. Other glared at Laberday, wanting more than anything to wash the leather couch with the professor's blood.

On the other hand, One's lips curled up just slightly, an endorsement to his adversary's prowess. "Tell me one thing, Laberday. Why did you humiliate Peck so badly?"

"Payback for his years of disservice to his country."

One and Other turned to leave. Ken threw a parting shot. "If it's any consolation, you've succeeded in shutting down my circus. I'm sure that will be comforting news to some." The front door closed behind the men.

Kenny breathed hard and then expelled a lethal blast of stale breath. He knew how close he had come to buying it. His threat to One and Other was mostly valid, save for one minor item—he hadn't yet worked out the part where the police would be handed the incriminating material had he been harmed.

Details, details. Fortunately for the professor, their fear of being discovered along with Peck's list of Beltway bad boys was enough to make them punt. *It doesn't make any difference how you get there, as long as you get there,* Ken contentedly reflected.

The professor triumphantly mixed the vodka gimlet he had craved a few hours earlier. Drink in hand, he returned to the couch and closed his eyes. Refreshing swallows of soothing alcohol molecules cascaded on a free ride to the farthest reaches of body tissue. When they invaded the penthouse, Ken's brain readily accepted the depressant, which, in turn, powered down the overworked organ. The result—free-range thoughts of self-adulation and sex.

A woman's image popped into Kendrick's head. Not just any woman. His body stiffened; his groin quivered. A small eruption of saliva welled up in his mouth. He had seen her at Nora Balfour's funeral. There was immediate attraction on his part, and he thought he had caught her giving him a second glance. However, she was spoken for, not that that's a legitimate measure in today's world and *especially* not in his world. But should she be off-limits considering recent history with the family?

Ken silently laughed at the thought. For the life he was leading, should any quest be off-limits? Of course not. Living on the edge kept his senses sharp. The highs came from scamming the unsuspecting in order to satisfy his cravings. And right now, he was craving her, and that's all that mattered.

CHAPTER 26

"Got a minute?" Casey poked his head into Mark's passenger-side window. "I need to talk." His near-perpetual smile had molted into worry lines.

Mark sensed the bad vibes. "Sure. Jump in."

Casey settled into the passenger's seat and said nothing for an uncomfortably long moment before speaking. "I'm worried about Sylkie. She's so fixated on proving Aaron is responsible for Nora's death it's like nothing else matters, not even me. I can't bring it up. Every time I try, she shuts down."

Mark put a hand on Casey's shoulder. "You know she loves you, Casey. Sylkie's been a different person since you came into her life. But you have to remember Nora was the last link to her family—a family that dissolved under tragic circumstances. Of course, she's going to seek justice for Nora's death. Support her. After all, maybe she's right about Aaron."

"What's your take on Aaron?"

"I can't, for the life of me, come up with any reason what anyone other than Aaron would have to gain from killing Nora. There was no sexual assault, so that rules out one possibility. It could a have been a stalker, but that's highly unlikely. And her death involved at least two assailants. The only other person she was close to was Professor Laberday, who, we know, was in Colorado at the time. By the way, I ran into him at Peck's 'hanging.'"

Casey looked surprised. "What was *he* doing there?"

"Said he was on his way to get something to eat."

An alert from dispatch ended the conversation. "Officer down. 1640 Melcrest, apartment 1C."

Casey waved a forward motion. "Let's go." He noticed Mark's face had turned the color of a turnip.

"What's wrong?"

"Brentsen, Forenza, and a couple of uniforms were dispatched to arrest a murder suspect."

"What's the story?"

"The guy was apparently involved in the convenience-store robbery Sylkie and I've been investigating. You were at the precinct the night we interviewed the other suspect. He clammed up about who his partner was. Not out of loyalty as much as self-preservation. However, his time in lockup gave him some 'religion.' He decided it wasn't worth it to take the rap as the shooter and offered up the other robber."

Mark and Casey pulled up to the apartment building, an ambulance on their tail. Mark rushed into the building and found Evan Forenza kneeling over Thor Brentsen, who was lying spread-eagle on the floor.

Forenza had a towel pressed on Brentsen's stomach. Mark put a hand on his shoulder. "Paramedics are on their way. How's he doing?"

"Lost a lot of blood."

Mark grabbed the big man's hand. "Hang in there, buddy. The medics are here. You're going to be all right." For the first time that Mark could recall, Thor Brentsen had nothing to say.

As the ambulance crew trotted down the hallway, Casey called out to Mark. "The shooter is two blocks south."

The cops that had been assisting Brentsen and Forenza were chasing the assailant and broadcasting their position over the police radio. Mark and Casey leapfrogged a block ahead of the chase in hopes of heading off the shooter.

Sure enough, they soon spotted a man with a shaved head and arms decorated with tattoos dash out between two houses, cross a front yard, and run into the street. Mark hit the brakes. He and Casey jumped out of the car, guns drawn.

The suspect didn't hesitate. He pulled out a handgun and pointed it at the lawmen. It was his last earthly act. Mark and Casey opened fire, their weapons aiming true. The assailant's feet went out from under him. He was dead before he hit the asphalt. The convenience-store robbery case was officially closed.

*****

Val Docket trudged up the stairs to Clayton Rimm's third-floor apartment. Two bottles nestled in a brown paper bag clanked together in unison with each step conquered. Docket could have used the building's elevator but talked himself into the rewards of exercise. Truth was, Val Docket was stalling and hoping the contents of the bottles—Malbec for Rimm, as he was a wino, and whiskey for himself—would cut the awkwardness of the conversation. *Didn't used to be like this. Clayton used to be a player. A first stringer.* Docket deduced old age had cursed his friend with a conscience.

"The paper bag can stay, but I'm not so sure about you," Clayton grinned as he held the door open. "You've been nothing but bad news lately." Val handed over the bag then removed his jacket and tossed it onto the back of the room's featured selection of furniture—a worn gray fabric couch. The air inside the apartment was blue with the lingering stench of a burned-at-the-stake dinner. Docket wondered why the fire alarm wasn't jumping off the ceiling.

Guest and host pulled chairs up to the kitchen table and took possession of their refreshments. Rimm uncorked his bottle and gurgled out a fair amount of the red liquid into a plastic glass.

"So, Val, what's on your mind? And please tell me this is a social visit. Bad news shouldn't follow good wine."

Docket shrugged. "Hope you like the wine."

Clayton pursed his lips. "You're saying bad news claims the night and the wine is the consolation prize? So be it. Bring it on." Clayton abruptly changed his mind. "Wait!" He raised his glass to his forehead in a visionary gesture. "Let me guess. You're here to share tidings concerning Senator Sam 'the Trapeze Man' Peck. I understand the good senator is scheduled to be the featured guest in a forthcoming congressional rendition of 'This Is Your Life.'"

Val grinned and shook a finger. "Aha! Been reading those tarot cards again, have ya? Yes, I'm afraid Sammy is about to be dragged into the spotlight by the overzealous Senator Sheridan, whom I've heard is motivated by revenge and about to challenge the dear man's ethics. Although Sam may have had a lapse or two of judgment, rumor has it he's seen the error of his ways and is willing to take his punishment—to a point. However, and I come hat in hand, I'm afraid he may need a little assistance from Justice to, let's say, help course him back to a productive life. And considering his age and faithful service to his country, a minimum of hardship on his road to recovery."

Rimm rolled his eyes. "What do you mean, revenge? What's Sheridan got against him?"

Val cleared his throat. "It's complicated."

Clayton poured more wine. "Meter's running."

"Last election cycle, Sheridan ran against a guy by the name of Clements. Peck raised money, a lot of it, on Clements's behalf through a PAC, which Peck helped found."

"Uh-huh," Rimm acknowledged, once again elevating his wineglass. "Let me take a shot at this. The money was exchanged for favors. I'll also wager Sam failed to disclose the source of the contributions to the PAC."

"You definitely missed your calling. My sources tell me the contributors are intensely interested in seeing the life stomped out of both the Dodd-Frank Wall Street Reform and Consumer Protection Act *and* the rumored re-emergence of Glass-Steagall, thus, I refer to our previous conversation concerning possible bribery charges."

Clayton's finger traced the rim of his glass. "And ole Sam grants their wish by twisting some arms to initiate legislation that will eviscerate Dodd-Frank."

"Hello—and from what I hear, Sam is satisfied in coming down with a good case of amnesia on the matter as long as he isn't pressed too hard."

"Sure, sure, but it sounds like Sam could be looking at, and I'm just guessing, federal charges of money laundering involving his PAC? Plus failure to disclose campaign contributions?"

Val crossed his hands over his belly. "And maybe more. The PAC he's tied in with is also being scrutinized. Something about accounting discrepancies. But look, Clayton, the reason I'm here is, if Justice does find enough evidence to bring down an indictment, I don't have to tell you it could, ah, have far-reaching repercussions. In Sam's world, this lack-of-judgment thing is just the tip of the iceberg."

"And he's the Titanic." Rimm drained his glass. "So are you asking for help from my end? I do believe I remember you disclaiming that possibility in our last conversation."

Docket tried to read his friend's face. Was he on board or not? Regardless, he had to push ahead. "Containment. Keep in mind the collateral damage this guy is capable of causing. Sam's more than willing to do some horse trading—you know, throw some small fish into the bucket so that all parties can give the impression that justice is being served." Val looked hard into Clayton. "Can do?"

Rimm hesitated and ultimately surrendered. "I'll keep a toe in the water, but don't expect miracles." He probed further. "You know, Val, I really don't understand why Peck is still alive. Why did this so-called ringmaster allow Sam to take a bow and be spirited off? I mean, he's killed all of his other victims. Why wasn't Peck dangling by his neck instead of his torso? Why the alternative ending?" Clayton pushed his chair back, sauntered over to the kitchen island, and retrieved a fresh bottle of Malbec.

Docket, now flying with Turkeys as in Wild, felt confident that Rimm was buying in. Clayton had a lot of sway in the higher circles of Washington. If anyone could direct Samuel Davis Peck's final years to a soft, inconspicuous landing, Clayton Rimm would be the man to seal the deal. For Val, it was essential to ensure Clayton's trust. And to get Clayton's trust, he really had no choice but to share what he knew. Docket waited for Rimm to reload his green-tinted plastic glass featuring the lone word "KOOL," stenciled in white. Had he been sober, disclosure would have been a push. However, they were both surfing on a crest of spirits, which enhanced an excessive amount of tongue wagging.

"Okay. Here's the whole ugly story as I know it: Someone in this town knows who the circus killer is. They contracted him [them] to take out Peck out of fear that Peck would lay bare his dirty dealings in order to save his own skin. Then the killer was supposed to get whacked after Peck was dead."

Rimm tilted his head back and stared at the ceiling. "Two problems solved, and everyone lives happily ever after. Except, the circus killer changed the ending."

Docket nodded. "Yes, yes, he did. He outsmarted the contractors. One smart fox he is."

Clayton leaned in close to Docket, close enough to give Val a good dose of wine breath. "So who *are* the contractors, Val?"

Docket retaliated, puffing a flock of Wild Turkeys back at Rimm. "Ya gotta understand, Clayton, this isn't firsthand information. I… I heard the contract originated out of DHS."

"Homeland Security? Oh, man." Rimm was incredulous. "I've said for a long time they're out of control, but this is way over the top. Who pulled the strings, and why?"

Docket could see Rimm was not taking this well. He had to get his convincing voice on—and fast. "Look, Clayton, the circus-acts killer *is* a domestic terrorist. And what makes it worse is the following he's garnered. I swear half the country sympathizes with him. Not good when the antihero becomes the hero. I know, we've already beaten the subject to death, but if the FBI had been doing its job…" Val stopped short, not wanting to anger the man whose help he was seeking.

Rimm dismissed the comment. "So now the government contracts assassinations to erase good old boys like Sammy and then assassinates the assassinator?"

"Of course not, Clayton. There's a rogue unit out there somewhere. My guess is either they have a terribly misguided sense of patriotism *or* they're doing the dirty work for someone that's keenly interested in having Peck's skeletons stay in the closet—except, in Sam's case, the closet would be the size of the Pentagon."

Rimm raised an eyebrow. "How's Sam taking all this?"

"Sam is scared stiff. He doesn't trust anyone. All he wants is to get the dogs called off. He told one of my lawyers he's compiled a secret document of all his questionable transactions over the years that will stay secret as long as there are no contracts out on him. He swears the document is loaded with enough firepower to blow the dome off the capitol building."

Rimm stared into his near-empty glass. It was way too late in the game for him to want to get involved in anything this ominous. Still, he was curious, so he pressed his friend again. "Who wants Sam dead, Val?"

Docket blew out a hearty laugh. "Clayton, get real. Sam's had more money pass through his hands in the last forty years than the Federal Reserve. The possibilities are endless as to who might want a permanent moratorium on his biography. But look, let's not speculate on what we don't know. All I'm trying to do is ensure that an old friend gets a fair shake, does some easy time, and then is allowed to retire in peace. Sam goes way back with us, and I think he deserves our loyalty. Do this for Sam, then go to your river—and be sure to save a spot for me."

Clayton Rimm stood and walked (staggered) over to his window overlooking the "shining city on a hill." "You know, Val, there are good people, a lot of good people in this town who truly want to do the right thing. They came here to serve their country, and they work at it every day." Clayton turned to his friend, his voice trailing off, "I so much want to be a part of them. Now. When it's too late." Rimm pushed out a sigh. "Okay, I'll do what I can." He raised his glass, breaking out into a broad smile. "To Sam...and the river."

"To Sam and the river," Docket chirruped.

CHAPTER 27

Plop! Plop! A volley of pebbles punched the water, creating a wave of mini-tsunamis that quickly scurried away from ground zero. Mark absently watched the tiny ripples disrupt the mirrored lake surface. He zipped his jacket against the cool fall air, welcomed by some but detested by those who foresaw the "s" word, snow, creeping into their forecasts. The serenity of the surroundings provided the right atmosphere to reflect on the unsolved circus murders, the death of Nora Balfour, *and* the shooting of his friend and colleague, Analius Brentsen. Fortunately, Brentsen would pull through. Unfortunately, he would never wear the badge again. His future included several months of PT, a permanent colostomy, and hopefully a long retirement. Every time something like this happened, Mark couldn't help but think—*But for the grace of God...*

The sound of a faint *smuck* directed Mark's attention to a stand of pike reeds several yards from the dock. Something had broken the surface, possibly a tullibee snatching a treat on its way to spawn over the rocky lake bottom on the far side of the weeds. Mark contemplated the simpler life of fish and their world. Food, sex, but then again, for the smaller varieties, there are the northern pike and muskies to think about. *I guess we all have our deals.*

The seasonal chill was herding away paltry attempts by the setting sun to stimulate warmth into the atmosphere, its parting golden rays piercing the deep-blue sky to create a near-heavenly apparition. Mark tossed the remaining pebbles en masse into the black water and started for the cabin. As he passed his woodpile, he took a hard look, the sight triggering a replay of the horrible dream he had experienced the night of the convenience-store robbery. In his nightmare, the woodpile was where the vicious killer, Tom Moore, had clubbed Mark's son, Brian, over the head. He shook away the all-too-vivid rerun.

Settling into the cabin, Mark piled a couple of birch logs atop the glowing embers in the woodstove and pulled up his rocker. The heat brought comfort against the invading night air, and the crackle of the burning logs kept him company. Mark cherished the time alone. Not that he was antisocial, but he had to admit he was a bit of a loner—another reason Mark missed his old partner, Jamie Littlebird. Jamie wasn't much of a talker, but when he did speak, his offerings were either relevant or humorous. The kind of person you could easily tolerate on an all-night stakeout or remain friends with on a two-week paddling trip into the Quetico.

Right now, though, Mark needed to "paddle" around inside of his head and tag something that would shed light on the murder cases. He was both annoyed and frustrated at the zero-to-none progress in either of these affairs. His professional side told him to concentrate on the circus killings, as it was his primary case, but his heart tugged him toward Nora Balfour's death because of the grief it was punishing on Sylkie. Mark tilted his head back and closed his eyes. *One case at a time.*

First up were the circus killings. The immediate question in that confounding case begged an answer as to why the killer didn't erase Senator Peck. And even stranger, what was that announcement about the "pictures" the night of Peck's faux hanging? The short answer was that someone must know the killer's identity, and *that* must somehow be attached to Peck's release. As for Peck, the FBI grilled him extensively, but no relevant information surfaced. He claimed he was blindfolded and drugged and said he couldn't pick the ringmaster out of a lineup—in his words—"of three army-dillos, his kidnapper, and a jacky-lope." There was a gaggle of explanations here, but the prospect Mark cuddled up to the most was that the circus killer was *supposed* to kill Peck but didn't for obviously self-serving reasons. If this was true, Mark realized he needed Maxwell and Renner's help.

There has to be a Washington, DC, connection here. The circus killer's last act before Peck's abduction was in Washington. Who may have found out—what? Mark made a mental note to lean on the FBI agents.

Mark then redirected his thoughts to Nora Balfour. Nora's death was filled with question marks. There was no rhyme or reason to kill Nora, yet it was obvious to Mark her death was the result of foul play. At the moment, speculation fingered her ex-husband, Aaron. Possible, but not a shred of evidence pointed in that direction.

Frustration threatened to overwhelm the deductive process. Efforts at picking apart the cases were not producing any tangible results. His drifting thoughts finally settled on a wicker basket across the room used to store magazines. He noticed a children's drawing book protruding above the rim. It was one of those connect-the-dot books, the open page featuring a partially outlined man wearing a coonskin cap. Nora's daughter, Margo, had authored the drawing on a recent visit. *Connect the dots... Connect the dots.*

Mark once again shut his eyes and encouraged his mind to wander. Soon the two crimes, strangely and without design, began to revolve around each other as if they were waltzing to a dark, sinister tune. As if they were somehow related. Though confused, Mark kept his foot in the door. Suddenly, lightning struck. *Connect the dots.*

A mental picture of Professor Kendrick Laberday flashed in Mark's mind like a target in a shooting gallery. Mark remembered seeing Laberday among the crowd the night of Peck's circus act. Laberday had been Nora Balfour's boyfriend. He was supposedly out of town when the Washington murders occurred. The investigation into Peck's "hanging" revealed that the warehouse had been rented to several customers, Vickers College among them. Laberday taught at Vickers. Access to the warehouse must have been obtained with a key, as there was no forced entry noted. Laberday, an economics professor, would understand the mechanics of the financial crisis, central to the circus killer's motives for murder. The unidentified man seen at the Admiral Suites shortly before the Dover murder was tall and thin, like Laberday. *Connect the dots.* Implausible as it seemed, it was a thread to follow.

Armed with a glimmer of hope and relieved that the little devil who had been pounding nails through his gut for days had finally put away his hammer, Mark was anxious to head back to town, which he would do at first light and start digging for solid clues. What Mark couldn't have foreseen was that the biggest clue would soon emerge from a very small package.

*****

Ken followed the red Mustang into the parking lot at Samson's Workout Center. His newest fantasy's itinerary had been the same for the past two days—from her job to the gym. Ken waited a few minutes and then grabbed his gym bag. He bought a membership and ducked into the locker room to change, and he was soon aiming for a workout device—and Brooke Pope.

Ken mounted the elliptical exercise machine next to Pope. With earbuds closing off the outside world, Brooke concentrated on ramping up her gait. Ken could not help but gorge on her profile. Yes, Brooke Pope was a whole new tier of conquest. He lusted at her yardstick-straight frame that supported perfectly arced curves. Compared to this woman, Rose Cherotte, a noble conquest for any man's passion was but a beggar to a billionaire. He had to get at that body. But would he? There was no doubt in Kenny's mind. His looks and charm had produced a lifetime of scores that would make most red-blooded of males secretly plead with the Almighty to be reincarnated in Kendrick Laberday's image. Ken pondered his approach shot and determined that the initial contact should be coy.

Scheming turned out to be a nonissue. Pope looked in his direction and smiled. Minutes and calories ticked by. Finally, Brooke stepped off her machine. Ken did the same, quite thankful the marathon was over. Brooke removed her earbuds and put out her hand.

"I remember you from the funeral. I'm Brooke Pope. Sorry, I forgot your name."

She was as delicious-looking as Ken had remembered, even though her jet-black hair was curled in soggy ringlets around the nape of her neck. Ken docked hands with her.

"Ken Laberday. I certainly remember you, Brooke. You shared some very kind words with me. Obviously, you understood how great my loss was."

"Well, Nora is fondly remembered by everyone she touched."

Ken noted the hollowness in her voice. He hoped *his* testament to Nora had been more convincing. "Yes, well, life goes on, I guess. So here we are trying to keep ahead of life's temptations and the forces of nature. Please excuse me if I'm out of place, but I can see you have done admirably in that department."

"Thanks for the compliment," Pope flatly answered. She then stepped in close, locking eyes with Ken. The hairs on the back of his neck rose to attention. He had expected Brooke to take a mental curtsy at the flattering remark. Instead, she eyed him with defiance. This woman was different, starting with the strange color of her eyes. A bluish-purple, almost violet. *Very intriguing,* he mused. *Come to me, eyes. Let's see how deep you are.*

A test of wills ensued. As they engaged in meaningless conversation, Brooke purposely drove her violets into Ken's smoky blacks. He felt a slight chill. Strange—he could see no bottom, only mesmerizing orbs of mystery. Who was this woman? A thought surged through him. *Could Brooke Pope possibly be a female version of me? Me, a male version of her? If so, surely a match made in heaven—or hell.*

Ken decided to test his theory. Skip the small talk and get to the point. However, before that arena was entered, there was one hurdle that needed to be cleared. "So how is Aaron doing? I imagine it must be hard. You know...the children are so small."

Brooke took a step back, allowing air to fill in between them. "Oh, Aaron will be all right. To tell you the truth, our relationship has become somewhat stale."

Ken saw a green light. "Something as traumatic as Nora's death would certainly be a cause of great stress. If you need to bend an ear, we could discuss it over a light dinner." Kenny pasted a thin smile. "Wouldn't want to reverse the effects of our workout, you know."

Brooke didn't return the smiley face. "No, I don't need to talk about it, and yes, let's have dinner." Obviously, the woman focused on what she wanted.

The diners matched orders of salmon, vegetables, and a salad. They left the restaurant cradling to-go boxes. The meal left Ken hungering for "dessert" dressed in white pants and a matching white sweater. He wanted to consume all of Brooke Pope, starting at the top and working his way down. Lust, as lust is meant to be enjoyed—no rules, no boundaries.

Ken turned to Brooke as they reached their cars. If his instincts were correct, this would be a night to remember. "Can I interest you in an after-dinner drink at my house?"

Brooke smiled (correction, smirked). Ken interpreted it as a telltale sign that their thoughts were in sync. "I'll follow you."

Kenny's groin was packed with love sticks of TNT, and Brooke Pope had just lit the fuse.

Ken made a quick sweep of the property as he turned into his driveway. There were no guarantees One or Other hadn't been reassigned back into his life. Thankfully, that whole ugly chapter would soon be ending, but for now, he needed to be on the lookout.

Ken escorted Brooke to the house and into his study. She took note of the wall covered with his degrees and awards, much as Nora had done. Ken pointed to the couch. "Please make yourself comfortable while I fix a 'Kendrick special' after-dinner drink."

"I don't think so." Brooke pulled Ken in close, unbuttoned his shirt, and pushed him onto the couch. They felt, they tasted, and they tussled like two wild dogs in a death grip over the last scrap of meat. Kenny wouldn't have been surprised to find bite marks on his neck. The episode was lust, pure lust. He was she; she was he. Beauty and the Beast; Beast and the Beauty. Come, enjoy, and devour. All too soon, it was over. Brooke let herself out.

Ken slumped in his desk chair, a soft light glowing from a table lamp across the room. It had been quite an experience, making love to that Brooke Pope. They'd both gotten what they wanted— quick and dirty sex. Brooke Pope was Rose Cherotte exponentially reincarnated. Though tiny quakes of satisfaction rumbled through their bodies as they undocked, it meant nothing. For people like Ken Laberday and Brooke Pope, there was never sensual, passionate fulfillment, only the proclamation of conquest followed by shallow gratification. Soon enough, Brooke's appetite for a "quick fix" would drive her to once again gorge on Ken like a jackal on a lion kill.

But yes, soon it would have to be. The days were short before a new chapter in Kendrick Laberday's deranged life would begin. That is, if the "grand plan" came to pass as planned.

Ken reached down and opened the drawer that held his mother's picture. He removed it and set it in front of him. He so much admired her beautiful features. Yes, quite perfect on the outside but quite dead on the inside—verification for those who believe that there is no such thing as a soul. At least not in every human. *Just once you could have hugged me, Mother. Just once you could have told me you loved me. But then I guess that's me also. After all, I am my mother's son.*

Ken refocused. There were plans to be finalized. He shoved the picture back in the drawer, slammed it shut, and closed his eyes. He needed to review his escape plan. It had to be thought out perfectly. Like a space-shuttle launch, failure wasn't an option. The first item of concern was his house. There were no assurances that the "O" boys wouldn't be paying him a surprise visit. Also, with Nora Balfour's death unsolved, the police may have him on their radar. As a countermeasure, Ken had rented a secluded country home several miles to the west of his property under an assumed name. The accommodations were spartan, but he needed the privacy to put the finishing touches on his final circus act—the grand finale.

If all went according to plan, Ken's final act would provide the exclamation point to his campaign. Right or wrong, Kendrick Laberday had struck a national nerve. Though public sentiment, for the most part, deplored his violent actions, Ken had succeeded in exposing festering wounds. Where Americans rated tooth extractions more popular than Congress and graded Wall Street moguls below the Bubonic Plague—including the rats that carried the disease— Ken Laberday saw himself as filling the void of the federal government's failure to protect its citizens from, well, their fellow citizens. Martyrdom aside, in the end, it was all about him because that's how psychopaths roll. And lest anyone forget his derring-do, the great ringmaster was determined to go out in style.

Ken's thoughts drifted to his exit strategy, and a good one it was. Soon he would be basking in sunny Venezuela. He had contacted an acquaintance teaching at the Universidad del Zulia in Maracaibo and who subsequently secured a professorship for him at the school. The setup was perfect, as the Venezuelan government was still having heartburn with the United States for backing the short-lived presidency of Pedro Carmona several years previous. The present regime would be delighted to have a reinvented Ken Laberday expound his expertise on the corruption of the American capitalist system. It would serve them well to deflect blame from their own corrupt institutions. And thanks to Senator Samuel Davis Peck, Ken now had enough money to live the good life. He also had little fear of being sent back to the United States because even though Venezuela and the United States do have an extradition treaty, the president of the country very seldom complies. As for female companionship? Well, both the climate and the women could be described in a word—*hot*!

CHAPTER 28

Cason opened Sylkie's front door to an orchestra of clanging pots and pans. However, loud as they were, their clamor failed to drown out the verbal assault directed at them.

"Who's winning?" Casey chuckled as he entered the kitchen. A frustrated, angry look from Sylkie signaled that levity had long since left the building.

"How am I supposed to store all this"—Sylkie waved an arm across a countertop stacked with kitchen hardware while pointing her other arm at a row of cupboards below—"into these already-over-stuffed cupboards?" The question was being directed at herself.

"You're not." Casey eased into the moment with a concerned look. "Sylkie, you have to give this up. I know how much Nora meant to you, but you can't hold onto everything she owned. Her memories are what matter, and there's no shortage of room in your heart for them." A clumsy attempt at physical embracement was rebuffed.

"You can't understand what I feel. Nora and I were like one. Being able to see and to touch things she owned keeps that memory strong. It's something I can identify with. It...all of it reminds me of her. And what about Margo and Danny? They'll want mementos from their mother."

Casey leaned against the counter. "What Margo and Danny need is a calm, rational aunt who will guide them to adulthood. It's a formula comprised of love and understanding, not regurgitating the past."

Sylkie flopped down onto a kitchen chair. "Why does it have to be like this?" She cried into her hands. "Of course, my priority will always be the kids. And I don't know what I would do without you, but…"

Casey pulled a chair alongside. "But what?"

The words did not come easy. "Oh, I don't know. Life can be so cruel. Sometimes I wonder if there truly is a grand plan like I was brought up to believe, or are we just products of random sex in an animal species that evolution will someday chalk up among its miscues?"

Casey rose and strode over to the coffeepot. "Want a cup?"

"No, thanks."

He poured one for himself and sat down next to Sylkie. Casey could not fathom the depth of her pain, and trying to jump-start the faith he knew she had deep inside would not serve any great purpose right now. Quietly being there for her was the better option. Before Casey even downed a sip of coffee, Sylkie buried her head into his shoulder and sobbed, drowning all her anger and hurt in a river of tears. They held each other for a long time in the kitchen piled high with pots and pans and utensils and boxes.

When they finally separated, Casey's shoulder was soaked with Sylkie's pain, oozing from a soul that had weathered more than a fair share of loss. Casey silently prayed that the void created by Nora's death would be filled with his presence.

"I talked to Mark tonight," Casey said, rubbing Sylkie's back. "I guess he wants to meet with us in the morning. Said he has some new ideas."

"Yeah, I know. He called earlier," Sylkie replied, wiping her eyes with a kitchen towel. "He said something about 'connecting dots.' I just hope these dots don't have the words *foreclosure records* stamped on them. I don't think I could stand one more day in that dog pen or stomach one more interview."

"And I don't think you should worry any more about this kitchen tonight. If we can find the stove, let's pop some corn and watch a movie."

Sylkie sighed and softened. "I can bite on that…and, Casey?"

"Yes?"

"I love you."

*****

Sylkie noted the extra bounce in Mark's step as he walked into the conference room. Whatever he was up to, she hoped "foreclosure," "records," "interview," or any synonyms thereof hadn't been invited to participate.

Mark thrust out a hand to Jim Renner. "Good to see you back, Jim."

"Good to be back in circulation," Renner nodded. "Fortunately, the bullet didn't cause much damage. I'm still hopping around, but I'm not in pain. Getting back to work will keep my mind off of it."

Sylkie tentatively pitched, "So, Mark, you mentioned something about 'connecting dots'?"

Mark grinned. "Yes, I did. Believe it or not, I got a revelation about our murder cases from a children's drawing book."

"You mean as opposed to looking into a crystal ball?" Casey grinned.

"Something like that. Strange as it sounds, I cannot separate the circus murders from Nora's death. I know it doesn't make sense, but in my mind, I keep seeing these dots. They start out in different places, but eventually they align to point at one particular person."

"And that person is…?" Renner straightened up.

"Professor Kendrick Laberday."

"Are you kidding?" Sylkie blurted out.

"Pure speculation, but here's my reasoning: Laberday was close to your sister. Because of his profession, he has insight into those who profited from the mortgage meltdown. The professor was supposedly out of town when the Washington, DC, murder took place. He was at the scene of Senator Peck's 'hanging.' The warehouse used in the Peck incident does business with the college where Laberday teaches. The unidentified man at the Admiral Suites was tall and thin like Laberday, and the facial sketch, although admittedly it requires a little imagination, does remotely resemble Laberday. Now look at this." Mark unrolled a map and tapped an index finger on a circled area. "I checked soil maps this morning. Laberday's property lies within the same soil type that was found on the vans used by the circus killer." Mark rolled the map back up. "I know it's not much to bite on, but all these little factoids are chasing each other around in my head."

Renner shook his head. "Mark, that's not even circumstantial evidence."

"I'm well aware of that. So talk me out of it, but throw out a better option. And think about this: if Aaron didn't kill your sister, who did?"

Cason and Sylkie exchanged glances. Casey said, "But Laberday was in Colorado when Nora died."

Mark raised an eyebrow. "Murder by proxy, maybe?"

"But why?" Sylkie looked shaken. "What possible motive could he have to kill my sister? She loved him with all her heart."

Mark flashed Sylkie a sympathetic look. "When you've been in this business as long as I have, you'll understand the true meaning of the adage, 'Truth is stranger than fiction.'" Mark looked around the room. "Willing to give it a shot?"

Everyone crawled into their own thoughts. Suddenly, Sylkie jumped up. "Maybe your 'dot' theory isn't so crazy."

Mark feigned hurt feelings. "I didn't think you think I'm crazy."

Sylkie waved him off. "The Lavonia murder—I know it was around the time of the Lavonia murder Nora told me that Ken was out of town for a few days. But I can't be positive of the exact timing."

"We'll check it out," Mark nodded.

"Okay, what's the plan?" Casey was starting to buy in.

Mark said, "Remember the strange statement the ringmaster gave about pictures being ready on the night of Peck's 'hanging?'"

"Yeah." Casey confirmed. "What about it?"

"I'm guessing the killer's identity was revealed when the Washington murder took place. And let's spread this out even further. Peck was the first target the circus murderer didn't kill. Why? I think there may have been a lot more to Peck's abduction than just another circus act." Mark looked hopefully at Casey and Jim Renner. "Could you guys do a little probing in DC? Maybe connect a few dots yourselves."

"As in uncovering a conspiracy or something?" Renner stroked his healing leg.

"Why not? The town's been known for one or two of those."

Casey nodded. "Or more."

"So what about us, Mr. Connect the Dots? I pray, don't banish me to foreclosure purgatory," Sylkie pleaded. "My eyes will fall out if I have to spend one more day pouring over records."

"Your prayers are answered." Mark winked. "Those days are over for now anyway. Let's concentrate on the good professor's personal life. Find out where Laberday does his banking. See what you can dig up about his finances from 2007 to the present."

Sylkie pumped a fist. "Finally, my get-out-of-jail card."

"And you?" Casey asked.

"I'm going to pay a visit to Laberday's property. I want to poke around when he's not there. I plan on interviewing him, and it would be nice to have some ammunition to shoot his way."

Casey looked concerned. "Do you truly feel there's a good probability Laberday is tied to both crimes?" He knew this must be playing on Sylkie's emotions, and he didn't want her to suffer through another disappointment.

"I admit it's a hunch. But every time I close my eyes and ponder these two cases, I see Nora Balfour on one side of a wall, the circus murder victims on the other, and Kendrick Laberday standing over them with a foot on each side. I can't seem to shake the picture."

Casey nodded. "Hopefully Jim and I can add a few brushstrokes of our own."

*****

Ken Laberday rubbed his hands together, ready for his first lecture of the day. Little did his students realize the professor would not be issuing them a final grade for the semester. Ken's triumphant departure was set to follow one last act—the grand finale. The setting was to be the Vickers College auditorium where Ken would speak on the fascinating topic of "Employing the Keynesian Model to Stimulate Economic Recovery." The lecture was scheduled to conclude a three-day jubilee honoring the college as the oldest surviving institution of higher learning in the state along with promoting its honored portfolio of renowned programs. Each department was scheduled to host an event, the economics department providing the finale on Saturday afternoon. Ken's lecture would not only draw students studying economics at the college but would also garner an obligatory presence from prominent people in the local, business, and financial world.

Ken began, "Last week, we completed the unit featuring, among other things, the argument for supply-side economics." Ken slowly paced in front of his students. "Today we will start a new subject, a subject for which you will not find a title in any economics book. I call it Darth Vader economics because it thrusts us into the dark side of capitalism. So why delve into such a controversial and, quite frankly, depressing topic? Because I believe it is the engine that has driven your life in one manner or the other for the past several years.

"Let's ask the question: 'Why are you sitting in front of me this morning?' I see a wide diversity of ages. That's a good thing in the respect that we should continue learning until the day we die. But again, why are *you* here? Retooling, maybe? Did your career wither on the vine? Might you be a victim of venture capitalism? How about a bottom line 'beheading,' where your company downsized, sending your work out of country, the savings providing seven-figure bonuses for its masterminds. And the reward for your loyalty? Unemployment compensation, food stamps, maybe visits to the local food shelf. You might be among the working poor. You juggle a part-time job with raising a family while struggling to keep up with college classes in hopes of getting a degree that will take years to pay off. And for this effort, you have been labeled as lazy ne'er-do-wells because you're forced to take government 'handouts.'"

Ken looked around the room. With the exception of those who were still close to the womb side of life, it was evident his words had hit home. Many in the room acknowledged his rant with nodding heads and understanding, tired eyes. A few students welled up tears. It could have been a wonderful bonding moment between an educator and his class, could have if the educator had been someone other than Kendrick Laberday. Of course, for Kenny, this was merely a manipulative maneuver to sway opinion and garner support for his circus of justice. To think otherwise would be to not understand the mind of a psychopath.

Satisfied he had all his cattle in the corral, Ken felt confident to continue his one-man assault on the holy grail of capitalism—wealth distribution (or lack of it). "And so, we shall explore the dark dungeons of American finance next time with my lecture entitled, 'Satan Lives in the Bull.'"

*****

Mark cautiously approached the Laberday property, keeping an eye out for any sign of activity. The professor's schedule had him in class most of the morning, more than enough time for Mark to give the place a good once-over. He parked in front of the garage and made his way around the building. Looking through a side window, Mark saw two empty stalls, reasonable confirmation that Laberday was not at home.

Mark noticed what looked like a rather well-used, rutted trail behind the garage and followed it to the machine shed. Finding the shed locked, he scanned the building for an entrance. A lone window provided the only opportunity to look inside. He picked up two dead branches and used them to separate the dried cocklebur bushes that were guarding the window. Reaching the shed with several brown burrs clinging to his pants, Mark peered through the window. A broken-out corner on one of the panes allowed the smell of old oil mixed with damp wood to pass through. What he didn't see intrigued Mark more than what he did observe. The contents inside consisted of a wooden door resting on sawhorses, a few pails strewn around, and a workbench with an attached vise. The building appeared to have been cleaned out rather than unused. *Unusual for a storage building to be completely empty,* Mark concluded. A call from Sylkie interrupted his retreat from the cocklebur forest.

"I think I may have something."

"Where are you?"

"I'm at a Wells Fargo bank where Laberday has an account. In 2006, he pulled out thirty thousand in personal savings plus borrowed another fifteen thousand to start an online tutorial school. In late 2008, the business failed."

"Ooh, yeah. I do believe you may have found motive. Good work, young la—I mean, Sergeant."

"So what now?"

"Tomorrow you and I are going to pay Professor Kendrick Laberday a long overdue visit."

CHAPTER 29

As the wheels of the 757 kissed the tarmac at Reagan National Airport, Casey Maxwell absently gazed out at a gray Washington, DC, sky, reflecting on his sudden kinship with Tony Bennett, who had left his heart in San Francisco. At the moment, his own pumper was wandering the green concourse at MSP International, looking to hitch a ride to Sylkie's condo. As the aircraft taxied to the terminal amid the glow of artificial lighting, Casey unceremoniously bounced Tony off the plane and rewound to the task at hand.

Casey glanced over at his partner. Jim Renner looked like he had swallowed an apple—whole. The poor guy was as comfortable in the air as a fly on a lizard's tongue.

Soon the two men were standing outside the terminal gate. Renner pulled out his cell phone. "I'm going to make a call, see if I can fast-track our mission."

Casey found the men's room. When he returned, Renner was stuffing his cell phone into his pocket. "I've got us a dinner date lined up tonight with an old friend. Ten gets us a buck he'll give us a lead or two."

"An insider?" Casey asked.

"Yeah, and with more connections than the computer running this airport."

*****

The night air was unwelcoming, filled with Chesapeake Bay chill as Jim and Casey sauntered into Fabrini's. The hostess led them to a table with a lone occupant, an older man with a ruddy complexion and gray hair that ringed an otherwise balding head and which begged for an appointment with the barber. The man stood as his dinner guests approached.

"Jim, it's good to see you." Clayton Rimm smiled, extending a hand.

"It's been way too long, Clayton." Renner grinned. He put a hand on Casey's shoulder. "Casey Maxwell... Clayton Rimm."

The men settled into chairs. Casey asked, "How do you two know each other?"

Renner explained, "Clayton worked in the New York State Attorney General's Office when I was starting my career with the FBI. We collaborated on several cases, struck up a relationship, and have been friends ever since."

Rimm added, "Friends that don't see near enough of each other. So what brings you fellows to the Sodom and Gomorrah of the Western Hemisphere?"

Renner smiled at Clayton's caustic quip. "We have some questions concerning Quinn Montague's death. Also, we'd like to interview Sam Peck."

"I see. So what do you want to know?"

"We're looking into the possibility that the killer's identity may have been compromised here in DC."

Rimm cleared his throat. Jim thought his friend looked pale. "Rumor has it that information concerning Montague's killer may have surfaced the day of his murder. I haven't been able to glean anything from it, but I can give you the name of someone to talk to."

Casey pulled out a pen and notebook. "Ready when you are."

"Go to the DC Police Department headquarters on Shepherd Street Northwest. Contact a Captain Robertson. Ask him about pictures."

"Pictures?" Casey asked.

"Yeah. There's some mystery surrounding the incident. Robertson claims there were pictures being taken at the time of the shooting, but no one seems to be able to find them. My people have looked into it but can't substantiate the claim." Rimm felt it was in their best interests not to divulge anything that Val Docket had told him.

"Life in the shining city on a hill," Casey interjected.

Rimm shot Casey an envious stare. "Ah, to be young again, to have it all ahead of you." Clayton winked. "I'm jealous, if you can't tell."

Renner ginned up a smile of his own. "You certainly have had your share of life's experiences, Clayton."

Rimm picked up his wine glass, then set it back down. "Yeah, and I've got one more coming up."

Casey cocked his head. "What's that?"

"I had some medical tests earlier this week. My doctor informed me I have cirrhosis of the liver."

Renner winced. "Clayton, I'm sorry. What, ah, is the prognosis?"

"He said six to nine months. Maybe a year if I take good care of myself."

Casey said, "Clayton, I…"

Rimm raised a palm. "It's okay. My main regret is that I was planning on buying some land in the country. Wish I hadn't waited so long…"—his voice trailed off—"…to take that dip."

"Let me know if there's anything I can do," Renner offered.

Rimm said, "There's something you both can do. Live your lives well. Be true to yourself. Love your families."

The evening ended on a solemn note. It would be Jim Renner's last conversation with Clayton Rimm.

*****

"The plan is to overlap questions concerning Nora's death with the circus killings," Mark instructed Sylkie as they drove to Wherland-Vickers College to interview Kendrick Laberday.

"And hopefully prove your hunch," Sylkie added.

"Hopefully. Sorry to involve you in Nora's case, but this is an exception. We're more or less trolling one case to snag another. Are you okay with it? I won't put you through it if you're uncomfortable."

"I'm fine. I promise to stay professional."

"Good enough. So are you missing him?"

"What?" Sylkie turned her head toward Mark, looking puzzled.

"Casey. You haven't seen him for almost twenty-four hours."

"I've lived all but a few months of my life without him. I think I can handle a couple of days."

Mark winked. "Say you miss him."

"Shut up. Okay. Yeah, I miss him. Satisfied?"

"I knew it."

After checking with the main office, Mark and Sylkie found their way to Kendrick Laberday's classroom. The entrance door had a slot window, through which Laberday caught a glimpse of Sylkie.

This is interesting, Ken noted. More curious than alarmed, he asked a student in the back of the room to open the door. "Please, come in," the professor motioned. The investigators tentatively stepped into the room and took seats in the back.

Ken resumed his lecture, "As I was saying, so now the country is in economic free fall later defined as the Great Recession. What to do? The Treasury Department and the Fed come to Congress with a desperate proposal. 'Give us a lot of money, and we will save the banks that are too big to fail. Plus, we will also help folks with underwater mortgages.' Only problem was that they 'forgot' to help the individual homeowners. They actually pulled this scam twice on Congress. Bottom line? Most of the fifty billion from the government sponsored Troubled Assets Relief Program went to bail out the big banks."

"So how did the big banks profit from the bailout?" a student asked.

"Good question. Pay attention. Now this will be on your final. The banks put some of the money in the Fed where it collected interest. They used some of it to subsidize a string of financial mergers. They also made use of some cheaper government loans to pay back the more expensive TARP loans." Ken closed his notebook. "That's all the time we have today. Wednesday's topic is titled, 'Saving Private Bankers.'"

As the class filed out, Mark and Sylkie made their way to the front of the room. "To what do I owe the pleasure of your visit this morning?" Ken stuck out a hand. Mark noted the calmness in his voice.

"Professor Laberday, we'd like to ask you a few questions concerning Nora Balfour's death."

Ken drew a puzzled look. "Ah, of course. I will be happy to answer your questions, but I don't understand. I mean, Nora's death *was* an accident, was it not? And why would you question me about it?"

Mark purposely ignored Laberday's queries. "Nora Balfour died under suspicious circumstances. We feel there may have been foul play involved."

Ken put a hand on his lecture podium as if he needed to brace himself. "Oh, this is terrible. I mean..." Ken turned to Sylkie. "Sergeant Maune, this must be very hard for you. I'm so sorry."

Sylkie didn't respond to the platitude. "You were on a trip in the Southwest at the time of Nora's death. Exactly where did you go?"

Ken made a mental note that the theatrics weren't working. Still, he feigned surprise. "Am I a suspect?"

Mark made direct eye contact. "Everyone's a suspect until a case is solved, Professor Laberday."

Ken said, "Well, then, let me think. My trip was planned around the Grand Canyon, and that's where I spent the majority of my vacation. So to answer your question, I was somewhere in or around the Canyon the days before Nora's death."

Sylkie asked, "Can you prove your route from here to the Grand Canyon with credit-card receipts or hotel registrations? Something to show where you were?"

"No can do. Remember I'm an economics professor. I am well aware of the pitfalls of overusing credit. I budget my money very carefully. I used cash for most of my trip." Ken pondered for a moment. "And, with the exception of my return trip, I camped out every night, an exercise I thoroughly enjoy. I guess that's not much help, is it?"

Sylkie pressed on. "I remember my sister saying that you also took a trip earlier in the summer to visit relatives. Can you tell us about that?"

Ken gave a puzzled look. *Time for a little offense.* "Why do you ask? How could that possibly have anything to do with Nora's death?"

It wasn't hard to detect the cool collectiveness in Laberday's persona. Mark determined the only way to get anything out of this guy was to crank up the heat.

"Professor Laberday, we feel that Nora Balfour's death and the circus murders could be connected. Please answer Sergeant Maune's question."

Ken hadn't expected the interrogation to take this direction. He was alarmed, but only mildly. These pests would soon be distant memories. "I don't believe this. You're actually trying to connect me to the circus murders?" Ken looked incredulous. "Oh, that's rich. I can't wait to share this with the faculty. Me—the circus killer? Rich indeed."

"Answer the question, Professor," Sylkie deadpanned.

"Of course. I'm sorry." Ken turned serious. "The truth is that I was at home. I, ah, suffer from depression. Two or three times a year, I get into a bad bout, where my only recourse is to isolate myself for a few days. I was ashamed to share my illness with Nora; I was trying to impress her, and so I lied about taking the trip. Actually, I never left my house. I have medication for it. I can show it to you if you like."

Mark and Sylkie looked at each other. "We'll be in touch." Mark motioned Sylkie to the door.

"You were unusually curt with him," Sylkie noted as Mark started the car. "That's not like you."

"I think that whole scene was an act on his part, and I wanted to send the message I wasn't buying it. There's something off-kilter with that guy. I sensed he was forcing his shock-and-surprise reaction to Nora's death. The lips were pleading emotion, but the eyes were vacant. And that, young la—Sergeant, leads me to a theory that could lock this puzzle into place."

"Go on."

"I've come across his type of behavior more often than you might think. I'm guessing that our Professor Laberday may be more surface than substance in the emotions he presents. I sensed that, as we were talking to him, he was plotting a way around us, and my crassness was intended to cast doubt on his story. If he picked up on that, it may lead him to an irrational move. It's worth a try."

"So you think his explanations were all BS?"

"Fresh from the bull itself."

"Bad."

"You asked."

Ken stared out his office window at the mighty Mississippi. The passing water with its random, swirling eddies at the edges and placid current in the middle normally instilled a calming effect. But not today. The conversation with Truitt and Maune had left him unsettled. His charm and intelligence unfailingly granted him a free pass for cruising past the fools in his world, but this encounter with Truitt was different. He got the distinct impression Truitt was deflecting his arrows of lies with disturbing accuracy. Ken knew he would have to be very careful in conducting his affairs in these final days before his departure.

CHAPTER 30

Sam Peck and his droopy red eyes greeted the two men standing at the door.

"What can I do for y'all?"

"Senator Peck, I'm Special Agent James Renner, and this is Special Agent Cason Maxwell. We'd like to ask you a few questions concerning your abduction."

Peck managed a weak nod. "C'mon in, have a seat." The senator dragged in behind the agents. "I've told the authorities everything I can recall about those insane days with that monster. I don't know what else I can add."

Casey cleared a newspaper's sports section from a chair. "We've read the transcript of your interview. We just have a couple of questions."

Peck waved a hand. "Give it a shot."

Jim Renner moved a plate of half-eaten *something* from the couch to an end table and sat down. "You stated you spent most of your time lying on a bed. Did you hear noises like cars going by or people talking—anything of that nature?"

"Mostly I didn't hear nothin' other than an occasional vehicle passing."

Casey continued, "Do you think you were in a private home?"

Peck scratched the back of his neck. "I'd say, yeah, more 'n' likely."

"Do you think you could identify your abductor's voice if you heard it again?"

"Already been asked that question, and the answer's the same—no. Like I said before, starting with the cabby that sprayed me in the face, I was so drugged up most of the time I could've been riding on the back of one of them icky-saurouses an' I wouldn't-a known the difference."

Casey pressed, "And I suppose you still have no idea why the killer made you his first live release."

Peck stared and said nothing. Finally, "Can't help you" dribbled out, barely above a whisper.

"Thanks for your time, Senator."

The agents' next stop was DC Police headquarters. A harried Captain Carl Robertson stuck out a brown hand and motioned to two chairs. "What can I do for you?"

The men sat, this time without having to pre-clean the furniture. Renner said, "Captain Robertson, we understand there were some pictures taken by a tourist at the time of Quinn Montague's murder. What can you tell us about that?"

Robertson frowned. "I should be asking *you* that question. Don't you people communicate with each other?"

"What do you mean?" Renner defensively countered.

"Well, it *was* a couple of FBI agents who took the camera's memory card."

Casey and Renner immediately experienced similar torpedo strikes to their midsections. Taking a moment to clear post-bombing residue from his throat, Casey responded, "Um, we have no knowledge of a card being confiscated by the FBI, so, ah, let's move on. What can you tell us about the card?"

Robertson narrowed his eyes. Renner envisioned the word *incompetent* being pointed at them. "Shortly after the Hummer incident, a tourist came up to my desk sergeant and said he was taking a picture of his wife at the intersection where the Hummer stopped. When the shooting began, he kept snapping pictures until the gunfire sent them scurrying for cover. As he was about to hand over the memory card, an FBI guy showed his badge, told him he was in charge of the investigation and confiscated the card."

Renner asked, "Did this FBI agent tell your sergeant his name?"

"No, he didn't, and in defense of my sergeant, you can imagine the pandemonium at the time. It was a pretty hectic scene."

"I'm sure it was." Casey nodded. "Anything else?"

Robertson stood. "That's it."

"I definitely wasn't enamored with Robertson's ending to that story," Casey opined as they left police headquarters. "I mean, if our boys had grabbed the memory card, we would have known about it, even if it didn't have much to offer."

"That's my guess." Jim Renner wasn't liking what his brain was thinking.

"But then who?"

"Dunno, but we're not helping ourselves by hanging around Murkysville. And in case you're thinking it, we're *not* checking in with headquarters. We're heading back to Minneapolis."

That plan was music to Casey's ears.

*****

Mark lay back in his recliner, absently flipping through TV channels. Attempts to divert his attention from the mission at hand proved fruitless as his thoughts kept floating back to the interview with Kendrick Laberday. Though the professor's looks and charm were eye candy to women, he was toxic in Mark's eyes. He sensed this guy was not on the level. However, intuitions don't make for good court prosecutions. He needed concrete evidence.

In the background, Mark could hear Margo and Danny playing a game of hide-and-seek. The children's father, Aaron, had increasingly gravitated toward becoming an absentee parent, and watching the children from time to time helped Liz fill the void of her own children leaving the nest. Of course, it was far from an ideal arrangement, as the kids needed a permanent, stable home with caring parents. Mark pondered how it was all going to turn out.

"Doesn't the children's giggling and bantering remind you of Maggie and Brian when they were small?" Liz reminisced, entering the room.

Yes, yes it did. Seemed like ages ago. "Yeah, I guess," Mark answered with a twinge of nostalgia.

"So how was the interview with Professor Laberday?"

"To tell you the truth, Liz, I have a real bad feeling about the guy."

A little voice found Mark's ear. "My mommy cried."

Mark whirled around. "What?"

Margo was standing in the entrance to the living room. "We drove by Professor Laberday's house, and my mommy cried. And then we almost hit a train."

Liz picked the little girl. Mark bounced out of his chair.

"Then my mommy went to heaven." Margo buried her head in Liz's neck.

"How about a snack?" Liz changed the subject. "Go get your brother. I have a fresh chocolate cake that needs to be sampled."

Margo ran off to get Danny. "What was that all about?" Liz stammered.

"I don't know, but if I had any doubts about Laberday, Margo just erased them. Something *did* happen between Nora and Laberday." Mark stroked his chin. "Out of the mouth of babes…"

"Are you going to tell Sylkie?"

"Absolutely not. She'd beat him to death. For her own protection, she is not to know about this. I'll handle it."

Mark felt more confident than ever of Kendrick Laberday's involvement in Nora Balfour's death. It was time for the endgame.

*****

Sweating, panting, twisting, and grabbing, Ken and Brooke played out wild love raptures on Ken's bed. Calories en masse floated off to wherever calories go, testifying to a more strenuous workout than either had pried out of a session at the gym. Finally, they reached the point of exertion exhaustion and rolled away from each other, replenishing their bodies with mouthfuls of air.

"I'm leaving Aaron," Brooke broke the silence.

Ken stared at the ceiling. "Why?"

"He bores me."

"Did you tell him that?"

"I spared him the long sword. I told him I felt suffocated, that I needed more space."

"What'd he say?"

"Doesn't matter."

Ken rolled over and propped his head on an elbow. "So where are you going to stay?" He ever so lightly ran a finger over her tummy. She responded with an equally light flinch. He hoped she wasn't going to propose to move in with him, an impossible proposition at this late stage of the game.

"If you think I'm setting my sights to bunk with you, don't flatter yourself. Good bed partners seldom make good roomies, and truthfully, I don't really like you that much out of bed."

Ken laughed out loud. "Ditto. And do you know why?"

"Because we're the same?"

"Because we're the same." Kenny completed his rollover.

Ken watched Brook's taillights disappear from his driveway. After all his conquests, far too many to count, he had finally met his equal. Brooke Pope simultaneously intoxicated him and caused him pause. To meet your alter ego face-to-face is a sobering experience. *So this is what I'm actually like—cold, hard, altruistic.* The concept felt numb to Ken. *What else is there in life? I need, I want, I take.* Natural enough to a psychopath.

The professor moved away from the window. The days were quickly disappearing before his departure to Venezuela, and there were obstacles blocking his path. First, there was this pest, Truitt, and his sidekick, Nora's sister. Then there were the "Bo Brothers." Ken had no illusions about One or Other's handlers being content with his blackmailing them via Senator Sam Peck's confessions. For sure, their paranoia would have the two morons attempting to complicate his life.

Ken contemplated the real possibility that his enemies would pursue him from both sides of the law. Fools. Unfortunately for them, in the end, there could be only one winner—*and hands down, it's going to be me.*

One last time, Ken sat at the desk in his study and stared at the sacred drawer that held his mother's picture. Though he struggled against revisiting the tormented saga that was his childhood, it was as if a spellbinding curse had him forever trapped into a strange and unyielding embrace with his mother's spirit. Seemingly on its own, the professor's hand reached into the drawer, removed the picture, and set it on the desk. Tonight his mother appeared to be smiling. *Is it a smile of pride, or are you mocking me?* Kendrick contemplated. *No matter, I am going to succeed, and I will do it without your smothering veil.*

Ken regained control of his hand and shoved the picture back in the drawer. He silently vowed to renew his attempts to dismiss her spirit just as she had silently abandoned him and his father one dark, unforgettable night.

*****

"Where are they?" Guy impatiently scanned the First Precinct parking lot from a window in the conference room.

"Relax," Mark cajoled. "They got back from DC late last night. They'll be here shortly."

Lompello shrugged. "They should have shown up by now. Young people don't need much sleep. Say, did I ever tell you about the time I was on this stakeout for three days and—"

"Yup, you did," Mark winked. "And you also used to remind me of the virtues of being patient."

Guy frowned. "Well, that was then. It's easier to be patient when the tape measure of life has a lot more inches in the direction you're going than where you've been."

Soon the door to the conference room swung open to Renner and Maxwell. "We've been waiting for you." Guy attempted a stern face.

Jim Renner didn't acknowledge the scold. Although he could be rather aloof, Mark liked the guy. For sure, he was 99 percent business; the remaining one percent, a mystery.

Mark and Guy were briefed on the Washington, DC, trip. Mark filled them in on the interview with Laberday. He was also able to relate Margo's story to them, as Sylkie was downstairs interviewing a sexual-assault victim.

Lompello summed up the session. "So, number one, we cannot count on any real assistance outside our group."

Casey nodded. "Looks like it."

Guy continued. "Okay, number two. Even though we lack evidence, Professor Kendrick Laberday is our best prospect as the circus killer and a prime suspect in Nora Balfour's death."

Casey shifted in his chair. There was nothing he wanted more than to be in on catching Nora's killer.

"So now we come to number three. How do we pull this together?"

Mark said, "I'd like to get a search warrant for Laberday's property. If Peck was right about being held someplace quiet, well, the professor lives in a quiet country atmosphere. There may be some lingering clues if Peck *was* there. Also, let's monitor Laberday's movements, twenty-four seven. I'm hoping our interview has shaken him enough to make a mistake."

Guy shot a look at Casey and Renner. "Sound like a plan to you guys?"

Renner nodded. "Do the search. We'll take first post."

*****

"This is ridiculous," Ken growled, pushing the door open.

Mark countered with little emotion, "Sorry to inconvenience you, Professor."

Laberday's eyes narrowed. "You'll be sorry when your department gets slapped with a lawsuit."

So no more Mr. Nice Guy? "Professor, you know that's not going to happen. I'm well within my rights." Mark *was* on rather shaky ground, but the options were few.

"Your rights?" Laberday protested. "No, you have it all wrong, Sergeant. You're violating *my* rights, my Fourth Amendment rights to be exact. You have no probable cause."

Mark got in Ken's face. *Time for a shot across the bow.* "Nora's little girl told me that shortly before Nora's death they drove in front of your house and Nora started crying. In fact, Nora got so upset she almost ran into a moving train. What was it that disturbed her, Professor? What did she see that made her so upset? Is there something here you don't want me to see?"

A direct hit. Suddenly, Nora's nosiness made sense. *She must have seen Rose and me together before we left for Washington, DC. I wonder what else Truitt knows.* Ken cleared his throat and adopted a more conciliatory tone. "I have nothing to hide, Sergeant. Feel free to look as long and hard as you like."

Mark painstakingly picked through every room in the house, searching for clues along with watching for hot and cold reactions from Ken. Finally, he reached the spare bedroom. It was clean, fresh smelling. Mark lifted the bed covers. A very new, perhaps brand-new, mattress lay resting on the box spring. The sheets, blanket, and bedspread also displayed new, crisp appearances.

"Nice room. Looks like you've made a recent upgrade to the bed."

Ken looked distracted. "Huh? Oh, yeah. I replace things as needed...and, of course, when I can afford them."

"I see." Mark sensed apprehensiveness.

The garage was next. Nothing there to warrant a closer look. As they exited the building, Mark pointed to the ruts leading to the machine shed. "Where do these tracks lead?" Mark feigned ignorance.

The question interrupted some very ugly thoughts on Ken's part concerning Mark. "There's an old machine shed back there. I never use it. It's mostly empty."

"Well, I guess I should take a look before I leave."

Ken opened the padlock securing the shed door. The oil-and-damp-dirt smell greeting them as they stepped inside trumped the whiff Mark had inhaled through the window on his previous visit. Mark poked along the inside walls, looking for signs of anything other than old. A small clump of metal slag caught his eye. Impossible to tell how long it had been there, but obviously someone had been cutting metal. He worked his way over to the wooden workbench at the far end of the shed. He closely inspected the shelves beneath the sturdy top. Something in the back of one of the shelves caught Mark's eye. He picked up a cutoff section of hydraulic hose with an attached fitting that looked fairly new. He set it on top of the bench.

"What's this?" Mark asked and feigned ignorance.

"It looks like a section of hose. I have no idea what it would be used for."

"Looks to me like it might be part of an hydraulics assembly."

"Oh." The anger in Ken was swelling like a volcano in eruption mode.

Mark purposely took his time inspecting the rest of the shed, as he could see it was irritating Laberday. Finally, he let the professor off the hook. "I guess I've seen enough."

On his way out of the building, Mark looked up and noticed fresh scrape marks on the center sill. He surmised a cable had been slung around the beam. Another clue that there had been recent activity in the building.

Mark made idle talk on the way back to the garage, not allowing the professor a hint of what he might be thinking. Ken barely responded. Reaching his car, Mark smiled and said, "I guess I'm satisfied...for now. Thanks for your time, Professor."

Ken stood in his driveway and watched Mark drive away, clueless as to what the pesky cop might have noticed or what he was thinking. *What did he mean by "for now"?*

Mark drove away, hoping he had put a few dents in Laberday's armor.

CHAPTER 31

Ken kick-shut his office door, his mood dramatically skewing to the downside following Mark's visit. Dark thoughts of adding a circus act with Truitt as the featured performer raced through his mind with NASCAR speed. Fortunately for the professor, neither administration nor faculty members were aware of the storm clouds gathering around him. When a rumor surfaced that the police had paid him a visit, Ken brushed it off as an inquiry pertaining to a robbery investigation in his neighborhood.

These cat-and-mouse games were, for sure, a distraction, but there was little he could do except take evasive measures, one of which was to play out after his last class of the day. Ken presumed he was on top of Mark Truitt's most-wanted list and would be closely monitored from here on in, and so he had worked out a ploy that should get Brooke Pope and him to his safe house without fear of being followed.

Reviewing the mechanics of the plan chippered his mood. Ken reminded himself that uncertainty invites failure. Conversely, confidence ensures success. *Stay focused. If you can't outfox that loser cop, get out of the game.* Ken's calculating, psychopathic mind reset. Chance for success? 100 percent. He mentally dared any would-be pursuers to tail him so he could prove his superior abilities. Though that wish would soon unfold in real life, at the moment, he had a paying audience to address.

Ken lectured to his afternoon economics class, "You have to understand knowledgeable people in the banking and real-estate world in the mid-2000s understood all too well the American housing market was in trouble. The 'well' of legitimate applicants was rapidly drying up. So did they close up shop? Not a chance. Instead they got very creative, finding new ways to shake the money tree by building mortgages for people who were financially insecure. Those mortgages were then bundled into bonds by investment institutions and sold to greedy—slash—foolish investors." Ken paused. "And how did bond departments of big corporations internally label their toxic creations? 'Nuclear Holocaust,' 'Subprime Meltdown,' 'Mike Tyson's Punch Out.' And to add insult to injury, not only did they pedal these securities, they bet against a number of them. Crazy."

A hand went up. "My parents lost their 401(k). Is it because of this?"

Ken nodded and feigned compassion. "401(k)s, pension funds, IRAs. The list is a long one."

"How many people have gone to jail for this?" another student questioned.

Ken cast a wry smile. "No senior banking official has been indicted. The government claims they can't show criminal intent."

"How about civil suits?"

Ken was loving this. "Forget it. The SEC tried. Corporate lawyers have carved the government's cases up for fish bait."

"So the ringmaster swoops in and takes a few swings at dark justice," a voice sarcastically zinged from the back of the room. "I know whose side I'm on." Heads nodded. "What do you say, Professor?"

Ken smiled. "Class dismissed."

Soon after, Kenny nonchalantly climbed into a car he had rented that morning. He pulled out of the parking lot and aimed for downtown Saint Paul. Looking into his rearview mirror, he was not at all surprised to observe a black SUV keeping pace several car lengths behind.

Renner and Maxwell followed at a safe distance behind both vehicles.

Exiting onto a downtown street, Ken drove for several blocks, finally entering a parking ramp connected to a professional building complex. Jim Renner noted that the SUV also turned into the parking ramp.

Ken parked his car on the second level and aimed for a building entrance. A stocky Hispanic-looking man jumped out of the SUV and followed Laberday. Cason put some air between them, bringing up the rear. Renner kept an eye on the SUV.

Ken found a stairway, walked down to the first floor, and exited onto a sidewalk. The Hispanic man trailed a fair distance behind. The professor ambled up to a bus stop and glanced at his watch. Casey watched the Hispanic man watching Laberday.

A shuttle bus soon pulled up to the curb. Its doors swung open, and Ken boarded. The marquee on the bus read "Mall of America." The Hispanic man talked into his jacket collar. Maxwell summoned Renner with his cell phone. Before long, the SUV showed up, and the Hispanic man jumped in.

"I think the SUV driver might be on to me," Renner warned as Casey closed the car door.

Maxwell shrugged. "Either way, forward ho."

The shuttle chugged its way out of Saint Paul, past the Minneapolis-Saint Paul International Airport, and on to the Mall of America, a 4.9-million-square-foot colossus and America's most-visited shopping mall.

The bus stopped in front of a main entrance. The SUV pulled in behind it. Renner drifted in a few car lengths behind the SUV.

Ken helped an older woman off the bus and escorted her into the mall. Both front doors of the SUV opened. The Hispanic man jumped out of the passenger side, angrily glanced toward Renner and Maxwell and started after Laberday. The SUV's driver burst out of his side and quickly advanced toward the FBI agents' car, waving a gun. Renner and Maxwell drew their service weapons, exited the car, and faced the man down.

"Guns down! Guns down!" One shouted.

Renner flashed his badge. "FBI."

"I said guns down!" One repeated, also showing a badge.

"No way! Casey, go!" Renner shouted.

"Move and your dead!" One growled, taking his eye off Renner and fixing his gun on Maxwell.

The threat was the opening Renner needed. His bullet pierced One's handgun; the gun flew to the pavement.

Other drew his gun and fired. Maxwell returned the favor. Casey's bullet caught Other under his chin. He whirled and fell against an entrance door. Renner threw One against his car and frisked him.

"I wasn't going to shoot," One groaned. "I only wanted to stall you. I couldn't be sure you really were who you claimed to be."

"Sorry. I failed telepathy class. Who are you?"

One didn't answer. He was soon hauled away by a couple of uniforms to a hospital. There was no hurry for quick-draw for Other. He would be attended to by the medical examiner.

Maxwell, looking very pale, leaned against their car and slowly pushed a finger through a bullet hole in his sport coat. His eyes told Renner he was more than a little shaken.

"Are you okay?"

Casey was trying to make sense of the moment. "I guess. The bullet came at an angle, pierced my sport coat from the inside out."

Renner put a hand on his shoulder. "There was nothing else you could do. He was aiming to take you out."

"But why the guns? There was no reason for the guns."

"For them, there was. Evidently their orders were to silence Laberday before we got to him—at all costs. Whatever Laberday knows, it's important enough to kill for. Anyway, this probably puts us off the case. Guess it'll be up to Mark and Sylkie now."

Casey slapped the car's hood. "I want to nail that creep. I want to help Sylkie get her sister's killer."

"Well, I hope you're good at moral support, because that's going to be the extent of our involvement. Depending on who was on the opposite side of the shoot-out, our next career choice may well include cars and soapy water."

*****

Ken pushed against the throng of people scurrying toward the source of the commotion. He had been aware of the SUV following him and got a glimpse of Other as he entered the mall. He didn't know who was on the other end of the shooting, but the altercation had provided the perfect diversion. Whatever the outcome, Ken hoped it involved One and Other being fitted with new body orifices. The important thing was that there was no one on his tail now. Another plan worked to perfection, aided perhaps with a dose of fate.

Ken walked up to level P4 and found his van. He looked around to be sure no one was following him. Satisfied, he climbed in and drove down the ramp. Flashing lights ahead turned him in the opposite direction. Ken presumed the commotion was a tribute to his evasive tactics. Also, he hoped it meant an end to the futile but pesky attempts of One and Other to rein him in. He kissed butterfly kudos to whoever had detoured them. Unintended consequences could prove such a blessing. It could also prove his cause was just. But for Kenny, it was a possibility not worth contemplating because he really didn't care about "just." He only cared about Kenny.

Ken was still congratulating himself on a job well done when he reached Brooke Pope's new apartment in St. Louis Park. On the way there, he had spent as much time looking to the rear as looking forward to make sure he wasn't being followed. Confident he had outsmarted the police paparazzi, he determined it was safe to resolve a hanging detail.

Responding to the call buzzer, Brooke bounded down the stairway with a gym bag and an overnight bag in hand. She looked delicious in black jeans, a green turtleneck, and a black leather jacket. Laberday wanted to devour her on the spot.

"You said you had a surprise." Brooke wrapped an arm around his. She teased, "It better be good, cuz I did what you asked and took a vacation day tomorrow."

Laberday chuckled, "I promise it will be. But before we get to that, I have a favor to ask. There's a rental car in Saint Paul I need you to pick up. You can drive it back here. Someone will be along to retrieve it."

"Someone?" Brooke sounded suspicious.

"A friend. He wants this done on the quiet." Brooke swallowed the lie.

"Like clandestine? Fun. So what's the surprise?"

"I hope you won't be disappointed. I rented a property north of Elk River with the option to purchase. I'm thinking it may be a good investment opportunity. Nothing fancy, but it does have possibilities. A creek meanders through a rather dense woods in the back of the property, and even though the trees are mostly bare right now, it still has late-season beauty with a carpet of leaves covering the ground. The house is a sixties-style rambler; nothing fancy but comfortable. I was hoping we could spend tomorrow morning looking for ways to make it into a comfortable home away from home. I want it to be yours as much as mine. Unfortunately, I have to be at the college later on in the day for jubilee festivities, but I promise the evening and weekend will be devoted to satisfying your every whim."

"Does it have a bed?"

"Oh yes."

"Take me there."

"First things first. We go get the car, tune up at the gym. After which, I will treat you to a fine dinner at Tony Roma's."

The legion of endorphins released courtesy of their gym workout also enhanced a strong appetite for food, drink, and—of course—sex. A great meal was followed by a trip to a liquor store where Ken bought a bottle of expensive scotch and Brooke picked out the fixings for margaritas.

The rental house proved to be unremarkable, as advertised. On one side of the structure, an addition stuck out like a boil. In the rear, a screened porch had been thrown together, at some point, with construction considerations obviously terminated at ground level as the floor swaggered sharply toward the center. Mercifully, the early darkness spared an even less rosy assessment.

Following the walk-around, Pope's sole comment was, "Got a match?"

Inside, Brooke's mood flexed to the upside. The house was fairly comfortable if one ignored the faint musty smell, and after several ounces of alcohol, the remaining shortcomings were reduced to a nonissue. Ken scratched up a fire in the stone fireplace and then turned on some soft-mood music. Brooke demanded heavy metal. Ken complied.

Alcohol was guzzled, stories were told, and truths were revealed. First, their lives, then their bodies were laid bare. Though nothing was left to the imagination this night, for Brooke Pope, the future was unimaginable.

*****

Following the shoot-out at the OK Corral of America, Maxwell and Renner spent a rather lively session of give-and-take with their supervisor. He handed them their heads (along with their posteriors) on the proverbial silver platter, and they selfishly took them back. First, they were pummeled with endless questions, followed by endless waiting to be pummeled by more questions while the supervisor talked to someone at FBI headquarters. In the end, and true to Renner's prediction, they were removed from active duty and placed on administrative leave. Their questions concerning the identities of the men they had encountered were met with silence, making them all the more suspicious because it confirmed their fears that they had shot two "company" men.

Mark and Guy showed up in support for the beleaguered lawmen. However, the supervisor didn't share their empathy and was not shy in making it clear their presence was not appreciated. As they were rudely ushered out, Guy felt it necessary to direct a barrage of unique Minneapolis police vernacular. In a word, the evening had been dreadful.

*****

Casey glanced at his watch and quietly closed Sylkie's front door. The house was dark, with the exception of a faint glow wafting from the living room. He peeked around the corner to see Sylkie nervously fingering a handkerchief. With reservation, he mustered a "hi."

"Aaron's taking the kids."

"Say again?"

"He's moving to Burlington, Vermont. Said he wants a fresh start, *and* he needs to get Margo and Danny away from me because I'm turning the kids against him."

"That's ridiculous. Where'd he get that idea?"

"Don't know. He said something about all women being she-devils. I think his anger is being directed mostly at Brooke. I got the impression she's left him."

"And so he's going to take it out on you and the children? Nice guy."

Sylkie blew into her handkerchief. "Margo and Danny are all I have left of Nora, and now I won't even have them. This sucks, Casey. My heart has fallen out, and I'm walking all over it." Sylkie jumped up off the couch and looked into Casey with pleading, desperate eyes. "So talk to me about faith, Casey. Tell me where the Great Healer is when you need him—or her. Tell me what I've done to deserve this."

Casey held eye contact and searched for the right words. Preaching probably wouldn't help. An honest exchange might. "If you were brought up as I, to believe we are all born with attached puppet strings of angel hair, you'll go nuts trying to figure out why the Great Puppeteer has you flailing around down here so much of the time."

Sylkie pushed out a heavy sigh. "Why does it have to be so god-awful mean on this lousy rock ball? What's the point?"

"Maybe it's about—we're born, we live, we die. No guarantees in between."

"So what's the message then—'Good luck, hope you make it'?"

"Or hang in there; maybe this messy flesh-and-blood part is just a flash in the pan. Think about it, Sylkie; when it comes down to it, isn't that the *real* message—the good part starts when we depart this 'rock ball.' That's where faith comes in, but I think you already know that."

Sylkie pulled close and buried her head deep in Casey's chest. "It's hard," she whispered. "It's so very hard."

Casey gently cupped her head in his hands. "I know it is. But when you pick your heart up off the floor, look it over carefully. I think you'll find a good dose of faith in there. Don't ever let go of that. As humans, in the end, that's all we have."

CHAPTER 32

"So what do we do now?" a red-eyed Sylkie Maune questioned Guy and Mark as they hashed over the recent turn of events.

Mark studied her with concern. "I think we'll call the professor in for a little chat. See what he was up to with his roundabout journey to the Mall of America."

Lompello cautioned, "Okay, but remember, he didn't do anything illegal with that hide-and-seek performance. And what about the feds? Think they'll want a piece of him?"

"I'm guessing they're trying to peel off the layers behind the two mystery men. As for Laberday, I'm envisioning a scenario where he's feeling the heat—not only from us but also from a darker side. I'm convinced he's coddling information that somebody with a lot of influence in Washington, DC, wants very badly, and I'd give Sylkie's next paycheck to know what it is."

Maune rolled her eyes. "Now that would be a bargain."

An hour later, Ken Laberday was making eye contact with Mark and Sylkie in the First Precinct's interview room. Even though it had cut into his plans for the day, he determined this was a good thing. Cooperating with their request should keep them off his back. All he needed was one more day.

"To what do I owe the pleasure of our interface today?" Laberday blandly asked.

"Oh, I think you have a pretty fair idea, Professor," Sylkie dryly answered. "What was the purpose for the diversion tactic in your trip from Vickers to the Mall of America yesterday?"

"Sergeant Maune, I have no idea what you're referring to. None of my activities yesterday included a 'diversion' tactic." The question jarred Laberday. He knew that the "O" boys had been on his tail, but he didn't know how that tied in with these people. However, it did allow him a guess as to who might have been on the other end of the gun battle outside the mall.

Mark jumped in. "Let me refresh your memory. You drove a car from your college to a parking lot in downtown Saint Paul. You then hopped on a shuttle bus to the mall. Wouldn't you call that a little strange?"

Laberday sighed. "I don't see the significance, but let me explain my travels in hopes you will stop looking at me as if I'm Jack the Ripper reincarnated.

"I drove my van to the mall yesterday morning. I then took a shuttle to a nearby Ace Car Rental lot. I rented a car and drove it to the college. In the afternoon, I drove to a parking ramp in downtown Saint Paul. I left the car there for…ah, for a lady. I then took a shuttle back to the mall. Later, she met me for dinner, and we spent the evening together. Does that satisfy your curiosity, Sergeants?"

"Not quite," Sylkie probed. "Who is the lady, and why did you rent her a car?"

"The answer to the first part of your question, Sergeant Maune, is—no."

"No, what?"

"No, I won't tell you who she is."

"Why not?"

Laberday squirmed in his chair for effect. "She's committed to someone. Our relationship must remain private. We…ah, didn't mean to get involved romantically; it would be devastating, you understand." Ken locked eyes with Mark and Sylkie to show he was not going to back down. "Now if you keep pressing me on this, I'll insist on contacting my lawyer." Laberday figured to prime Brooke as his lady friend if absolutely necessary, but he was thinking checkmate here.

Mark had changed directions. "Where did you have dinner, and can you prove it?"

"Tony Roma's, and yes, I can prove it. The bill is on my credit-card account."

Sylkie sarcastically pointed out, "You said you don't like to use credit cards."

Laberday shrugged. "I make exceptions. I was short of cash."

The investigators realized this was going nowhere. It wasn't hard to see that Laberday lied as naturally as the rest of us breathe. Lies and deception are a trademark characteristic of psychopaths, and this man appeared to be an expert at inventing his own reality. However, for the record, Mark pressed on. "What's the story on the rental car?"

Ken attempted a convincing smile. "My friend is having car problems, and I was just making her life a little less complicated."

Sylkie asked, "Who were the men following you?"

"What men?"

"C'mon, Professor," Mark interjected. "You know who we're talking about, and I don't think their intention was to invite to you out for a night at the Orpheum Theater."

Ken exhaled deeply. "And do you know what I think, Truitt? I think you've hit the ditch. Seems to me like you people have a lot of murders to solve, but none of that's going to happen as long as you focus your misguided accusations on innocent people like me."

Mark and Sylkie threw each other a glance. Mark said, "I guess that will be all, Professor. We have no more questions."

Laberday was convinced he had provided an adequate alibi. As this was the last time he would have to suffer these two yahoos, he threw a parting shot. "So, Truitt, has my presumed but totally misplaced guilt finally ceased to flow through the backwaters of your overly suspicious mind, or am I still riding the current?"

Mark calmly answered, "We'll be in touch."

*****

"Did he give you anything to chew on?" Lompello questioned Mark and Sylkie as they slid into chairs in his office.

Sylkie said, "Well, there's the rental car. If it's still in the parking ramp, we'll know his story was a lie."

Mark shook his head. "It's not there. Casey called me before he got to your place last night. Told me the whole story. I had the Saint Paul police check the parking ramp. The car was gone."

Sylkie tried again. "I suppose we could have pressed for the name of his friend or look at his dinner bill."

"He wouldn't have told the story if he couldn't back it up. And having a girlfriend is not a crime. It's better to let him think he's one up on us—"

Sylkie finished the thought, "Which may give him an air of false confidence and lead him to make a mistake."

"We're walking a tight line here," Guy reflected. "But I agree with the logic."

Mark stood and paced, clearly frustrated. "The man never leaves a trail. Who can get away with all the crap we think he's responsible for and doesn't leave a trail? I was going to have his car bugged when he was in here for the interview. Do you know how he got here? A cab. It's like he's reading my mind."

Guy scraped a tiny gob of something off his desk with a paper clip. "So what now?"

"Well,"—Mark scratched his head—"I know he's not liking our attention. I'm afraid he's going to bolt."

Sylkie punished the armrest on her chair. "If we lose him, we lose the chance to solve my sister's murder. On the other hand, if he stays put, whoever is after him will get another shot—and we lose the chance to solve my sister's murder."

Guy shook his head. "He may not like our close encounters, yet that may be keeping him alive."

Mark said, "We'll have to do some rescheduling, but by tomorrow night, we'll have an eye on Laberday around the clock."

Lompello's office door creaked open. Maxwell and Renner filed in. "Are we interrupting anything?"

Mark smiled. "Hey, aren't you guys on administrative leave?"

"Screw 'em. They're playing dodgeball with us." The men found chairs.

Renner had a distant look and appeared preoccupied. Sylkie picked up on it. "Looks like you're holding up a heavy weight."

Renner managed a weak smile. "Sorry. I, ah, got word a little while ago that a friend of mine passed away."

Casey added, "I met the fellow when Jim and I were in DC. Nice man. Poor guy had liver disease."

"Tough way to go," Sylkie reflected.

Renner shifted in his chair. "Actually, he died in a drowning accident. Clayton—that was his name—was fly-fishing in a river in West Virginia when it happened. Kind of strange though."

"Why is that?" Mark queried.

"I never knew Clayton to be an outdoor enthusiast." Renner pulled in a deep breath. "So any new developments on your end?"

Guy ran a hand through a wave of thick white hair. "I was about to ask you the same question."

Casey offered, "Well, the men we shot sported badges belonging to Homeland Security. But everything surrounding the incident is murky. The deceased and the injured man were ferried out of the Twin Cities within a couple hours of the shooting. Just like that, gone to who knows where. And no explanation."

"Did they leave any evidence behind?" Mark asked.

Renner shook his head. "Nothing. It's like they never existed."

Sylkie frowned. "Who authorized their release?"

"They were released to the custody of the Department of Homeland Security. The secretary signed the order."

"Palmer Cheshire signed the release? What's that about?"

"This is getting way too involved." Mark was thinking out loud.

Renner put up a couple of fingers. "Two things intrigue me. One, why were these men following Laberday? Are they the men he had pictures of? Two, the fact that Casey and I aren't getting leaned on harder leads me to believe that someone(s) wants the whole incident to quietly blow over. I can envision a relatively painless end to this by blaming the shooting on the dead guy. Believe me, the truth can get buried so deep in the politics of these agencies its final resting place may well be in the earth's lower mantle."

"Okay, let's move on," Guy advised. "Keep Laberday close and keep him alive."

Casey put a hand on Sylkie's forearm. "Do they know about Aaron?"

Sylkie shook her head. "No, I haven't said anything."

"What about Aaron?" Mark asked.

"Aaron's moving to Burlington, Vermont. He's taking the kids with him."

"Oh, no. I'm sorry, Sylkie." Guy's perpetual scowl morphed into a look of concern. A moment of awkward silence ensued.

Casey broke the spell. "Is it okay if Sylkie takes an early lunch?"

Lompello waved Sylkie and Maxwell out of his office. "I don't want to see you back here till Monday morning."

"How 'bout me, boss?" Mark teased.

"Seems to me I'm short some paperwork from you that needs to be in by the end of the day. Better get busy."

"I love you too."

*****

Kenny whistled the old Dave Clark Five tune "Catch Us If You Can" as he tooled along I-94 between Minneapolis and Saint Paul. Destination—Vickers. It had been a good session with those misfits at the First Precinct. Although Ken was convinced they couldn't solve a carjacking if they were in the car when it was stolen, he thought it best to park his van downtown, as it contained props for his final circus act, and take a cab to precinct headquarters. His only concern was the possibility of replacements for the goons who had tried to take him down, and that worry would evaporate in another thirty-six hours. With that thought in mind, the professor called up the Rolling Stones for what else? "Time Is On My Side."

Laberday's mood was still upbeat as he parked his van in the college parking lot. He grabbed a briefcase from the passenger seat and walked to his office, isolating himself for the remainder of the afternoon. The campus was active with jubilee activities that would continue for a few more hours, whereupon he could get down to business. In the meantime, he fine-tuned what was to be his farewell speech—a speech that would include spectacular visual aids.

Finally, the halls of the old college fell silent. Ken checked his watch. It should be another two hours before the custodian worked his way to the auditorium, the site of the grand finale. *Plenty of time to install the necessary gimmicks.* Ken grabbed the briefcase and locked his office.

The upper end of the auditorium was accessed through two ancient oak doors, one on each side of the room. A similar door was located at the room's lower end and accessed by a hallway that served as an emergency exit. A fourth door, further down the hallway, opened to the stage and was out of view of the audience.

Reaching the entrance to the auditorium, Ken scanned the area to make sure no one was around. Finding the coast clear, he went to work on the two main entrance doors. Near the top and bottom edge of each door, he drilled two one-inch holes. He then drilled matching holes of a slightly smaller size into the doorjambs. He inserted a bullet plug into each hole he had drilled in the doors. The plugs were designed to be remotely ignited and were propelled by a tiny amount of propane gas. One half of the propelled plug would stick into the doorjamb, and the other half, along with its casing, would remain in the door. The plugs weren't designed to hold back the Fifth Infantry, only to corral the audience in the auditorium for a short period. Finally, he covered the holes with tape, colored to match the doors and jambs.

Having finished his work on the upper doors, Ken aimed for the door at the bottom end of the auditorium, where he installed a similar device. He then screwed on an old-fashioned barrel-bolt security guard to the inside of the stage access door, which would eliminate the possibility of being blindsided during the performance. So far, so good. Next, he familiarized himself with the electrical panel. He was pleased with the options.

Reaching into his briefcase, Ken removed several tiny bundles of harmless though noisy explosives and hid them around the auditorium. With that task completed, he checked his watch. About an hour remained before the custodian would show up.

Ken hurried outside, climbed into his van, and drove around the building to the maintenance room outside access door. He opened the van's rear doors and removed several sections of what appeared to be a cage. It took a few trips to carry the entire package of light-weight aluminum green-painted sections through the maintenance room and into the hallway that ran alongside the auditorium. He then carried the sections through the stage door and onto the stage.

With all the pieces on-site, the professor slipped behind one of the curtain halves and pressed a large black button mounted under the electrical panel. A whirring sound triggered a section of stage floor to drop slightly and then retreat under the stage. Ken walked over and peered into the trap room below. A platform operated by hydraulics stared back at him. He pressed another button, and the platform rose to stage-floor level. He connected the cage sections and then fastened the unit to the platform. With the centerpiece of his final act now in place, Ken reset the floor. He then descended a set of stairs at the back of the stage and opened an access door to the trap room. He set the briefcase inside the room. Mission accomplished, with several minutes to spare.

Ken took a moment to look out over the empty auditorium. The russet-colored seats, about four hundred in all, staked their claim as being the only modern adornments in the hall. The white lathe and plaster walls were interrupted in their continuity by thick square posts milled in a bygone era. Menacing-looking dragonheads that cradled the room's sidelights sprouted from the posts. Vintage chandeliers dripping with prisms and pendeloques floated silently below a domed gold-colored ceiling.

There was history, so much history in this room. Eloquent speeches given by prominent people of the day. Spellbinding lectures from some of the country's most famous educators. Plays and concerts too numerous to mention. But that would all be dwarfed by the history to be made here tomorrow. Though possessing a dead soul, Kendrick Laberday felt a twinge of superiority in that the great ring-master was about to trump them all.

Ken started to walk from the stage and then abruptly stopped. Out of nowhere, he was struck with a flash of inspiration, in layman's term, a brain fart. Although his plans had been impeccably thought out, he concluded a little extra insurance would be good—just in case. Kenny slapped his hands together and disappeared into the night.

*****

Washington, DC

Deep within the recesses of a nondescript concrete building, two men squared off. The man who called the meeting spoke in somber tones. His thinning grayish-yellow hair, deeply crevassed face, and dark half-moons that buoyed uninteresting eyes would have one guess, either undertaker or terminal patient. The stench of tobacco smoke wicking from his clothes lobbied the case for terminal patient.

The man on the opposite side of the table was clean-cut, muscular, and had a bandaged right hand. To Kendrick Laberday, the man was known as One. His real name was Leon Harris.

"How many ways do you want me to tell the story, Marlin?" Harris lamented.

"Look, Leon, I'm trying to wrap my head around this, and your explanation doesn't warrant even half a wrap. Rule number one is invisibility. What part of that concept didn't you and Fabian understand? I mean, you may as well have hired a high-school marching band to accompany you to the Mall of America to draw more attention, and how could you forget the local TV stations?"

Harris hated failure, his own or anyone else's. But what he hated even more was being berated by the likes of Marlin Terrie. Terrie was a career bureaucrat whose visions of grandeur far exceeded his abilities. Harris wasn't sure if Terrie's motivation truly was, as he claimed, a patriotic desire to align himself with those forced to take radical measures to preserve our embattled republic, or if he sold himself out to spite a hierarchy that had dead-ended his career. Harris didn't much care. He had his own agenda, which was waving at him from Terrie's shirt pocket. And which probably reeked of stale cigarette smoke. What Harris couldn't stomach was the verbal tongue lash-ing being administered from one who would quickly succumb from ineptitude if assigned to the field himself.

"Leon, do you realize how hard it was to get the secretary to defuse the incident? We... I had all I could do to convince him it was all a terribly unfortunate misunderstanding, and for the good of both agencies, the incident needed to die a quiet death. I mean, albeit Fabian's passing, the incident had all the makings for a *Keystone Cops* comedy."

Harris momentarily stared at Terrie, attempting to determine if Marlin was providing cover for Secretary Cheshire or if Cheshire truly was unaware of the clandestine operation flourishing on his watch. Terrie's eyes didn't betray his explanation.

"Look, Marlin, we agreed Laberday was a flight risk, did we not?"

"Yes."

"And we agreed on the necessity to call his bluff that our pictures, along with Peck's information, would miraculously be sent to the police if we took him out. Isn't that correct?"

Terrie scowled, "You should have made that call the first night you confronted him. You could have beaten it out of him. He's no hardened combatant; he would've cracked."

Harris had all he could do from reaching over the table and wring Terrie's leathery neck. "Yeah, and if we were wrong, you would have washed your hands of the whole expedition. Of course, there would have been the lingering problem of some very high-profile people left compromised, not to mention the pictures and audio Laberday supposedly has of Fabian and me. Think the hammer wouldn't have come down on you too? Don't kid yourself, Marlin, there are no favorite sons in our little 'family.'"

Terrie kicked back in his chair and reached for a smoke.

"Don't even think about lighting up." Harris thrust a finger.

"Okay, Okay." Terrie flashed a palm. He knew Harris was volatile and decided not to push the envelope. "Just tell me what happened, Leon. I've got answers to provide. There are a lot of people very deep into this Peck thing. I mean, if certain information were to come out, it could start a chain reaction that would… Well, put it this way, they are *very* dependent on our success."

"I don't know what else to tell you, Marlin. I just wanted to divert those FBI guys long enough for Fabian to get in the mall and follow Laberday."

"You could have let the chase die."

Harris winced. Valid point. "I'll give you that. But we were exposed, and I didn't know who was following us until they flashed their badges. Sure, looking back, we should have aborted, but we were desperate. You gotta remember, Marlin, we had staked out Laberday's house the two previous evenings, and he hadn't shown up. And being that he took a bus to the mall, I was hoping he'd lead us to an accomplice, you know, someone who would be a good lead to the info and pictures. It seemed logical at the time. For sure, we didn't want to lose sight of him. We couldn't take the chance he was going to disappear. You can't say it wasn't reasonable to assume he was up to something being that he wasn't staying at his house."

Terrie rubbed his chin, which made the deep crevasses on his face writhe like snakes. "I guess I can understand your position, Leon. You were trying to complete your objective. And an important one it is." Terrie suddenly seemed preoccupied. A moment later, he picked up the conversation again. "You know why people like Laberday disgust me, Leon? They focus their misguided hatred on the very people they should be hailing as heroes. Why can't they understand this country escaped a full-fledged depression in 2008 only because of the astuteness of knowledgeable and brave people, not only in government but also in the business community? They had the insight to do what was necessary to bring the country back from the brink of collapse."

Terrie looked at Harris for confirmation. Harris denied him the satisfaction. Terrie pushed on. "Do you know who the real villains are, Leon? Shameless people like this Senator Sheridan who's going after Sam Peck. And why? I'll tell you why—their own selfish ambitions. They cry crony capitalism, but it's a tough world out there. So what if Peck has done some gray wheeling and dealing in his day?

I mean, patriotic acts like securing the continuance of an outdated military base is not only good for morale, it's good for business."

Harris marveled at how Terrie could look him in the eye with all sincerity and defend the actions of the very man he had put a contract on. Maybe it was his way of transferring guilt. The guy was, after all, strange and maybe a little wacko. Regardless, he wasn't interested in a pep talk.

"Don't waste your moralizing on me, Marlin."

Terrie either didn't hear Harris or pretended not to. "Do you know who else shares the blame, Leon? All those defaulters who lied on their mortgage applications so they could buy houses they couldn't afford. They're the ones really at fault for causing the Great Recession. Leon, listen to me; the country is still hanging on by a thread economically. It wouldn't take much to kick the weak financial legs out from under us, and in that vein, it's more important than ever that Laberday be taken out. The business community needs to be looking forward, not over their shoulder for a crazed killer."

"Okay, but…"

"No, let me finish. It's not your call to question; it's your job to keep the country safe and to keep it free from chaos—the kind of chaos that could result from the next economic catastrophe like this redistribution of wealth crap some are espousing. That's your job, Leon, and I wouldn't ask you to do something that wasn't in the country's best interests. Okay? Are you okay with that?"

Harris stared into Marlin Terrie's dull, bureaucratic eyes. He also stared at the bulging envelope in Terrie's shirt pocket. "So what's the plan?"

CHAPTER 33

The final day

Smiling and shaking hands with the gathering audience, Ken Laberday was the center of attention in the Vickers main auditorium lobby, a prelude to his being the center of attention in the auditorium itself. He glanced at his watch. 4:40 p.m. It had already been a very long day, as Kenny had been up long before dawn to prepare and install one of the final pieces in his farewell act. However, Ken looked fresh as a daisy and unfairly handsome in his Ralph Lauren black-vested suit, his stamina bolstered by grand thoughts of an equally grand future. Additionally, his ego was severely stroked via the second and third glances cast his way by a diverse age group of flirting attendees.

Ken kept on the lookout for one woman of particular interest. She was a major contributor to the college and an essential piece of his grand plan. Katie McKourley owned a very successful investment firm in the Twin Cities and was a longtime acquaintance of Ken. It was obvious she was fond of Ken in more than just a casual way, but her very public position and prudent loyalty to her multimillionaire husband kept any thoughts of a cozy relationship in check. McKourley had made a small fortune as an independent broker, marrying bundles of mortgage securities to eager buyers for a generous middleman fee. Her business strategies handsomely enriched her personal pot of gold and solidifying her participation in today's circus of justice.

Finally, McKourley stepped into the lobby. Tall and blond, with a frame leaning more toward robust than feminine, Katie looked the part of her take-charge personality in her red skirt, white blouse, and matching red jacket. Ken maneuvered his way through the crowd and was soon shaking McKourley's extended hand. With no time to waste, Ken got down to business.

"Katie, I'm so sorry to have to ask this of you. But the student who was supposed to help present my lecture became ill this afternoon, and I need some help in the latter part of the presentation. It requires an intimate knowledge of the derivatives market, and there is no one I can recruit at this late date. Would you be kind enough to help me?" Ken surmised that being a big booster of the college coupled with her affection for him would nudge Katie's answer to the affirmative.

"Why, of course I will, Ken. What do you want me to do?"

"Come with me. It'll only take a few minutes to fill you in."

McKourley followed Ken down the hallway that ran alongside the auditorium. Entering through the stage door, Laberday directed her behind the curtain and then down the stairway to the back of the stage. She was about to ask where they were going when Ken sprayed a gentle mist in her face while wrapping his hand over her mouth. McKourley immediately fell back into his arms. Ken opened the small door that accessed the trap room and dragged her inside. He pulled out a syringe and injected a doping agent into Katie. He then placed her into the cage opposite of "Sleeping Beauty," who looked quite peaceful as well as alluring in her circus attire. The performers were now in place and awaiting their cue.

The professor was greeted with a healthy round of applause as he stepped out from behind the curtain. Ken graciously smiled and nodded, taking a moment to adjust papers on the podium. A student usher closed the access doors at the back of the room. The auditorium was three-quarters full. The audience was a mixture of students, college alumni, educators from other institutions, supporters from the business community, and a smattering of interested (and curious) attendees from the general public. Ken noted how the business crowd had pulled together like metal filings on a magnet.

Everything looked perfect, just as he had imagined it. Then a curious thing happened—a clear-cut image of his mother drifted into his mind's eye. Just like that, there she was staring at him. *Are you here to support me or criticize me, Mother?* Like it or not, his mother would always be with her boy, casting a critical eye.

"Good afternoon, ladies and gentlemen. I thank you so much for coming to this, our final event of Jubilee Week at Wherland-Vickers. Let's see… I believe your programs show that my lecture is titled, 'Keynesian Economics as It Relates to a Sustained Economic Recovery.' However, since there has been such an overwhelming interest shown by my economics students concerning accusations hurled at our financial and political communities in reference to the attention given to recent events involving this so-called circus killer, I think I will leave the mending of the economy to a future discussion and instead concentrate on the darker side of the equation. In fact, I'm sure the change in topics will provide much better theater for this afternoon's discourse." Scattered laughter broke out. The new theme found immediate approval among the attendees. The guests in the business section who knew the professor personally fully expected him to vaporize any accusations of wrongdoing by the heavyweights of the financial world.

Ken dug into a short speech on the pros and cons of the ringmaster's indictments. As there was no reason to delay the "real" show, Laberday kept his comments to a minimum. He finished with, "If we dig deep into the focus of this…ah…the cause for Mr. Ringmaster's contempt, well, maybe he legitimizes his actions with this logic: Think back to 9/11. Foreign terrorists invaded our country, committed horrific acts of death, and destroyed two buildings that symbolized the very heart and soul of our country's financial fabric. In retaliation for that insidious assault, our government started two wars, will spend up to six trillion dollars to finance them. And in which, many thousands of our fine men and women have been killed or wounded. That's seventy-five thousand dollars for every household folks, which, of course, means nothing compared to the heartbreak in many of those households.

"Now consider the subprime-mortgage crisis where the few and the greedy have erased up to twenty-two trillion dollars from the overall economy and vaporized over eight million jobs. And the misery this reprehensible devastation has caused? Incalculable!"

Ken paused and let his words sink in. "So how has the government responded?" Laberday thrust out his arms in a theatrical gesture. "Why, they rewarded the homegrown 'terrorists' with more seed money to plot their next acts of thievery." Kenny pitched up his voice. "I ask you, where is the justice!"

Murmurs rumbled through the audience. Heads nodded. The business crowd fidgeted in their seats. A few stood to leave.

"Excuse me one moment, folks. I have something very special prepared for you. Please stay seated; I will be right back."

Ken ducked behind the curtain and secured the stage door. He activated a small electronic device. The student usher in the back of the room heard four small pops. Abruptly, Ken reappeared wearing black riding boots, a red jacket with gold buttons, and a black top hat and wielding a whip. Calliope music drifted from the stage out onto the audience. The props, designed for distraction, hit their mark. A confounded audience riveted their attention on the ringmaster. The lone exception was the student usher who was pushing on an exit door. It held tight.

"Please keep your seats," Ken admonished. "If everyone stays put, no one will get hurt. I have explosive devices planted around the room. Don't make me use them." Text messages bounced off one another on their way out of the auditorium.

Mark and Sylkie were following up on a domestic brawl that resulted in a homicide when an alert blared over their police radio. Mark turned to his partner. "Did the dispatcher say Wherland-Vickers College?"

"He sure did."

"We can be there in minutes."

"Think our favorite professor is up to something?"

"Does a goose have feathers?"

"You hold him; I'll pluck him."

"Easy, young la—partner. Let's concentrate on bag, book, *then* ruffle as necessary."

"Spose."

Ken walked to the front of the stage and peered out into a half-mesmerized, half-frightened audience. He took a deep breath and swelled his brain with the ingredients for the sales job of his life. He had but a pinprick of time to sell his story of martyrdom— his parting shot at convincing the world he was neither murderer nor maniac but lonely avenger for the faceless millions of Americans heartlessly cut loose from the American dream by the barons of financial butchery.

"A few moments ago, I asked, 'Where is the justice?' Well, my friends, *I* am the justice; the justice is *me*! I have sacrificed myself for the good of our precious country. I have exposed those who have driven so many to the depths of despair." Ken paused, allowing his bottomless dark eyes to take stock. Yes! He had their attention.

"And what is *my* stake in this?" The ringmaster clenched a fist and put it to his chest, and with all the false sincerity he could muster, he said, "Because, my friends, I suffer your loss... I feel your hurt... I *am* your pain. Now it is up to the good and honest citizens of our nation to carry the torch, to reign in the unbridled greed that is destroying our democracy!"

Satisfied with his plea to manipulate himself from heavy to hero, the professor decided it was time to depart for greener pastures. Kenny backed up to the curtain and ducked behind it. He pressed the button that activated the false floor and then quickly reappeared as the floor retreated.

"Ladieees and gentlemen, I present to you the infamous 'cage of revenge.' Feast your eyes upon the great ringmaster's version of deserved justice for those who would force you into financial slavery."

The cage slowly rose into view, exposing a sleeping Katie McKourley on one side and the beautiful and scantily clad Brooke Pope, who was in a similar state, on the opposite side. Brooke was clothed in brilliant yellow skimpy shorts and a bikini top of the same color, the choice of clothing a ploy to focus the audience's attention on the deadly skit. But the features that trumped all were the long metal fingernails sharpened to a point and glued to Brooke's nails. They were meant to do damage—a great deal of damage. Ken had given Brooke a hallucinogenic drug that would cause her to lash out at any moving object, and her nearest object was Katie McKourley.

The cage came to rest at floor level. Ken quickly injected both women with a stimulant to pull them out of their semiconscious state. He cracked his whip. The snap echoed throughout the auditorium. He then switched off all auditorium lights, with the exception of a set of intense white stage lights directed on the cage.

"A fight to the finish folks, the circus of justice—grand finale!" McKourley awoke to the horror staring at her from across the cage. Both women stood. McKourley smartly took off her jacket and wrapped it around an arm. Katie was bigger and heftier than Brooke and had an attitude to match her size. She would not go down easily.

Brooke pounced. McKourley deflected Pope's right hand with her jacket, but Brooke's left hand slashed across Katie's midsection, tearing her blouse and drawing first blood. Ken delayed his departure long enough to savor a taste of the crowd's pleasure. Although some, mostly women, were hiding their eyes, the majority focused on the cage. Laberday knew that blood lust ranks high on the human-pleasure scale. So does scantily clad women, one of which was becoming more undressed and bloodied with every swipe of those deadly nails.

Kenny could hear banging on the outside of the entrance doors. Time to exit "stage left." He electronically set off the noisy but harmless explosives hidden in the auditorium, along with activating several smoke bombs he had placed on the stage. The crowd panicked and herded to the exits. Ken discarded his circus coat and hat and jumped off the back of the stage. He yanked a pre-loosened grill from an air duct and climbed inside. He wriggled through thirty feet of ductwork until he reached the maintenance room, the access doors to which he had previously secured. Pushing off a second grill, Ken dropped to the floor.

He threw open the outside service door and looked around. Ahead of him was a long sloping hill. At the bottom of the hill, a tree-lined path followed the Mississippi River. Floodlights cast a dim glow onto the path. Wailing sirens mixed with urgent shouts for help echoed from the other side of the building. Laberday saw no one in his field of vision.

Ken quickly made his way down the hill. A short jaunt along the path would bring him to a canoe storage building. The plan was to paddle a canoe a half-mile downstream to a municipal landing where he had parked his van. Perfect plan. Well thought out. Nothing to get in his way...except...

Except for the two figures that emerged out of the semidarkness. "Evening, Professor. Out for a walk?"

Ken pulled up, dismayed but not defeated. "How'd you know, Truitt?"

"When we got the call about the strange goings-on at the college, I knew it had to be you. Scanning the scene when we arrived, I was thinking 'diversion.' You would've realized the place would be crawling with cops within minutes. Then I remembered something you said in our last interview about 'my misplaced accusations about you that were flowing through the backwaters of my mind.' Backwater, flowing—maybe the river. Darn those subliminal messages, huh? Your way out—but tonight, not so much."

Laberday cast a thin smile. "That's impressive, Truitt. You're not the gumshoe I took you for. Look, I'd like to stay and chat, but you do understand I'm in a bit of a hurry."

"Sorry, Professor, as of now, you're on our time."

"Oh, I don't think so." Ken reached into his pants pocket. Mark and Sylkie drew their guns. "No need for weapons, Sergeants. I just want to show you something that is sure to pique your interest." The professor produced a cell phone. He opened it and set it on the ground. Sylkie peered at it and quickly snatched it up.

"Bastard!"

"Yes, Sergeant Maune, it's your niece and nephew. Sorry I couldn't get them to smile for the picture."

"How...?"

"I, ah, 'borrowed' them earlier today. By the way, your ex-brother-in-law is most likely still secured to his bed. I assure you, Sergeant Maune, much as I dislike children, it is not my intention to bring harm to them. They are merely my insurance policy, quite safe in a locked room with plenty of provisions. I promised them their aunt Sylkie would be picking them up later tonight. Now you don't want to disappoint them, do you? Oh, and for good measure, I have a bomb planted in a public place that is timed to detonate unless I'm allowed to be on my way."

Ken looked at Mark, then Sylkie. "You *have* made a promise to protect and serve, have you not?"

Mark's decision was immediate. "When will you tell us where the children are and where the bomb is?"

"Give me your number. I'll call you before midnight. Promise."

Sylkie got nose to nose with Laberday. "You better follow through. If anything happens to them, I swear…"

Ken cut her off and rolled his eyes. "Yeah, yeah, I know. You'll dismember me one appendage at a time. Oh, by the way, not that I care what you think of me so much as I want to keep my glowing image intact, but for the record, I did *not* kill your sister."

Sylkie cast a suspicious look. "So…who did kill her?"

"Your ex-brother-in-law and Brooke Pope."

"What?" Sylkie's heart bounced off her rib cage.

Ken said, "I have to admit I was surprised also. I thought the two goons that wanted me to kill Senator Peck did her in. Evidently Brooke and Aaron beat them to it."

Mark pulled closer. "How do you know that?"

Laberday frowned. "Look, I do need to go, but very quickly, a couple of nights ago, after Brooke had downed enough margaritas to satisfy a Jimmy Buffett concert crowd, she opened up about killing Nora for the insurance money. I guess it was a Bonnie and Clyde moment for her, as I had already fessed up about my new profession."

Sylkie felt a twinge of hope. "How can we prove it?"

"Brooke told me she's petrified of wasting away in jail. She'll cough up Aaron like a chunk of lodged steak if you let her plea-bargain. She said Aaron did all the planning for the murder. But then, why don't you hear it from Brooke herself?" Laberday reached in a pocket and handed a tape to Sylkie. "I was going to mail this to you."

Sylkie stared at it. "Why…?"

For a fleeting instant, the professor's dark, menacing eyes softened. "Nora, ah..." Then his mother's image flashed, and the door closed.

The man who, moments before, had been Sylkie's worst nightmare had suddenly become something of a benefactor. He had unlocked the door separating her from Margo and Danny. There was now a way where they could be together again. She suddenly found it harder to despise Professor Kendrick Laberday.

"Now are you going to let me go or not?" Laberday impatiently demanded once again on his game.

Mark stepped aside. "Later."

"I don't think so. Oh, and if anyone's interested, I'm holding information that some very important individuals would not want to be shared with the public. So let us all live in peace."

Flashing the peace sign, Ken smiled and disappeared into the night.

The Vickers parking lot mirrored a scene from a science-fiction flick where everyone was running from an ominous alien creature. The cops desperately searched for Kendrick Laberday. Snarling traffic bottled up the parking area, and ambulance crews flashed a path through them all to take Katie McKourley, a now-sedated Brooke Pope, and a few slow folks who got trampled to the hospital. Though McKourley looked like she had been introduced to a giant paper shredder, her wounds were mostly superficial. Her body would retain some scarring, but her ego emerged unscathed, as she had dealt Brooke Pope two very black eyes. The unfortunate Brooke would regret hooking up with the ringmaster, as she would awaken to charges of accessory to murder.

Shortly after the melee at Vickers, Aaron Balfour was released from his bondage of duct tape in exchange for a new form of bondage at the Hennepin County Jail.

*****

Mark, Sylkie, Casey Maxwell, Jim Renner, Guy Lompello, and Liz Truitt gathered in the First Precinct conference room, suffering the excruciating wait to hear from Kendrick Laberday. They hoped. They prayed. Liz held close to Sylkie. The ordeal was as hard for Liz as anyone, as she was fully invested in Margo and Danny.

"So what about this bomb Laberday said he planted?" Guy growled. "Think he's telling the truth?"

"I'd say no," Sylkie answered. "I think he threw it out as an add-on so we'd be sure to let him go."

Casey leaned back in his chair and folded his hands behind his neck. "I wonder what his escape plan is. Think he's leaving the country, Mark?"

"I can't see him staying in country. Too many people want a piece of him."

Sitting like a ticking time bomb in the middle of the conference-room table, Mark's cell phone became the center of everyone's universe. It was nearing nine p.m.

"Brentsen was in the other day," Guy offered, more to make conversation than as a statement of significance. "Cleaned out his desk; said he felt okay. He was struggling to get around though."

Mark said, "I had lunch with him last week. Gonna miss his stories, even if most of them were 'enhanced.'"

Ten p.m. No call.

Liz brewed a second pot of coffee.

Eleven o'clock. Mark's phone sat silent. Sylkie was getting more frantic by the minute. Trembling, she uttered, "I can't stand this. Where are they? Mark, are you sure Laberday's property was thoroughly checked out?"

"Yes, I'm sure, Sylkie. Every building was scoured; the grounds were gone over inch by inch. Even the surrounding woods have been searched. The children are not there."

Eleven thirty. The phone remained agonizingly quiet.

Eleven forty-five. The group crowded around the table. Sylkie crossed her arms and lay her head on them. Guy Lompello looked like he was about to cry.

Mark stared at the phone, willing it to ring. At eleven fifty-four, he got his wish. Mark reached for the phone and nervously flipped the cover.

"The children are at 1096 Raven's Point Drive, Elk River. There is no bomb. The good people of the Twin Cities are safe. Happy trails, Truitt."

CHAPTER 34

Seven months later

Minnesota fishing wisdom holds to the adage that when the leaves on the poplar trees are the size of mouse ears, the walleyes will end their spawning cycle and turn their attention to the fisherman's lure. Such was the state of the leaves at the Truitt cabin the day of the wedding. The setting was picture-perfect—deep-blue cloudless sky, wavelets lightly lapping at the sand, and a warm breeze dripping with the fragrance of spring flowers. Save for a few renegade dandelions, the grounds were camera-ready for the ceremony.

The minister—young and a little hot under his collar as a healthy spring sun rose above the treetops—took his place in front of the small group of attendees lining the processional route. First to walk down the "aisle" were Margo and Danny, flinging flower petals along the path. Next, Liz made her way to the front as the maid of honor, followed by Jim Renner, Casey's best man. Casey Maxwell fell in behind Renner.

Finally, Sylkie, looking radiant in her wedding gown, walked down the aisle arm in arm with Mark, who had the honor of giving her away. Casey looked on with admiration at his soon-to-be wife. Sylkie's eyes reflected the same glow back at him. Margo and Danny took opposite sides of the couple. It was the moment of conception for the new family, where, once again, two little children would have a mom and a dad.

Guy blew into his handkerchief.

The collective mood was jovial, yet there was a degree of somberness in remembrance of Nora Balfour. The attendees silently reflected as their faith guided them on the presence of Nora's spirit.

The vows were about to be exchanged when a beautiful black-and-white striped zebra swallowtail butterfly, far-removed from its usual summer habitat, lit on the minister's Book of Worship. Just for an instant. Just long enough to catch the preacher's attention and give him pause. The momentary silence focused everyone's attention on the minister, at which point, the butterfly returned to the air, merrily dancing its way in a whirr of black and white to the upper reaches of nearby birch trees.

Black—the color of Cason's suit. White—the color of Sylkie's gown. The newlyweds were inseparable as the colors on the butterfly's wings.

Black—the symbol of evil. White—the symbol of good. As the butterfly flew higher, the sun's reflection off its white strips all but drowned out the black.

As quickly as it had appeared, the butterfly was gone.

Guy blew hard into his handkerchief.

*****

Maracaibo, Venezuela

Ken Laberday stepped onto his patio and into another lazy, humid morning. The temperature would climb to ninety today, too hot for Ken's comfort. He was contemplating a move to the more temperate and decidedly less volatile climate of Uruguay, although he would have to be careful, as that government was friendly with the United States. It seemed a good option sometime down the road. Under the world's radar for the most part, the country should be a good place to become invisible.

The undeniable counterpoint was that living there was comfortable. A good teaching job, a decent place to live, and a new woman every couple of months. And the Venezuelan government turned a blind eye to the American who went by the name of Professor Joshua Callen. As long as he continued to rail against the corrupt American business model, Professor Callen was a welcome guest. Yes, all in all, life in Venezuela was what he had hoped for.

Hoped for? Most certainly. Satisfied? Not! Why? Because Kendrick Laberday's mundane existence was counter to how psychopaths roll. Kenny's craving for stimulation and manipulation was far from being met in his new, passive lifestyle. He readily owned up to the fact he had reveled in his dark role as ringmaster and enjoyed the adrenaline rush in the cat-and-mouse game with Mark Truitt. In a word, Ken Laberday was bored with his new and unexciting life.

Fortunately, what was done could be undone. Ken's ace in the hole was Senator Samuel Peck's reluctant confession. How to exploit that time bomb? For sure, his disclosure of the corruption so flagrant from the sacred halls of Congress and the gilded towers of Wall Street would skyrocket him back into the limelight. He would throw out bits of information in exchange for money and pleasure and then scurry and hide. No doubt the competition would be fierce for information to expose the corruptness of his home country's power brokers. Yes, the name Kendrick Laberday would soon be synonymous with forcing a government to bare its deceitful soul before its citizens, and the list of safe harbors to welcome this "decent" man who only wanted to restore the concept of democracy to the United States would be a long one.

But as always, the endgame wasn't about honesty and integrity—it was about Kenny.

*****

Laberday and his live-in had just settled in for breakfast when the doorbell rang. The woman answered the door. "Joshua, this man has a registered letter for you to sign," she called out.

Showing displeasure that his breakfast had been interrupted, Ken grumbled his way to the door. The smiling man held out a clipboard with an attached piece of paper and a pen. Ken gruffly grabbed the clipboard and picked up the pen, and then out of nowhere, two men appeared and pushed Laberday back into the house. Clipboard man held a gun on the woman while the other two put a hood over Ken's head and herded him into a waiting truck.

Several days later, two boys walking along the shore of Lake Maracaibo spied a bundle of clothes lying on the beach. As they got closer, it became gruesomely apparent the bundle was actually a body. It was not a pretty sight. Waves had pushed the dead man's pants legs up to his knees, exposing gray bloated calves. The rest of the decaying mass was caked with sand, including the man's hair. His face had several nasty gashes and was discolored and swollen. Flies buzzed the body, scouting for places to lay their eggs.

The boys cautiously circled the remains with every intention of alerting the police *after* they had checked for items of value. One of the boys noticed a bulge in the man's back pocket and gingerly removed a wallet. He opened it, looked around, and then pocketed several bolivar banknotes. Searching further, he spied a Venezuelan driver's license.

"*Como se llama?*" The boy pointed to the license and handed the wallet to his friend.

The second boy removed the driver's license and studied it. "Jos-hu-a... Cal-len," he sounded out.

"Gringo."

The boy stuffed the license back into the wallet and threw it on the body.

*****

Ah, yes. Playa del Carmen, Mexico, in the fall. What a great place to be, and no one was enjoying the warm breezes wafting from the ocean more than the two vacationers stretched out on cots, occasionally taking a dip in the pool beside them. The woman's swim attire left little to the imagination, which gifted her a near-complete body tan. The gentleman was still in the early stages of skin-color enhancement, as he had been rather busy doing, well, other things. However, Kendrick would have plenty of time to catch up on that now that he was confident that all tracks to his former life had been erased. His acquaintance in Venezuela had proved quite useful not only in resettling Ken but also in staging his fake death and then ferrying Ken's ultimate lifeline—the damaging information provided by Senator Peck—to a safe location.

What a deal. Life was great! Ken called the server and ordered a margarita then turned over to even out his tan. His thoughts filtered back to whole ordeal. He mentally took a bow for his brilliance in pulling off the gig and how he had blindsided everyone—well, maybe except for Mark Truitt. He had to admit the guy was nobody's fool. The other person who briefly popped up was Nora Balfour. He couldn't excuse himself for letting that little no-account throw such a large grenade into his plans. He reminded himself of his mother's warnings. For certain, it wouldn't happen again.

Ken put a match to a San Cristobal La Punta cigar. The server set the margarita on the little table next to him. Time for a celebratory puff and a drink. The liquid slid down smoothly for the first few seconds. And then it didn't. First, there was the burning in his gut, followed by violent convulsions that blocked desperate attempts to bring in air. Forty-five seconds at the most, it was over. The girl nonchalantly stood and walked away.

On a third-floor apartment above the pool, window curtains quietly fell back into place. Leon Harris turned from the curtains and nodded to Laberday's Venezuelan acquaintance. The man stepped up to Harris and handed him a briefcase. Harris returned the offer with a thick envelope. Friendships aside, everyone needs money.

Call Leon Harris One, or call him Other. But never call him out. Many went to sleep that night thankful that their government, or a least part of it, was watching out for them. As for Kendrick Laberday's post-partum memorial—

You're lazy, Kendrick. You will always fail because you don't crave perfection. You settle for mediocrity. Get away from me, lazy boy.

ABOUT THE AUTHOR

For David Zini, closing the door on a long career in the mining industry in northern Minnesota allowed a new door to open. Having little previous writing experience, but long a fan of mystery/thriller novels, David aspired to write a novel of his own. He determined to focus on creating a unique brand for his writing, both in content and in the characters he creates. David's premise to center his novels around real-life events are meant to draw the reader into the story and go along for the ride. Out of that foundation came his first novel, *Waterfall*.

Positive feedback from *Waterfall* encouraged David to continue onto a second novel. With experiences learned in hand, writing Circus Acts turned out to be way more fun than work. He encourages anyone who has the itch to write a book—novel, memoir, or whatever—to go ahead and put fingers to the keyboard or pen to paper. "You don't have to be polished, just start writing!"

CPSIA information can be obtained
at www.ICGtesting.com
Printed in the USA
LVHW030846281121
704653LV00001B/173